1/23

D1032732

SCOT IN A TRAP

Also by Catriona McPherson

Last Ditch mysteries

SCOT FREE *
SCOT AND SODA *
SCOT ON THE ROCKS *
SCOT MIST *
SCOT IN A TRAP *

Dandy Gilver mysteries

AFTER THE ARMISTICE BALL
THE BURRY MAN'S DAY
BURY HER DEEP
THE WINTER GROUND
THE PROPER TREATMENT OF BLOODSTAINS
AN UNSUITABLE DAY FOR A MURDER
A BOTHERSOME NUMBER OF CORPSES
A DEADLY MEASURE OF BRIMSTONE
THE REEK OF RED HERRINGS
THE UNPLEASANTNESS IN THE BALLROOM
A MOST MISLEADING HABIT
A SPOT OF TOIL AND TROUBLE
A STEP SO GRAVE
THE TURNING TIDE
THE MIRROR DANCE

Novels

AS SHE LEFT IT *
THE DAY SHE DIED *
COME TO HARM *
THE CHILD GARDEN
QUIET NEIGHBORS *
THE WEIGHT OF ANGELS
GO TO MY GRAVE
STRANGERS AT THE GATE
A GINGERBREAD HOUSE *
IN PLACE OF FEAR

* *available from Severn House*

SCOT IN A TRAP

Catriona McPherson

**SEVERN
HOUSE**

First world edition published in Great Britain and the USA in 2022
by Severn House, an imprint of Canongate Books Ltd,
14 High Street, Edinburgh EH1 1TE.

Trade paperback edition first published in Great Britain and the USA in 2023
by Severn House, an imprint of Canongate Books Ltd.

severnhouse.com

Copyright © Catriona McPherson, 2022

All rights reserved including the right of reproduction in whole or in part in any
form. The right of Catriona McPherson to be identified as the author of this work
has been asserted in accordance with the Copyright, Designs & Patents Act 1988.

British Library Cataloguing-in-Publication Data
A CIP catalogue record for this title is available from the British Library.

ISBN-13: 978-1-4483-0768-5 (cased)
ISBN-13: 978-1-4483-0785-2 (trade paper)
ISBN-13: 978-1-4483-0784-5 (e-book)

This is a work of fiction. Names, characters, places and incidents
are either the product of the author's imagination or are used fictitiously.
Except where actual historical events and characters are being described
for the storyline of this novel, all situations in this publication are
fictitious and any resemblance to actual persons, living or dead,
business establishments, events or locales is purely coincidental.

All Severn House titles are printed on acid-free paper.

MIX
Paper from
responsible sources
FSC
www.fsc.org   FSC® C013056

Typeset by Palimpsest Book Production Ltd.,
Falkirk, Stirlingshire, Scotland.
Printed and bound in Great Britain by
TJ Books, Padstow, Cornwall.

To Neil McRoberts.
Three's the charm.

ONE

'Should I slice some pears?' I asked.

'No!' bellowed Noleen.

'*Can* I slice some pears?'

'*No!*' bellowed Noleen again, if a bellow can be that high-pitched.

'There's no need to shout,' I told her. 'We're supposed to be staying calm, remember.'

'So don't drive me up the fucking wall and out through the fucking chimney, blathering on about fucking fruit!'

'It's just . . .' I tried. But there was no way to explain it to someone who didn't see it. I couldn't *not* see it. On the many surfaces around the kitchen of the owners' flat of the Last Ditch Motel, where Noleen and I were currently incarcerated, there were – and I will try not to miss anything out, but I can't promise: a vat of Mexican wedding soup big enough to drown the entire bridal party, except that it was so thick everyone could walk across it to the edge of the pot even in stilettoes; two commercial (surely) bakers' trays of rolls that smelled like cakes and definitely had sugar on the top; three washing-up-basin-sized bowls of alleged mashed potato, which were actually cream and melted butter held together with just enough potato starch to mean you'd need a spoon to serve them rather than a jug with a spout; three similarly sized bowls of mashed yams reeking of what I hoped was nutmeg but feared was cinnamon and topped with full-sized burnt marshmallows, i.e. not the dinky ones from cups of cocoa but ones you'd have to bite in half or risk needing a Heimlich if you tried to breathe while chewing; a casserole dish (apparently – my first guess had been paddling pool) of stuffing (apparently – my first guess, having seen the cranberries, walnuts, and orange peel, had been cake-mix); a wheelbarrow without its wheels (Noleen called it a dish, but seriously) of pure, cheese-topped, butter-slicked extra-thick cream which allegedly had vegetables in it (onions and green beans if you were gullible enough to believe that); five shoebox-sized tureens full of jam which I was supposed to call sauce; and of course a mysterious object roughly the size of a suitcase you wouldn't be allowed to carry on, which was probably a turkey but couldn't be identified since every square inch of it was wrapped in bacon and it smelled only of maple syrup from the cake crumbs (supposedly breadcrumbs, but I've watched every episode of bread week in that tent and this was cake) bursting out of it like a baking-soda volcano at both ends.

So it seemed to me that, if we were going to start with sliceable soup and carry on to whole cakes, crumbled cakes, cheese, butter, cream, marshmallows, jam and maple syrup with some meat and veg thrown on as a kind of garnish, maybe we needed to finish with an alternative to the five pies that were perched all around: on the breakfast bar; on both bar stools; in a trio on the windowsill, on the . . . Hang on, that's six. There was a pumpkin pie on the breakfast bar, two pecan pies on the stools, a cherry lattice, a chocolate cream and a key lime on the windowsill. Yes, six. And an apple cobbler on top of the microwave. As I was saying, it seemed to me that maybe we needed a lighter alternative to seve . . . Eight! There was a cheesecake in the dishrack – alternative to eight – Nine! I had just spotted a peach flan by the coffeemaker – alternative to nine (and counting because I hadn't opened any cupboards) pies for pudding.

'OK,' I said. 'I won't slice anything now and if anyone feels like something light I'll hop up and do it then.'

'No one will.'

'I might.'

'Ungrateful.'

'Oh for God's sake,' I said.

'Stay calm,' said Noleen, with an infuriating smirk.

'I'm going to go and see how they're getting on setting the table,' I said.

'Of course you are,' said Noleen. 'Because how could a bunch of Americans possibly set out silverware and drinking vessels to the satisfaction of Your Majesty? Why, we'd just tip the swill in the trough and get on our knees if we didn't have you to help, wouldn't we?'

'Stay calm,' I said, then I nipped out of earshot before she could come back at me.

She had a point. This was my second Thanksgiving in my new country and last year I was somewhat obnoxious about the paper tablecloths and red Solo cups. I cringed to remember. I was converted after the end of the meal when Noleen's wife Kathi stood up and said, 'Now for my famous tablecloth trick!' and, instead of whipping the cloth off and leaving the empty bottles and glasses standing, bundled the whole lot up and took it out to the bin, saying 'Clean-up? Check!' over her shoulder.

And it did look pretty. We were having Thanksgiving dinner in the fairy-light-strewn forecourt of the motel, where three patio heaters were warming the long trestle table that had been there since spring and had seen many an impromptu lockdown party as the summer wore into autumn and winter beckoned. Tonight, it was bedecked with fold-out paper turkeys, real autumn leaves, every kind of pumpkin, gourd and squash that ever inspired a *Star Trek* alien, and the red Solo cups that fitted right in to the colour scheme.

'Hey!' said Todd, as he spotted me. 'How you doing?'

'Calm,' I said. 'You?'

'Same. Calm.'

'How's Roger?'

'Sleeping,' said Todd. 'Calmly.'

Roger, Todd's husband, was a paediatrician in Sacramento. He'd been in the COVID wards for a while, but things in Northern California were slightly better now and he was back saving babies and fending off grateful mums. He had managed to get Thanksgiving off on holiday by promising to work Christmas, and so far he looked like sleeping the clock round until it was time to go back again in the morning.

'Did Meera and Arif get here?' I asked Todd.

He beamed and pointed to where two adults and two children were collecting more fallen leaves at the edge of the motel car park. They were more of our lockdown buddies from the spring. They had met here while each of them was leaving a horrendous marriage and I had worried that their relationship could never be more than a rebound. But it was however-many months later now and they were going strong.

However-many months? I smacked myself on the forehead as I had the thought. Idiot! It was nine months later. Obviously.

'Mosquito?' said Todd, taking a big leap away from me. It was balletic in its execution but hysterical in origin. Todd has a severe case of kleptoparasitosis. He is mortally afraid of insects anywhere near him. Even imaginary ones. I assumed Kathi had fumigated the entire forecourt and car park this afternoon to help him relax.

'Just a brain fart,' I said. 'I was trying to smack some sense into myself.'

'Oh honey,' said Todd. 'Don't do *that*. You'll get a concussion.'

'Any sign of José and Maria?' I said, ignoring him. They were almost the last of our former lockdown gang and had swiftly become general abuelo and abuela to every kid – and adult, if I'm honest – who lived at the Ditch. They'd been back home again for a few months but their actual grandchildren were going to Disneyland for the holiday and, as José had said, 'rats ain't cute just cause they got pants on', so they were up for this reunion, complete except that we were going to have to do without Sergeant Molly Rankinson of the Cuento PD because she had pulled the shift, and we were also short Barb Truman, Todd's mom, because she was in Vegas, very much her spiritual home.

That left college-dude Dylan, his six-year-old stepson Diego, and the woman who brought them together in video-playing, junk-food-eating, sticker-collecting bliss, the final permanent Ditch resident, the focus of everyone's extreme anxiety, the reason for everyone's totally bogus and unconvincing attempts to pretend we were in any way the least tiny little bit calm, the currently nine months, two weeks and three days pregnant time-bomb whose tick was twisting the rest of us into unsustainable cork-screws of terror, tighter every minute.

'Della!' Todd squeaked in a voice I'd previously only heard emitting from the neck of a balloon.

'What?' I shouted. 'Shit! Where? What? Oh my God!'

'Della?' said Noleen, blatting out of the owners' flat with a ladle in her hand. 'Fuck! What? Shit!'

'I just . . . She's . . . I didn't . . .' said Todd. 'Here she comes, I mean. I was just saying hello.'

'Dickwad,' said Noleen, banging back into the flat again.

'Jesus, Todd,' I said, bending over to try to get some blood back into my head before I fainted.

'Wow,' said Della, waddling up to where we were standing. 'Will you calm down? Don't you remember me saying the one thing you could all do is calm down?'

I stood up. 'Sorry.'

Della waved my apology away with a languid hand then rested it on her belly. This was as perfectly round and easily as big as the ideal pumpkin everyone who visits a pumpkin patch is secretly searching for, her belly *button* a respectable stalk. And yet she had been gliding about so serenely she looked like she was on rails for the last six weeks. Even her blinking seemed to have slowed down.

In contrast, Dylan, who had been glued to her side at all times since her due date, was twitching like a shorted fuse, one eye flickering, a pulse beating visibly in his neck and a vein throbbing on his forehead. His hands shook, his lips quivered, his knees didn't quite knock but they weren't far off. He had even come to see me professionally a week ago.

'I can't be your therapist, Dill,' I'd told him. 'I'm your friend. But I can refer you.'

'She can't do this,' Dylan had said, completely ignoring me. 'It's insane. It's unsafe. It's illegal.'

'It's not any of those things,' I said. 'It's a good idea. She has had a baby before and it was straightforward. She's young and healthy. The pregnancy has been textbook trouble-free. There's a doctor here at all times.'

'A fired anaesthesiologist.'

'Anaesthetists are doctors,' I said. 'And he's on the psych suspension because of the bug thing, as you well know. It's nothing to do with how good a practitioner he is. Anyway, there's another doctor, a literal baby doctor, whenever he's not working.'

'And when he is?'

'It's still not a fantastic plan to go to hospital if you can help it at the moment.'

'And if you can't?'

'And, most importantly,' I said, because he wasn't the only one who could ignore people, 'this is what she wants.'

'So you're OK with it?'

'I am not Della's therapist. It's not up to me to be OK with anything.'

'How about as a friend?'

'As a friend,' I said, 'I feel like I'm getting to the top of the biggest drop on the biggest rollercoaster in the world and I'm not allowed to check if I'm wearing a seatbelt. I could *kill* her for doing this to us all.'

'Thank you!' said Dylan.

'But you can't tell her I said so.'

'Thank you for nothing,' said Dylan. 'God, I wish I could relax. Did you know she made me stop smoking?'

'Made you, eh? How did she do that?' I had wondered. Dylan was never going to be exactly thrusting but he'd seemed a bit less vague recently.

'She asked and I agreed.'

'Sneaky,' I said. 'What a power move.'

'Yeah, yeah,' said Dylan. 'You got any beer?'

Then we had shared a beer or lots and daydreamed about tonight, when Della would be sitting at Thanksgiving dinner cuddling their brand-new bundle of joy and eating small careful bites of lukewarm food she took care not to drop on the baby en route from plate to lips.

And now it *was* tonight and there *she* was, sitting at the head of the table, balancing a bowl of dip on her belly – no hands – perfectly calm while everyone else grew ulcers and cracked their back teeth from the clenching. I hoped she didn't need to do any fancy breathing exercises for extra oxygen when labour finally did kick in, because while we waited the rest of us had exhausted the world's supply.

TWO

Noleen ate a bit of pear. I had layered alternating slices of golden-skinned, creamy-fleshed Asian pears and red-skinned, white-fleshed pear pears on a plain blue plate, decorated them with a scattering of pomegranate seeds and put it right by her elbow. (I come down hard on passive-aggression if any of my clients display it, but I'm only human.)

I raised my glass and inclined my head at her while she was still chewing and if she hadn't been sitting too close to Kathi to get away with it, she'd have spat the lot into her napkin. Not that Kathi is a Miss Manners type. No, it's just that if a germaphobe saw someone spitting into a napkin after a Thanksgiving dinner it would go like this: Noleen is vomiting; Noleen has salmonella; our dinner was poisonous; we're all going to die. Or, Noleen is vomiting; Noleen has a stomach virus; everyone at this table has contracted a stomach virus from Noleen; we're all going to wish we were dead.

Noleen loves Kathi far too much to do that to her, even though that meant me smirking at her. Considering this, I smiled even wider; there was a lot of love round this table tonight. Roger loves Todd enough to live in a motel, when his doctor's salary should see them in an aspirational monstrosity of black tiles and white carpets. (The thing is Kathi loves cleanliness so much that she keeps the Last Ditch too sterile for insects, and so just right for Todd.) Meera and Arif clearly adored one another nine months in, and Arif loved her kids and they loved him and that's all lovely. José and Maria? Married for sixty years. That speaks for itself, surely.

A year ago I would have been sitting up this end of the table, hunched in my bitterness, shrivelling from lack of affection, twisting myself out of shape in my efforts to deny how sour others' happiness made me. Not any more.

Not that I've suddenly become a better person or anything. It's just that I met someone, and I liked him, and then I loved him, and I trusted him almost completely, except for two things. One, telling him the truth about my past and why I became a therapist, and two, where an ornithologist who works days at the state bird reserve and nights in a phone shop for a bit of pocket money got the cash for the diamond he put on my finger. I held my hand up and turned it this way and that to see how it sparkled in the fairy lights.

'Oh puke,' said Noleen, which re-balanced things between us. I ignored her and looked beyond my finger to where my beloved was sitting, on the other side of the table from me. He winked

at me and waggled his ears, making his glasses jiggle up and
down. I winked back and rolled my tongue since I can't waggle
my ears and I don't wear glasses.

'Oh dry heaves,' said Noleen. 'What the fu-hel-heck was that?'

'Smooth,' said Roger. He's great at not swearing in front of
kids because of work but he won't share the secret.

'And I can't even say "Get a room",' Noleen added. 'Because
you've got a room. I should know.'

This was true. Usually I live on a houseboat moored on the
eponymous slough behind the Last Ditch, but when Della
persuaded us all that she really meant to have this baby at
home, I offered it to her as labour ward, delivery suite and
neo-natal retreat, on account of the motel just beginning to get
some passing trade again, and the walls not being that thick,
and agonal screams tending to put the tourists off something
rotten. So, when her due date rolled round, she moved aboard,
along with Dylan and Diego, and I moved into the two adjoining
rooms they usually occupy. Only, Diego's got two big kittens
(and a rabbit, and an aquarium full of seahorses and assorted
other fancy water dwellers) and it turned out that Taylor was
allergic to cats. So I got a third room out of Noleen and Kathi's
business. It didn't seem like a big deal two weeks and three
days ago, when the kid was expected to pop out of Della any
day. Now though, dollar signs were beginning to pop out of
Noleen's eyes and I had heard her muttering about the rabbit
having more space than any other resident, which was true
because the kittens tended to leave by the bathroom window
at daybreak and only come back when they were hungry.

But it couldn't be long now. I stole a glance up the table at
Della. Or rather what I could see of her, which was roughly the
front two thirds of the pumpkin. She was rubbing it ruminatively
with both hands, but then she had just put away a pretty decent
pile of dinner for someone whose stomach must be squeezed in
behind her lungs. She had definitely had three kinds of pie. Anyway,
she wasn't the only one rubbing their belly and *she* wasn't groaning.

'OK,' she said when a lull came in the conversation. 'Does
anyone have any plans for the rest of the evening?'

'Anything you want,' Dylan said, but then ruined it by saying,
'Fortnite?' He does keep trying.

'Charades?' said Todd, but his heart wasn't in it. He only plays charades with costumes and he had eaten too many slices of skinless turkey breast, green beans with the cream wiped off, and pie-insides minus the pastry to go struggling into form-fitting fancy-dress right now. And he doesn't have any other kind. So many catsuits, so few kaftans.

'Poker?' said Noleen. She keeps trying too.

'Twister?' said Diego. Oh, to have the constitution of a seven-year-old.

'Wingspan?' said Taylor.

'What's that?' piped up Bob, one of Meera's kids.

'You draw a hand of bird cards and compete to build a habitat for them,' Taylor said. He is weird about anything with feathers.

Kathi doesn't blow raspberries because of the threat of droplet dispersal, but on this occasion she didn't frown when Noleen blew a doozy.

'What do *you* want to do, Della?' Todd said.

'Well,' said Della, 'I'm pretty sure I'm in labour so I thought I'd have a baby.'

No one said a word. We had all been scolded and mocked so roundly for failing to stay calm and thereby making it harder for Della to stay calm, and impossible for Dylan to get within a mile of calm, that we couldn't navigate to a new stage of being.

'Wh-what would you like us to do, Della?' I said.

'Huh?' said Della. 'Didn't you hear what I just said. I'm having the baby. I want you to panic, of course. Come on, people! It's time to freak out. Let's go!'

No sooner said than done. Well, Roger uncoiled himself from his chair, did a couple of hamstring stretches and switched his phone off. But he was the only one. Todd galloped up the stairs to his room taking them three at a time, I assume to change into the midwife outfit he had no doubt picked out weeks ago. Taylor downed a glass of wine in one gulp and started choking. José and Maria leapt up, grabbed one of Della's hands each and started firing Spanish at her like a pair of machine guns. I couldn't tell if it was blessings, prayers, advice, or demands that she stop the nonsense and go to the ER. Noleen and Kathi, both headed somewhere fast, bounced off each other's fronts like clowns.

Meera and Arif tried to stop Bob and his sister Joan re-enacting it before one of them cracked a skull. Diego stood up on his chair and started shouting, 'I get to choose the name. I get to choose the name.' I hadn't heard about any such agreement and I couldn't decide whether it was typical seven-year-old self-absorption to open negotiations right now, or typical Diego genius to know that Dylan and his mommy might agree to anything just to get him to stop shouting.

'Sure, sure, sure,' Dylan said.

'Dylan said "sure",' Diego shouted. 'Everyone heard him.' The kid was going to end up running the world.

'What are you going to call it, honeybun?' I asked.

'Tomash, if it's a boy,' said Diego.

'Tomash? With an SH?' I said.

'He's the manager of Beroe Stara Zagora,' Diego explained. Or so he probably thought.

'Bulgarian soccer team,' Dylan actually explained. 'Cool. Tomash. Strong name.'

Because when I said Roger was the only person not panicking as requested, I had forgotten someone: Dylan was suddenly as calm as a painting of lilies.

'And if it's a girl?' I said.

'Chihiro,' said Diego.

'You can't call a baby Churro,' I said. 'No matter how much you love churros. I love pork pies, but if I ever had a kid, I'd have to look past it.'

'Chi-hi-ro,' said Diego.

'Chihiro Ogino,' Dylan explained. Or so he probably thought.

'From *Spirited Away*,' said Taylor. 'Anime classic. Good name, Diego. Bold choice. Lucky baby.'

'You,' I told him, 'are perfect in every way.' And I got away with it because no one, not even Taylor, was listening.

The panic subsided pretty quickly and before long it was just Taylor, Diego and me left on the forecourt. Arif and Meera had taken their kids home, José and Maria had gone to church to pray, Noleen and Kathi had gone to the owners' flat to google 'homebirth' which was their version of praying, and Roger, Dylan and Della had gone to my boat with Todd in tow. He had changed into lavender scrubs and removed all studs and rings from his many piercings. Roger, in contrast, was rolling his sleeves up as they went round the end of the motel but otherwise looked ready to sacrifice a lot of cashmere.

'Where do you want to sleep, baby boy?' I asked Diego. 'Understanding that "alone in your room" isn't an option. You can come and sleep with me or I can come and sleep with you. Or I can sleep through the open door in your mommy's room. Or you can go in with Gramma Nolly and Gramma Kathi.'

'Can I sleep on the boat with Mama and Dylan?'

'Not tonight,' I said. 'Tomorrow you can sleep on the boat with Mama and Dylan and Tomash or Chihiro. But not tonight.'

'Can I sleep in your bed? In the middle? And we can watch a film that Mama wouldn't let me watch? Like *Pan's Labyrinth*? Because I won't be scared because you're there?'

'Not *Pan's Labyrinth*.' He does have eyes bigger and darker than cups of espresso viewed from above and he knows how to work them too, but I'm not a complete pushover.

'*Jaws*?'

'Nope.'

'*The Nightmare Before Christmas*?'

'Um, OK.'

'Wait though. I meant *On Elm Street*.'

'Absolutely not.'

'Can I carry you into our room, Diego?' said Taylor.

Diego agreed. Taylor lifted him up, draped him over one shoulder and meandered roughly in the direction of Room 103, bouncing a little as he went and singing softly. Diego was gone before I opened the door.

It was surprisingly easy to get to sleep with a sugar-drunk seven-year-old tossing and turning and twisting up the blankets in between us. I was only awake for long enough to hear Taylor start to snore gently and then I was off, dreaming of a shipwreck and needing to make a lifeboat out of bath sheets but they were all in the wash, which I took to be anxiety about what was happening on board and an undertone of worry about what exactly people used all the towels for during a birth, along with a hope that Della had set herself up with her own and wasn't currently leaking all over mine.

It wasn't the dream that woke me though. It was a noise, and a very odd one. My first thought was that I'd heard the sound it makes when you punch your hand into a bowl of raw risen dough. DOOFT! That kind of thing, but louder. My eyes snapped open and in the light from my phone on the bedside table I saw the glint of Taylor's eyes, also wide. We stared at each other over Diego's tousled head on the pillow between us.

'What the hell was that?' Taylor whispered.

'I have no idea,' I whispered back.

Then we heard another sound, one that took no puzzling out at all. From behind the motel, drifting in the open bathroom window came the distant shriek of a freshly disturbed and mightily pissed-off brand-new tiny human.

THREE

Friday 27 November

Diego could have smashed his piggybank, spent every cent inside it, and still not been able to *rent* a toss about a new baby at three o'clock in the morning. He flailed and moaned as Taylor carried him round the side of the motel and up the steps to the porch of the houseboat. 'Noooo! Leee me loooone! Dormiiiiidoooooh!' So we laid him down on a couch in the living room and, even though that meant we had no excuse to go breenging in, in we breenged. Well, Taylor barged because he doesn't know what 'breenge' means but I breenged like a pro.

'It's only us,' I said in my meekest voice, peeping round the door of my spare bedroom, half-hunched over, as if walking in a permanent bow meant I wasn't really poking my nose in minutes after the baby drew its first breath. Then I straightened up. Kathi and Noleen had beaten us to it and were sitting on either side of Della in the box-bed, gazing down at the dishevelled bundle in her arms. Roger and Todd were hugging and beaming off to the side. Dylan was leaning against the opposite wall looking . . . God, I would love to say proud and capable, but Dylan looked as if someone had just hit him over the head with a shovel and he hadn't quite passed out yet.

'You did it!' I said to Della. She was sweaty and knackered-looking with big purple bags under her eyes and hands-down the ugliest industrial bra that had ever been invented by an engineer who'd never met a woman, but her smile threatened to meet round the back, as she looked down into the bundle and then back at Taylor and me.

'No options,' she said. 'Nine months too late to take a different path.'

'She was amazing!' said Roger. 'Breathed her way through the whole thing. We could have gone for a burger and let her get on with it.'

'How are you feeling?' Taylor said. He had trained for this moment. *I* had trained him. We had agreed to ask three questions about Della before we homed in on the real star of the show. It's basic manners. It was my turn now.

'Can I see the baby?' I said. No one had trained me.

Kathi patted the bed near her legs; clearly she wasn't going to get up and give me her place. So I sidled in as close as I could and Della turned the bundle to face me.

It wasn't washed yet so it was still pretty waxy and blood-streaked and it had a huge blot of blood right in the middle of its downy forehead. Below that, two sets of tiny stumpy eyelashes were stuck together with God knows what and one crumpled little fist – the size, shape and colour of an overripe passion fruit – sat bunched under a button-sized chin.

'Awwwwww,' I said and I semi-meant it. 'What is it?'

'It's a baby, Lexy,' said Todd. 'Rude!'

'Bugger off,' I told him. 'Is it a boy or a girl?'

'It's a girl,' said Dylan. 'Chihiro Muelenbelt.'

'And you're raising her Hindu?' It was a pretty decent joke, I reckoned, because that blood splot really did look like a bindi. And Todd had cracked a joke already so I assumed we were being ourselves. So I was kind of surprised at the gasp of shock that ran round the room.

Noleen turned from gazing at the baby and said, 'The hell is wrong with you?'

'What?' I said.

'She's perfect,' said Kathi.

'What? I never said she wasn't!'

'She's the most beautiful baby I've ever seen,' said Todd.

'What? I didn't say otherwise!'

'A stork bite is lucky,' said Kathi.

'She's been kissed by angels,' said Noleen.

'And if you say different,' said Todd, 'so help me God, I will cut you.'

'*What?*' I said. 'What are you all banging on about?'

'Leagsaidh,' said Roger. And he really did call me 'Leagsaidh'. I can always tell. 'Nevi or haemangioma are harmless and quick to fade. The only negative aspect of this perfectly normal occurrence is that sometimes, some under-evolved, thoughtless, or plain mean people can ask intrusive questions and make inappropriate jokes.'

'Seriously,' I said. 'What?'

'Chi-chi has a strawberry birthmark and you're an idiot,' Todd said.

But here's the thing. Della hadn't heard what I'd said. She hadn't been listening. If the rest of them hadn't scolded me so thoroughly she'd have been none the wiser. And she almost missed it even at that, on account of being more bothered about stopping 'Chi-chi' before it took hold than whatever I had been wittering on about.

But not quite. 'Wait,' she said. 'Stork bite? Angel kiss? Strawberry birthmark?' She rounded on Roger. That's to say, her eyes swivelled his way. She was too exhausted to move anything else. 'You said it was a—'

'Nevus,' said Roger. 'It is. It will be gone before you know it.'

'A birthmark,' said Della. 'Bad luck.'

'Nope,' said Kathi. 'Incredibly good luck. Like . . .'

'Being shat on by a pigeon?' I said.

'Or a four-leaf clover,' said Noleen. 'Maybe. Huh? Leagsaidh?' She was at it too.

'Sorry,' I said. But I'd done *some* good. I'd kick-started Dylan. He pushed himself up off the wall, lifted the baby out of Della's arms and said, 'She doesn't need luck. She's got me.' Then he looked down and started crying big hot soppy tears right onto her face, which woke her up and made her wave her arms and legs and wail like a siren for milk, or a bath, or for everyone to get out.

Della clapped her hands on the cups of the horrific bra and motioned for Dylan to hand the baby back over. 'Before I burst,' she said.

Which seemed like our cue to go. 'Leave Diego where he is,' Dylan said. 'We want him to be here when he wakes up. He should meet her.' So it was just Taylor and me who made our way back round to the motel, with Kathi and Noleen following.

'Makes you think,' Noleen said.

'Sure does,' said Kathi.

That was about as philosophical as they ever got.

'I've never seen a brand-new baby before,' said Taylor.

'Me neither,' I said. 'Did everyone really think she was cute? Now it's just us. I mean, she was . . . small. And small is kind of automatically cute, but . . .'

Noleen poked me hard in the back. 'What a night to find out your friend is a sociopath,' she said. 'Of course, she's really cute. Babies are cute even when they're ugly. Even when they look like Alfred Hitchcock. Chihiro is extra-extra cute. Jeez, Lexy.'

'Kathi?' I said.

'She was filthy and stinky and you missed the part where a little bit of meconium came out, Lexy, and still I could have eaten her up like a Cinnabon.'

'Huh,' I said. I didn't want to know what meconium was or where it had come out of. As we emerged into the security lights of the motel forecourt, I turned and winked at Taylor. 'Looks like it's just us.'

'It's just you, Lex,' Taylor said. 'I thought she was more adorable than a duckling.'

'Huh,' I said again. 'Oh well.'

'Oh well?' said Noleen. 'You think it doesn't matter that you're missing a core piece of basic humanity? The urge to nurture and care for a helpless infant? How do you think the species survived the savannah? I'll tell you. Because there were plenty of us and not too many of you.'

Now this was going a bit far, in my opinion. 'It's not as if I'm saying she's the spawn of Satan,' I said. 'Stop over-reacti—' But there was that gasp again, just like before. 'What have I said now?' I might have sounded whiny; it was after three o'clock in the morning and everyone was ganging up on me.

'Angel's kiss,' said Noleen. 'Or stork bite. Or strawberry birth-mark. Or even nevus. Or that other thing Roger said. But you will *not* call that sweet little dot on that sweet little girl's head the mark of the devil around me and live to say it twice. OK?'

'Oh for God's sake,' I said. 'I didn't say anything of the sort!'

'Because did you hear Della fretting about bad luck?' said Kathi.

'And have you heard of baby blues?' added Noleen.

'I've studied post-partum depression, actually,' I said, reaching for haughty.

'Well, someone musta graded that class on a curve,' said Noleen.

'I'm just surprised at you two gushing over a baby like this,' I said.

'Why?' said Kathi, with a warning note in her voice.

'Because I'm an idiot,' I said.

'Damn straight,' said Noleen. 'To make up for it, how about you do room service in the morning? If I'm disturbed while I'm trying to sleep I can get cranky.'

I bit my lip on the observation that she couldn't have had a decent night's sleep in the entire eighteen months I had known her, because she had been in a bad mood every single day, like she was constantly at the cursing-the-world stage of having just stubbed her toe.

'Room service?' I said.

'Added value,' said Kathi. 'Getting the business back. The guy in Room 102 wants coffee and scrambled eggs at seven.'

'It will be my pleasure,' I said. 'Where are the eggs?'

'In your fridge or at the market,' said Noleen and ushered Kathi in the owners' flat door.

What is it with Americans and eggs? Don't get me wrong – a fried egg is one of the ten constituent parts of a good cooked breakfast where I come from, but not by any means the main event. If that song, you know the one, had arisen in the folk tradition of *my* land, the answer to the question 'How D'ya Like Your Eggs in the Morning' wouldn't have mentioned kisses. And the song would never have been a hit because trying to fit 'with some bacon, sausage, black pudding, tattie scones, beans, tomatoes, fried bread, haggis and mushrooms, please' into a rhyme scheme would have killed it dead.

But over here, everyone starts with eggs and adds on this and that as optional extras. So, gazing into Della's eggless fridge at half six the next morning, I knew I couldn't blag my way through my room service gig with hot toast and butter. I would have to hit the Lode and buy a dozen.

Well, it would give me a chance to lay in some balloons and flowers and one of those really expensive bumpy cards you have to put extra stamps on. I had some serious making up to do after my moronic gaffes the night before, even if Noleen's dark warnings about Della's mental health were a total over-reaction. I kissed Taylor's head, the only bit of him showing over the bedclothes, and let myself out into a beautiful pink and gold morning; Chihiro Muelenbelt's first whole day on this earth full of people who were climbing over themselves to love her.

I made a decent fist of the eggs, even if I say so myself. They weren't bobbles in water and they weren't snot; they were pillowy mounds of glossy fluff and the coffee was scalding hot and black as sin. I balanced the tray in one hand – the Ditch would have to spring for some baker's trays if Noleen was serious about room service – and tapped gently on the door with the other, calling out 'Breakfast!' in a Fifties house-wife sort of way.

Silence.

'Room service!' I called. Shouted really, I suppose. And my tap turned into a smart knock.

Silence.

'Hey!' I shouted into the hinge. 'Your scrambled eggs and coffee are ready and I'm coming in.' I manhandled the master key out of my back jeans pocket and unlocked the door. 'Sir?' I said, which was more than he deserved, in my opinion. If Night-Time You is going to ask someone to get up at the crack of dawn on Thanksgiving Boxing Day, then Next-Morning You needs to follow through on it. This guy evidently didn't agree. He was out for the count, lying flat on his back with his arms flung wide. He wasn't snoring – I'll give him that – and few are the men of his size who can sleep flat on their backs quite so quietly.

'Sir?' I said again. He really was most extraordinarily silent. And very motionless. I put the tray down on the table by the window and tiptoed closer to the bed. 'I'll just leave it there then,' I said, when I was not quite close enough to see his face. I told myself I didn't want to recognize him if I ran into him later. That's what I told myself. I even took care to close the door quietly and turn the key without any clunking.

It was a shame about the eggs, though. So I let myself into the office at one end of the horseshoe and slipped behind Noleen's counter. There were lots of things I didn't know how to do with her hotel reception switchboard. (It was so out of date it barely qualified as a computer, although technically it was manipulated by pushing buttons rather than throwing switches and plugging in jacks.) But over the months I had picked up how to call a room. I lifted the handset, cradled it into my neck and called Room 102. It was probably better this way, I told myself. He would wake up to the sound of the telephone and I could say, 'Your breakfast is on the table, sir.' Smooth and professional.

The phone was ringing. I cleared my throat ready to speak to him.

And then, well, who knows? I wasn't aware of time passing. I wasn't even fully aware of the sound of the phone ringing in my ear. I was just . . . waiting.

Taylor throwing the office door open and barging in jolted me back to life. 'Nol—' he said, bleary-eyed and gravel-voiced. Then, 'Oh! Lexy. Listen, can you hang up and call the guy in the room next to us? His phone's been going for five solid minutes and he's not answering. He must be in the shower.'

That was it! In the time it took me to get from his room to the office and put the call through, he had woken up, not noticed the breakfast tray and gone for a nice, long, hot, noisy shower. Of course!

'Although, I can't hear the water,' Taylor said, shaking his head as if to chase off the last wisps of sleep. 'Maybe he checked out. Can you kill the call from the switchboard?'

'Yup,' I said, and hung up the phone. 'That should do it.'

Taylor put his head out into the forecourt and listened for a moment. 'Cool,' he said, and yawned. 'I'm going back to bed. You coming?'

I could go back to bed. That was certainly an option. I could lie in Taylor's arms and drift off to sleep. I could wake again in a few hours in a different world. Maybe.

Or maybe not.

'We should look in on him,' I found myself saying. 'Make sure he's OK.'

'Why?' said Taylor. Then, 'Wait, weren't you supposed to be making him breakfast? Good thing he checked out early.' He yawned again and started scratching his belly through his T-shirt. 'He might have ended up giving Noleen a one-star rating for missing eggs.'

'Taylor,' I said, 'can you stop saying "checked out", please?'

Taylor is a morning person. Probably all ornithologists are, because what would be the point of rocking up at the hide just before lunch to find nothing but splats of poop and a few stray feathers. Still, we'd had a big dinner and a trip to the boat at three o'clock in the morning and he had just been rudely awakened. So it was only now that he stopped yawning and scratching and, instead, actually looked at me.

'Are you OK?'

'I'm not sure,' I said. 'I'm kind of hoping not. I'm kind of hoping I'm having a waking nightmare or a hallucination or something.'

'What?'

I came out from behind the counter and beckoned for him to follow me. Then I locked the office and walked with all the purpose I could muster, to Room 102. I put the master key back in the door.

'Hang on,' Taylor said. 'Shouldn't you knock and shout "Housekeeping". He might not have checked out after all.' I moaned. 'Sorry! But he might be on the john with the door open, or dancing around in a bowtie and nothing else.'

I had the door open now and I gestured for Taylor to go in ahead of me. The air smelled of eggs and coffee and something else. And it was so quiet. I could hear Taylor breathing and I could hear my own heart beating, but that was it.

I took Taylor's hand and together we stepped forward to the bedside.

'*That* isn't a bindi,' I said. 'Or even a strawberry birthmark.'

'No,' said Taylor. 'That's a bullet hole.'

'That's what I thought,' I said. 'You were right. He checked out, didn't he?'

FOUR

'I'm sorry,' Noleen said. She was sitting beside me in the plastic chairs just outside the office door, the place we were using as a lounge, months after the lockdown lifted because it still wasn't a great idea to cuddle up indoors.

I looked down at my hand, which Noleen was chafing between hers. I didn't think I'd ever had my hand chafed before. It was the sort of thing that only happened in Victorian novels. Like being picked up by the scruff of your neck and thrown out of a window only happened in cartoons.

'What have you got to be sorry for?' I said. 'You weren't to know.'

'I should have known,' Noleen said. 'We've talked about it often enough.'

'*You've* talked about it often enough,' Kathi said. She was on my other side but she wasn't chafing my other hand, because she didn't have any disinfectant wipes to run over my skin before she touched me. 'You talked and I begged you not to because it wasn't a real possibility.'

'And yet here we are,' said Noleen. 'Lexy, can I get you a cup of coffee? Slice of pie?'

'Slice of *pie*?'

'It's breakfast time the day after Thanksgiving,' said Taylor. 'It's in the constitution. You gotta have a slice of pie.'

'I can't imagine eating anything ever again as long as I live,' I said. Whenever I shut my eyes, even to blink, all I could see was his face, mouth slack, eyes not quite shut, and that fathomless black hole in the middle of his forehead looking like a portal to hell.

'You're only saying that,' said Todd, 'because you've never seen a gastric feeding tube.'

'Jesus,' said Kathi, but his instincts were good and I managed a gruff laugh.

'That's better,' Todd said. 'So. Go for broke? Cherry?'

This time Noleen laughed; she's got a pretty sick sense of humour. 'Key lime,' I said. 'I might need to work up to red food.'

Todd bustled off to his fridge where all the last course leftovers had been stashed, on account of his claim that he'd be able to resist sugar in the night, unlike turkey wings. I hadn't said there was more sugar in the glaze on that turkey than in half the pies anyway. I had thought it though.

After he'd gone, the rest of us sat in silence except for Noleen saying yet again, 'And not a word to Della, right?' as if one of us might have had a rethink after we'd agreed to it the first four times she gave it an airing.

'Right,' said Kathi.

'Because there's no such thing as luck,' said Noleen. 'Good or bad.'

'Right,' said Taylor.

And then we sat in silence for real as we watched the coroner's van idling at the open door of Room 102. Somewhere beyond that door, Sergeant Molly Rankinson of the Cuento PD detective unit was having the worst imaginable trip down memory lane. She had lived in one of our rooms for six weeks in the spring, so she had laid her head in an identical bed to the one where the dead guy had laid his so very finally.

'That fucker,' said Noleen. 'Not to speak ill of the dead. But when he was alive and he didn't want to be alive and he decided he'd come to *my* motel and put a bullet in his head and ask for freaking room service to make sure we found him? That was some grade-A fuckery.'

'Poor guy,' I said. 'But yeah.'

'Although,' said Taylor, 'how *would* you do it? You can't let your family find you. It's not fair to the commuters to throw yourself on the railroad tracks.'

'Or the driver,' said Kathi.

'Jumping off a bridge, or a cliff?' I said. 'Shame for the RNLI, mind you.'

'The who?' said Noleen.

'Coast Guard Auxiliaries,' Taylor explained.

'I think if you want to kill yourself,' Noleen said, 'you should feed yourself to hogs. No mess, no clean up, respects the food chain, good for the planet.'

'You can't be serious,' I said. 'What about the people who buy the bacon?'

'Ignorance is bliss.'

'You're insane,' Kathi told her.

'OK,' said Noleen. 'What's your bright idea?'

'Pretty much what he did,' said Kathi. 'With two amendments. He can shoot himself in the head in a motel room, by all means, if he leaves enough cash for a professional cleaning.'

'What?' I said. 'You wouldn't trust a professional cleaner to take care of a crime scene. Would you?' Maybe, I thought, she was getting better.

'Of course not,' Kathi said. 'But they could go in and get the place clean enough for me to go in and clean it.'

'I don't understand how he didn't wake everyone up,' Noleen said. 'It's not the Ritz round here but it's not so sketchy that we sleep through gunfire.'

As she spoke, a thought formed in my mind and I looked over at Taylor to see if it was forming in his too. It wasn't. It had formed. He was staring at me aghast.

Kathi didn't notice the looks on our faces as she kept talking. 'And the second amendment, no pun intended, is he shouldn't have arranged for someone to come in and find him.' She was facing away from the activity around Room 102, so she didn't notice what was going on behind her. She kept speaking, unawares. 'He should have pinned a note to the door. "Call The Cops". That would have been the polite thing to do instead of grossing out innocent bystanders.' She had completely failed to read the expressions on all of our faces, or even the throat-slashing gesture Noleen was frantically signalling.

'What about grossing out innocent cops?' said Molly, from two inches behind Kathi's head.

'You signed up for corpses when you took the badge,' Kathi said, recovering quickly. 'Lexy's a psychotherapist. She only signed up for whining. And I run a laundromat. I top out at lint.'

'Enh,' said Molly. She sat down beside us and let her breath go in a long creaking groan. 'It would have been kind of dumb anyway. If you just shot someone and got away with it, you're not going to stop at the door and pat your pockets for a thumb tack. Give some witness the chance to think "Say, what's that suspicious individual doing over there?", are you?'

We all frowned. Taylor spoke. 'Huh?'

'Huh, what?' said Molly. 'Pinning the note before the deed was done would be even dumber.'

'Wait, huh?' said Noleen. 'Who stopped at the door? What are you talking about?'

'Huh?' said Molly. It was catching. 'I'm talking about that dead guy in your motel room over there. Boy, you must be having a busy morning if that dropped off the radar.'

'I think what they mean,' Kathi said, 'is why are you talking about someone walking away? Isn't it a suicide?'

'Oh sure,' said Molly. 'It *could* be a suicide.' She paused. 'With an invisible gun.' She paused again. 'But I'm leaning towards murder with a visible gun that someone took away when they left, I'll be honest with you. So. Security cameras any better around here, Mrs Muntzes?' Kathi scowled. It was a fair enough mode of address – she was Mrs Muntz and so was Noleen – but put them together and it sounded like a wind-up. 'I'm guessing there are no witnesses. We can't say for sure until we do the autopsy, but the doc there thinks it was the middle of the night sometime. Kinda weird no one heard it, as one of my guys just said. But then he doesn't know about *you* guys's drinking.'

It was time for me to talk. It was past time, actually. I glanced at Taylor to see if he would rather speak up instead. He looked away.

'Three a.m.,' I said. 'It was three a.m. We heard it.'

'It was three a.m.,' said Taylor, getting in on the act now I'd done the hard bit. 'And he used a silencer.'

I squeezed my eyes shut. That sound! That sound I thought was a fist going into a bowl of dough. It echoed through my head for the thousandth time.

'You sure?' said Molly. 'You look at the clock?'

'Not immediately,' I said. 'I heard a funny noise – we both did – and we woke up. And we were just wondering what it was and waiting to see if there was going to be any more, and then the baby started crying.'

'Baby?' said Molly. And then, 'Oh hey, Della had her baby? When?'

It was November and we were outside and none of us had eaten. So there were lots of reasons for the sudden attack of shivers that ran round the four Ditchers as we sat there.

'Three a.m. last night,' said Taylor.

'One goes out, one comes in,' said Kathi.

'But not a freaking word to Della,' said Noleen. 'And Molly? That includes you.'

Of course Molly needed to grill Taylor and me for another twenty minutes before she was done. She got rid of Noleen and Kathi and then set to worrying us like a terrier with a new chew toy.

'What did you think the noise was?' she asked us. We explained that Taylor thought it was an inflatable with a ripcord, in contrast to my bowl of dough.

'How the hell do you know what punched dough sounds like?' said Molly. 'Does it even make a noise?' Like there were automatic inflatables going up like pufferfish at the Ditch on a random evening.

'Yes, it makes a noise,' I said. 'Just not a loud one. So, you know, silencer.'

She breathed in and out a few times as if she'd learned it as a technique on a course, but she moved on without a follow-up. What else did we hear? Neither of us heard anything. Not a door, not a step, not a car starting. And certainly when we got outside minutes later with a comatose Diego, we didn't see anything.

'Which is why I thought it was suicide,' I said.

'Suicides don't shoot themselves in the middle of the forehead,' said Molly. 'They shoot themselves in the temple or through the roof of the mouth.'

'Hercule Poirot shot himself dead centre,' I informed her.

She made a clicking noise in one side of her mouth and cocked a finger pistol at me. 'Good point,' she said. 'But he was OCD about symmetry, wasn't he? And what was the other thing . . .? Oh yeah. He was fictional.'

'So do you think it was a professional hit?' said Taylor. 'Silenced weapon, silent assassin.'

'You mean like a cat burglar?' said Molly. 'You've been watching too many cop shows. Anyway, nothing about the vic says "mob hit" to me.'

'Who was he?' I said, to make her stop scoring points off my boyfriend.

'I ask the questions,' Molly said. She glanced down at her notebook, scowled and said nothing.

'Was your next question going to address who he was?' I said.

She scowled harder and twisted her mouth in an effort to think up an alternative. I saw it hit her brain when it came. God, I hope she doesn't play poker. 'So did you have any dealings with Mr Lassiter over the course of yesterday?'

Taylor snorted.

'Wow,' I said. 'That was masterful. I don't think either of us noticed you sliding his name in there. I know I didn't. Did you, Taylor?'

'Not me,' Taylor said. 'How did you do that, Molly? That can't be taught.'

She waited us out, saying nothing.

'I didn't meet him,' I said, eventually. 'I suggested to Noleen that we should maybe invite him to join us for dinner – we had enough to feed an extra twenty – but she told me he had already declined.'

'Weird thing to do on Thanksgiving,' said Taylor. 'Seems like he must have been a strange kind of guy.'

'Oh he was a very strange guy when it came to Thanksgiving,' Molly said. 'We know that.'

'I don't think that's fair,' I said. 'He told Noleen he was tired from driving and he was going to bed for an early night. Besides . . .'

'Besides what?' said Molly.

'Nothing,' I said. 'It's normal to sleep when you're tired.'

'Some chance of that,' Molly said. 'With you all squawking and baying right outside his door.' It sounded heartfelt; in the spring when Molly was living here she had spent quite a few nights in her room doing paperwork, occasionally coming out on to the walkway to rant at us about noise ordinances and official warnings.

'I wondered about that when Diego started shouting,' I said. 'But Noleen said the guy had assured her he had noise-cancelling headphones and an ocean-sounds download. Hey!'

'Yup,' said Molly. 'Mrs Muntz reported that conversation to me too.'

'Where were they?' I said. 'He wasn't wearing a set of Bosies when I saw him this morning. Taylor, were they on the floor by the bed?'

'They could have been,' Taylor said. 'I didn't look. Or I would have known the gun was missing.'

'They weren't,' said Molly. 'So this cat burglar of yours is more likely an opportunist thief, Mr Aaronovitch.'

'I didn't say "cat burglar",' Taylor pointed out. 'You said "cat burglar".' But he *had* said silent assassin, so I wasn't going to bat for him.

'Since you've moved on to this morning anyway, Lexy,' Molly said, then she paused. 'When did you and Mr Aaronovitch find Mr Lassiter?'

'Seven twenty,' said Taylor.

'Talk me through it,' said Molly.

'We opened his door and went in and saw him and called you,' Taylor said.

'Yeah, great. I figured. But what I meant is talk me through how you two ended up busting in to the guy's room with the master key four hours and twenty minutes after you heard the shot. Right away, I can see. If you had put your brains into commission and ruled out a lifeboat and a . . . I still don't buy that dough thing. So that would track. Or I could see someone busting in after a day or two when things got nasty. But why then? What made you think he was in trouble? You did think he was in trouble, right? You didn't bust in for some other reason, did you? I mean, this place had its quirks when I was here, but Mr Lassiter was a paying guest, right?'

'Um,' I said. 'We did bust in because we thought – at least, I thought – Mr Lassiter was in trouble. Or maybe, actually, that his troubles were all over.'

Taylor said nothing, but he shot me a look out of the side of his eye that evidently spoke volumes to Molly.

'Just tell me,' she said. 'Don't make me wear you down, Lexy.'

I resented that and considered telling her as much, but I've been worn down by Molly before. To a nubbin. And it's best avoided if you can manage it.

'I took him his breakfast,' I said.

'Business that bad?'

'As a favour to Noleen, not for wages. He had requested eggs and coffee at seven a.m. and I obliged.'

'Seven twenty, you said.' Molly thumbed back through her notebook.

'No,' I told her. 'Seven. I got up at six to do it. And at seven I tried to wake him. I failed.'

'Yeah you would.'

'So I went in and put the tray down and called his name a couple of times and then left.'

Molly frowned. 'You went in at seven? And you didn't call me? You got Mr Aaronovitch instead and showed him the corpse?'

'It wasn't like that. I couldn't wake the guy up. So I went to the office to phone his room. Who sleeps through a ringing telephone, right?'

'Same people who sleep through bangs on the door and strangers at their bedside,' said Molly. 'Corpses.'

'But it rang and rang,' I said. 'And then Taylor came to the office.'

'Because the phone had been ringing for like five solid minutes,' Taylor said. 'And I wanted Noleen to kill the call. I had banged on the wall with my shoe already and that didn't work.'

'Corpses,' said Molly, shaking her head. 'I tell you.'

'And when Taylor arrived,' I said, 'I kind of woke up and got past the stage of denial and faced what I had seen. Or not seen, exactly, because it was low light. But heard. Or rather not heard. Him breathing. You know.'

'I do,' said Molly. 'I've seen corpses before and not one of them ever breathes worth a damn. So. You went into the room, saw the corpse, left the room, told no one, phoned the room, let the phone ring for five minutes, and then took Mr Aaronovitch to view the corpse. Then finally called the cops.'

'No,' I said. 'I didn't take Taylor to view the corpse. I took Taylor to see if the guy in Room 102 was OK. Totally different thing.'

'Yeah but, babe,' said Taylor. I do wish he wouldn't call me babe in front of other people. 'That's not true, is it?' Molly's eyebrows went up as mine came thundering down, like they were playing on a seesaw, the four of them. 'Because I was saying "maybe he's checked out" and you said "please stop saying 'checked out'", remember? And I asked if you were OK and you said you didn't think you were and you thought you were having some kind of psychotic break, remember?'

'No, I do not!' I said. 'I might have said nightmare or flashback or something. I did not say I was having a psychotic break.'

'Flashback to what?' said Molly.

'Nothing,' I said. Then I shut my mouth so completely that it made a smacking sound.

'So you remember Ms Campbell claiming she was having an episode of psychosis, Mr Aaronovitch? An episode which would explain why she didn't react to finding Mr Lassiter's body. But you now deny making this claim, Ms Campbell?'

'Wait, what?' said Taylor. 'What do you mean "claim"? This is all getting a little too . . . should Lexy get a lawyer?'

'I don't need a lawyer,' I said.

'Boy, if I had a dollar for every time I've heard that,' said Molly.

'I wasn't making claims,' I said. 'I was grasping at straws. Any way to account for how still he was and why he wouldn't wake up, without having to say he was dead. I can't explain it. I just went into a retreat from reality. Briefly. It's over now. I'm fine. I get it. Menzies Lassiter is dead. No biggie. We've all got to go sometime.'

There was a long silence. Not a dead silence like in Menzies's room, though. This was a whistling, susurrating silence, filled with the sound of Taylor breathing and Molly making notes with her scratchy ballpoint pen.

When she was finished, she looked up, smiled, and said, 'I didn't tell you his first name.'

'Did-didn't you?' I said. 'I'm sure you did.'

'She didn't,' said Taylor. 'Did Noleen tell you? Sometime this morning?'

'Uhh,' I said.

'Or last night after he checked in?'

'No,' said Molly. 'She didn't. She couldn't have. He checked in under a false name. A ludicrously bogus false name, by the way – Klatshovk.'

I said nothing. I didn't know any lawyers and I couldn't afford one anyway, but at least I said nothing.

'Or let's start from here,' said Molly. 'Ms Campbell, what made you say that Mr Lassiter wasn't so strange for not caring that it was Thanksgiving yesterday?'

I said more nothing.

'And might it be related to the reason a name spelled "Men-zees" is pronounced "Ming-iss"? Thanks for that tip, by the way.'

'You're welcome,' I said. 'Yes, it is related. It wasn't Thanksgiving for Mr Klatshovk. What the hell kind of name is that supposed to be anyway? It sounds like an anagram.'

'How was it not Thanksgiving?' said Taylor. 'What else could it be?'

'Thursday,' I said.

'Huh?' said Taylor.

'He's not American. He's Scottish. He's from Edinburgh.'

'Yes, he is, isn't he?' said Molly. 'But Edinburgh is a big place, relatively speaking, isn't it? I mean, Scotland is an itty-bitty country, but the capital city isn't Dog Patch. So how do you know who he is, just from looking at his corpse in a hotel bedroom. Even twice.'

'Because,' I said, 'I recognized him. He's an ex-boyfriend. He was . . . sorry, Taylor but . . . he was my first love.'

FIVE

I t was so long ago that looking back seemed more like spying on an episode in another person's life than remembering a bit of my own. I was seventeen; Menzies was eighteen. I was just about to burst out of my hated down-the-street high school like I'd been fired out of a pistol; Menzies was progressing steadily and confidently through the sixth year at

the poshest of Edinburgh's many posh private schools. He had
floppy hair and baggy clothes; I had gelled spikes and skin-
tight spandex.

But we found each other anyway.

Looking back, I can see that I was his bit of rough. It would
have killed my mum to know that and I wish I'd taken the chance
to tell her. And what was Menzies to me? Quite simply, the first
boy who laughed because I was funny instead of laughing because
he was making fun of me. So I fell in love. Hard. Taking the
phone into the coat cupboard to talk to him without my mum
passing seventeen times on fake housekeeping errands hard.
Changing from my school uniform on the train en route to meet
him on a Friday afternoon even though he wore his, even the tie,
right through the pizza and pints that made up our typical
date hard. Most of all, keeping him away from my city, my house,
and my mother hard.

Not because I thought she would disapprove. Oh God no. But
because I knew she would approve so lavishly she might start
picking out curtain material for our starter home.

Of course it couldn't last. The not-meeting my mother, I mean.
That summer, one of his cousins got married and I was invited
along with him and his parents. I was a fixture in their house by
now: Menzies's charming friend from Dundee. 'Charming' the
way people say a house is charming, when what they mean is it
could do with ten grand spent on it but they're trying to be kind.
Or they're the estate agent and they need a sale.

I wanted to go. The wedding was in a stately home – actually
a country house hotel, but what did I know? – in the Borders.
But to get away for a weekend with 'a boy', my parents had to
vet him. Check him for motorbike accessories and offensive
tattoos, I'm guessing. So he came for tea.

The thing my mum couldn't forgive me for was letting her
think that motorbikes and tattoos were the issue. If I had even
said his name clearly enough for her to hear – Menzies – she'd
have known better. Menzies is a golden retriever in a basket by
the Aga name, a muddy green wellies in the porch name, a broke
this year so we're borrowing a house in Corsica for the summer
name. But, for some reason, when I told my mum I was going
to a Beastie Boys concert in Glasgow with a boy I'd met at

Alison's birthday party, I mumbled so badly she thought I'd said Wayne. And Wayne is a ferret cages out on the balcony because they go for your wee brother's asthma name, a pile of stinky trainers behind the door of the flat name, a broke again this year so we're borrowing our nana's neighbour's caravan at Berwick name.

So she didn't put any effort into the spread. It was Thursday and that meant egg and chips, with beans for my dad and me and peas for my mum, in case she farted at her book club. There was a bottle of sauce on the table, and a pot of tea, not to mention a plate of bread and butter. It was my favourite dinner of the week, ever since my mum had put a stop to fish fingers. That was the book club's fault too: those women could spritz a deli-bought sardine with lemon juice like there was no tomorrow, but a fish finger in a pan of oil? Fainting couches all round. Or at least a lot of sniffing and a plug-in Glade.

Give Menzies his due, he didn't raise an eyebrow when the directions I'd sent him brought him to the cul-de-sac at the top of the estate where my mum and dad's pride and joy of a chalet bungalow sat in its ring of pink gravel chips (easier than grass), its hanging baskets ablaze with trailing fuchsia.

'Come in,' I said. 'Em, can you take your shoes off?'

'Like Japan?' Menzies said, hopping about obligingly to tug off one and then the other scruffy brown brogue. 'Bugger it. I've got holes in both socks. Can I borrow slippers?'

My mum heard the last bit. The coarse language, the admission of threadbare poverty (she thought), and the threat of sharing verrucas and God knows what else with my dad via purloined footwear.

'Excuse me, Wayne,' she said, sweeping out of the kitchen in her Bisto apron, 'but please don't—' She stopped dead.

'Who's Wayne?' said Menzies, coming forward. 'Menzies Lassiter, Mrs Campbell. How d'you do?'

My mum was transfixed. Menzies was *so* tall and *so* posh, with his accent like melting toffee and his hair like . . . actually, more melting toffee . . . that she ground to a halt, as the store of disapproval and superiority she had been working up for Wayne, ever since she'd heard about this visit, washed so inappropriately over basically Hugh Grant standing large as life in her hallway.

'Lexy,' she said faintly. 'Why did you tell me your boyfriend was•called Wayne?'

'I didn't,' I told her. 'I didn't even say he was my boyfriend.'

'I *was* very nearly called Woolton,' Menzies said. 'After my grandfather's favourite horse. But they had to shoot it just before I was born and my father thought it was a bad omen.'

This sentence summed up Menzies's entire life. It also showed what a basically decent guy he was. And he *was*. Otherwise I couldn't have borne to be around anyone who sounded like such an absolute Bertie Wooster without even trying.

It had an electrifying effect on my mum. She whipped off the Bisto apron, smoothed her hair and came breezing forward with a second stab at a greeting delivered in a completely different voice. 'Welcome to our home, Menzies,' she said. 'We've heard so much about you.'

'Me and Wayne both, eh?' Menzies said.

'Mum,' I said. 'Is something burning?'

'If you'll excuse me, Menzies,' my mum said, standing with one hand on the kitchen door like a starlet in a *Carry On* film. 'I'll just go and see what I can rustle up for tea. Dinner. Supper. Ahem. Our evening meal.' Then she went stamping off into the back of the house, screeching for my dad as if her hair was on fire. 'Keith! Keith! Come and help me! What are we going to do?'

'She's um . . .' Menzies said.

'She is,' I agreed.

'So's mine. You've been lulled, Lexy. But wait till you see her at this bloody wedding. She always loses her mind at family dos. Thank God you'll be there to dilute her for me.'

My mum and dad combined couldn't work out how to turn chips and egg with beans or peas and a plate of bread and butter into a baron of beef, so we sat down twenty minutes later to the Campbell Family Thursday Night Special. Menzies hoovered it all down like any other teenage boy, lost points with my mum for making a butty, gained points with my dad for the same, and turned into even more of the ideal boyfriend as far as I was concerned by going straight to golf as a conversation opener. He was too posh for football; my dad was too not-posh-enough for rugby; darts and snooker would have been patronizing; curling and rowing would have been weird. Menzies knew all that somehow. 'I haven't been in Dundee since they added the new holes at Carnoustie,' he said. 'Have you had a round yet, Mr C?'

Of course, he had probably seen the golf bag in the hall and the gloves in the bowl on the hatstand, and besides that there's something creepy about any eighteen-year-old still at school who can converse so effortlessly with adult strangers – it's all a bit young Tories network to be true – but my dad had just made his own egg and chip butty using Menzies as cover and he was now an official goner, same as me.

'Have you always golfed?' he asked. 'Or just since you moved up here to its home?'

'Moved up . . .?' Menzies said. 'I live in Edinburgh.' He gave me an arch look. 'You've not exactly been boring everyone stiff going on about me, have you Lexy?'

'I think he means—' I began.

'I mean moved up to Scotland,' my dad said. 'You sound like a southerner to me.'

I had forgotten about that. If I'd remembered I wouldn't have given Noleen such a hard time once she rejoined Taylor and me sitting there in the lounge with Molly. Or at least I'd have known she didn't deserve the hard time I was giving her.

As things stood, I said, 'How come you didn't mention him checking in, Nolly?'

'Huh? I did. I told you he was there, didn't want to share our dinner and was looking for eggs at the crack of seven. I mentioned him plenty.'

Technically. 'You didn't tell me he was a compatriot.'

'Are you kidding?' said Noleen. 'I wouldn't dare tell you some English dude was a fellow countryman. After all the times you flayed me for saying Scottish and English were the same thing? I learned my lesson after the big Miriam Margolyes meltdown.'

'Menzies Lassiter is as Scottish as I am,' I said.

'No way,' Noleen said. 'Guy sounded like a reject from the royal family.'

I nodded. That was the perfect way to describe the sound of Menzies's voice. He only sounded Scottish – i.e. as if he'd inhaled a fly and was trying to hork it back up again – when he said 'loch' and 'Auchtermuchty'. Otherwise, reject royal was spot-on.

Unless he had done the northern equivalent of turning Mockney as the years went by. Moxburn, if you will. I wouldn't know. I hadn't spoken to him a single time since we broke up eight wild months after our first meeting. I hadn't laid eyes on him since I turned away on that dark rainy street and stumbled off, weeping.

It sounds more Gothic than it should. Of course it was dark; it was Scotland in winter. Ditto the rain. But the weeping was real. I remember hot tears mixing with cold raindrops on my cheeks, cheap eyeliner blinding me so that I stepped into a pothole puddle up to my ankle in my new strappy party shoes and had to throw them away.

It wasn't raining now, and Cuento in late November might see California natives muffled up like Nanook of the North, but it wasn't really cold either. Today my tears felt pretty much ambient temperature as they began to trickle down my face.

'Aw, honey,' said Kathi.

'He called me Scully,' I said.

'Like from *Monsters, Inc.*?' said Molly. 'Rude.'

'SCULL-y,' I said. 'And I called him Mulder. Because he signed up to do a degree in parapsychology and I told him it was bullshit.'

'And so you broke up?' said Taylor.

'Not over that,' I said. The trickling tears picked up a bit of speed and volume until they were coursing down my cheeks and plopping off my jaw into my lap.

'So, Lexy,' said Molly. 'You gotta appreciate that, under the circumstances, I have a lot of questions for you.' She was speaking very gently. It wouldn't have been an exaggeration to call it 'tenderly'. That's how hard I was crying.

'Yeah,' I said. 'I know. I get that. Can I have a couple of minutes to—'

'And plus she hasn't had any breakfast yet,' Noleen said, gesturing to Todd who was making his careful way back downstairs, tray laden with plates of pie, bowls of cream and the inevitable jug of mimosas.

'So long as you come in sometime this morning,' Molly said.

'Come in?' That dried my tears right up. 'Come in to the station?'

'Nothing to be alarmed about,' Molly said.

'Nothing to be alarmed about because it's not happening,' said Taylor. 'Lexy didn't kill this guy. We were both in bed asleep when we heard the shot. She has a rock-solid alibi, remember?'

'I don't need a rock-solid alibi,' I said. 'I haven't clapped eyes on Menzies for years. Is it weird that he died in the next room to where I was sleeping? Yes it is. Does that mean his death is anything to do with me? No it doesn't.'

'Oh come on!' Molly said. 'You're trying to tell me him being here is nothing to do with *you* being here? No offence, Mrs Muntzes, but this place isn't exactly a destination. You don't hear people on the plane from Heathrow saying, "If you've only got a week in California, don't miss the Last Ditch Motel in Cuento."'

'I'll come to the station,' I said. 'I've got nothing to hide and I want to help any way I can. I agree, Molly: this must have something to do with home one way or another.'

Home. As if saying the word had ripped open space-time, my phone buzzed in my back pocket. I checked the screen and had to suppress a sigh. It was my dad's number, which meant it was my mum. (She wouldn't upgrade her phone to anything that could cope with a video call. He would never call me.)

'Hi, Mum,' I said, dinking the button and plastering a smile on my face.

Todd stood up and made off. My mother is his Kryptonite.

'You sound tired,' my mum said, like she always does. She never seems to realize that I only sound tired because she's just phoned me. Taylor calls this a case of smelly nose. 'And you shouldn't wear that pink eyeshadow,' she added. 'It makes you look as if you've been crying.'

'I have been crying,' I said, thinking that plunging in and getting it over with was probably the easiest way through. 'Mum, do you remember Menzies Lassiter?'

'Do *you* remember Menzies Lassiter?' my mum said. 'Have you spared a thought for him all these years you've been running about with heaven knows who, eloping, divorcing, taking up with Whatsisname—'

'You know his name.'

'—Aaron.' She paused to let me correct her. She's hopeless at mind games. If she'd really got it wrong she would have breezed past and I'd have had to interrupt her. After a long silence, she carried on. 'Working in a phone shop, Lexy. I mean, I ask you.'

'Only for money,' I said. 'Mum, I'm taking you off video so the call doesn't drop while I'm walking.' When I was far enough away that Taylor wouldn't hear me, I said, 'He's an ornithologist. You know this, Mother.'

'Oh! Mother now, is it?' she said. Which is the sort of thing I thought people only said in Seventies sitcoms or Alan Bennett monologues. 'And there was Dr Brandon with his own practice. I've seen the photographs on the website, Lexy. That waiting room looked like a spa hotel.' She had loved my brief marriage to an American dentist and his blinding white teeth.

'He slept with his ex-wife before our first anniversary,' I reminded her.

'And Ross, with his own fleet.'

'Three vans, Mum. Which he uses to deliver more skunk than fruit and veg. You told me that. His name was in the paper.' She had clipped out the breathless court report from the *Dundee Courier* and sent it to me in my birthday card.

'And Simon. Isn't he in shipping now?'

'He's in ferries,' I said. 'He manages the bar on the CalMac Rothesay run. Do you go about saying "he's in shipping" when you're telling your knitting bee about the ones that got away?'

'Book club,' she said. She sighed a long, hefty sigh. 'And of course dear Menzies. A scientist. He's been on *Autumnwatch*, you know.'

'Eh?' I said. 'He's a parapsychologist, Mum. He's a huckster. What the hell was he doing on *Autumnwatch*?'

'Halloween special,' she told me. 'I tried to film it on your dad's phone to send it to you but it wouldn't go.'

Thank God my dad's phone didn't have enough juice to send a file that big.

'Anyway,' my mum said, 'I thought you might be interested to know that he's single again.'

'Couldn't be less interested if . . . Hang on, how do you know that? He didn't broadcast it in his telly segment, did he? Cheesy.'

'No of course not,' my mum said. 'He told me.'

'You ran into him? Recently?'

I had wandered all the way over to the chain-link fence around the swimming pool. I let myself in and tucked the phone under one ear while I lifted the long-handled scooper and started dredging last night's crop of fallen leaves off the surface of the water. It's always better to be doing something with my hands and half of my attention whenever my mum's about to say something infuriating. And I had a strong suspicion that today she was going to regale me with a lot of guff she'd told Menzies while he tried to get away from her on the street.

'Mum?' I said. 'I asked if you ran into him.'

'In a sense,' she said.

'In what sense?'

'In the sense of he came to the house to talk to your dad and me.'

'That is not a sense of running into someone.'

'Oh pick, pick, pick,' she said. And then, 'Lexy.'

'What?'

'I'm telling her now.'

It was one of her more annoying habits – and there are plenty to choose from – that she holds two conversations, one in the room and one down the phone, and makes zero effort to help you tell them apart.

'He came to see us, Lexy. *You* put it on speaker if you want it on speaker. If I start hitting buttons who knows what could happen. What a state he was in. She's not saying anything.'

'Mum, hand the phone to Dad and get him to put it on speaker. I want everyone at this end to hear this too.' I chucked the pool scooper down and beetled back over to where Molly and the others were waiting. 'My mum,' I said. 'Menzies has recently visited and he was – I quote – "in a state".'

'Why are you telling me?' my mum said. 'I just told you.'

'I'm telling Taylor and Noleen and Kathi and Molly,' I said.

'It's very rude to have two conversations at once,' said my mum. 'But yes, he was in a terrible state. He misses you, Lexy.'

'Eh?' It had been seventeen years, half a lifetime, since I stumbled away from Menzies and ruined my party shoes.

'He never stopped caring for you, you know.'

Molly was writing in her notebook. If pressed, I would imagine that she was writing 'dig around really deep between the mattress and the box spring and double-check for gun', because it was sounding more and more likely that Menzies had killed himself. It hung together as a story. If he had suffered some kind of early midlife crisis or mini-stroke and got a bee in his bonnet about a random ex-girlfriend from his schooldays, then he might just conceivably have decided to make the grand gesture of killing himself where she would know about it. There was only one puzzle about it. And it wasn't that much of a puzzle, if I was honest.

'Mum? How did he find me?'

'He was always such a clever boy.'

'Mum? What did you tell him?'

'Nothing!'

'Except?'

'I didn't tell him anything.'

'Judith,' said my dad.

'Dad, what did she tell him?'

'Keith!' said my mum. 'Lexy, I didn't tell him anything. I just told him you had got married and moved away but it didn't work out so you got divorced and you didn't have a job any more and you were living in temporary accommodation in a sewer.'

'Wow,' I said. 'Are you serious?'

'No, of course I didn't say that. I said you had moved to California where you were running your own successful business and living on board your yacht.'

I think I preferred the first one.

'But you didn't tell him where I live, did you?'

'No.'

'Judith.'

'Dad?'

'Keith!'

'She told him you lived at the Last Ditch Motel in Cuento, CA, round the back and over the slough.'

'Keith, how *could* you?'

'But you *did*.'

'There's such a thing as family loyalty, you know,' my mum said. And she said it without any irony whatsoever.

'Well, it might interest you to know that he came over,' I told her.

'Oh, Lexy! Oh I am glad! Oh where do you think you'll do it?'

Molly wasn't writing in her notebook any more. She was gesturing to me to hand over the phone.

'Do what?' Taylor said.

'Hold the wedding, I assume,' I told him, as I chucked the phone to Molly. 'Don't worry about it. Just let it wash over you.'

'I knew we should have told her,' Taylor said. We were planning a trip home for Christmas to break the happy news to my parents and let him see the old country.

Molly was talking, off speaker, in her best official voice. 'We can arrange a time that suits you, Mrs Campbell. But I will need to speak to you in some detail about Mr Lassiter's visit and anything he might have said about his plans.'

We could all hear my mum squawking.

'Or, if you'd rather, a police officer from your local area can come to the house and we'll listen in on a video call.'

The squawking got higher and faster. I could only imagine what my mum would make of the police at her door.

'Because he's dead,' Molly said. 'He *did* come here, and he checked into the motel and then he was murdered. So, as I'm sure you appreciate, we're keen to hear all about his recent movements. What? Yes, but I need to speak to you again afterwards to arrange a time.' She put the phone over her chest and beckoned to me. 'She needs a quick word. See if you can calm her down. Don't tell her any more about the case.'

'She's never had a quick word since she learned to talk,' I said. 'And a Xanax burrito with Temazepam salsa couldn't calm her down. And I can't tell her any more about the case because I don't know anything that you didn't just tell her anyway.'

Then I took the phone. 'Mum?'

She was sobbing. 'Oh, that poor boy! Oh his poor mother! Poor Perdita and Anselm!' She had never met Menzies's parents but they had such unbelievably posh names that she always took every chance she got to drop them. 'He was so young and so handsome.' Like death is only for ugly people. 'His shirts alone!' Like death is only for scruffy people. 'Now, Lexy, you have to try to be strong. Surround yourself with friends and let them take care of you.' I took the phone away from my ear and stared at it. That didn't sound like my mother at all. 'Don't do anything hasty,' she said. 'Don't go shacking up with that phone shop man on the rebound, whatever you do.'

SIX

B efore anyone could do anything, before Molly could get my mum to shut up (or get on to Interpol to haul her off), before I could straighten her out about the meaning of 'rebound' (or summon a demon to reach down the phone and throttle her), before Taylor could ask me what she had said to make my face go brick red and my ears purple, and before I had the time to face the fact that coincidence hadn't sent Menzies here to die, nor the universe, nor a private investigator he might have employed, but rather my own mother . . . before any of that, a procession arrived.

There was no other word for it. Todd came first, appearing around the office end of the motel swaggering like an extra in *The Lion King*. Then came Diego carrying the Golden Eagle kite I had helped him pick out as his big brother present. After him, Dylan's bum wiggled into view because he was walking backwards, a bit hunched over, holding back the branches of the bird cherry and oleander. Finally, the main event: Della, walking slightly gingerly but not actually wincing, and in her arms a bundle of the palest powder pink. A noisy, struggling bundle. Hiro was awake and was not happy, either about that or about another matter, but definitely about something.

Della was wearing powder-pink too. She had also had a blow-dry and was clearly in light make-up. Or what passed for light make-up with you-know-who. Light make-up for me means a bit of mascara and a bit of lip gloss. Light make-up for Todd means only three shades of contour and no stick-on lashes. He was going easy on her. He had even let her wear Uggs. Pale pink ones, to match the rest of the ensemble.

Roger came last. He looked knackered, I have to say. And I understood. Not only had he delivered the baby but presumably he had also tried to keep Todd off Della's back. He had failed (pale pink, blow-dry, contour) but he had worn himself out in the effort. What a guy.

'Here she comes!' said Noleen. 'Happy birthday, Baby Girl!'

'Welcome to the world!' said Kathi.

'Lucky world to have you!' Taylor said.

'Yay!' I said. Lame, but there was nothing else left.

'What is it?' said Della, totally failing to be in a fug of hormones and exhaustion and thereby miss the plain fact that something was up today at the Last Ditch. Something beyond the hotly anticipated arrival of Miss Chihiro Muelenbelt, that is.

If they were serious about that.

'So . . . Chihiro, is it?' I said, going over to look at the raging little spitfire contained in the puff of pink blankets, hoping to refocus Della's attention. 'But not Chi-chi?'

Della did indeed look down again. And melt. 'Hiro,' she said, smiling. Hiro glared up at her and shrieked. She hated her name, apparently.

'You didn't need to de-camp,' I said. 'You could have stayed aboard as long as you wanted.

Della shrugged, shy and proud at the same time. 'I wanted to come show her off,' she said. 'She's so beautiful. I want everyone to see her. How many guests are checked in, Noleen? I could go door-to-door. And hey! Molly's here.'

'Molly is in fact here,' I said. 'Molly, come and see the baby!' I signalled frantically with my eyes that Molly was most definitely not to tell Della the reason for her presence. And give her her due, she picked it up and ran with it.

'Try and keep me away from a newborn baby!' she said, walking over and shoving her notebook in her back pocket. 'You handing out hugs, Little Miss?' she asked, when she was close enough. 'Or is that not . . .?' she said, stepping back. 'Not that I don't . . .' she added, stepping forward again. I had never seen Molly flummoxed. It was so bad she even turned to me. 'What's the protocol here, Lexy?'

It was almost impossible to say. Back home, random strangers chooked babies under the chin, planted kisses on their heads and tucked coins under their pillows with gay abandon. It's an added benefit to having a baby in Scotland. As soon as you're recovered from the birth and able to trawl up and down the high street pushing the pram, you can turn a tidy profit. I had sort of forgotten about it until this morning, but it was obviously still deep in my psyche, because it felt strange beyond belief to see a new baby and *not* see everyone in the vicinity patting their pockets for loose change. My own fingers were itching.

But setting aside the hygiene challenge of used coins near babies' faces, there was still a yawning divide between our two lands. There, a cuddle of the baby was a given, like getting a slice of cake at a party, or having to be in photos at a wedding. Not getting a turn at holding a new baby would have been as rude as watching someone eat their entire birthday cake themselves, or being told to stay in the church until the photographer was gone in case you bombed the happy couple and ruined the album. Here, as I have found out to my cost, it's not like that. Here, if you haven't washed your hands and taken your temperature and recently laundered your clothes and confirmed that you haven't consumed peanuts or alcohol, or smoked anything in the last twenty-four hours, you might – *might*, mind – get to touch a baby's foot. Through a sock.

But then Della was Mexican. And they're more Scottish than the rest of the locals. Mexican babies talk to strangers and don't get bundled away and given scoldings. Mexican babies wave to you in the street and bat their eyes. They stand up backwards in their cinema seats and ask for some of your popcorn. Basically, Mexican kids recruit a village to raise them wherever they go.

But, on the other hand, at the moment, Molly was off desk-duty, back mixing with the public again, and Hiro was not quite twelve hours old yet.

'Your guess is as good as mine,' I said.

Della broke the awkward moment by lifting Hiro clear and dumping the whole frothing pink bundle into Molly's arms.

'Hey!' said Kathi. 'She cut in line!'

'You held her hours ago!' said Todd.

'We restart every time,' said Noleen. 'That's widely accepted. It's me first, then Kathi, then Lexy, then—'

'*Me* first!' said Diego, so loud Hiro stopped crying in fright, then started again even louder. Who's *that* asshole, she demanded to know.

'But Noleen,' I said. 'Molly has come all this way and taken time out of her busy shift to meet the new arrival.'

'Why is there a truck backed up to the room next to ours?' said Dylan, who had somehow managed to peel his eyes off his daughter for a moment. 'Wait, is that the coro . . .?'

Della must have heard the note in his voice even though he had managed to swallow the question half-asked. She looked up too. 'Is that the coroner's truck?' she said. Then she turned to Diego. 'Go see how long that kite-tail is, Papi. Bet it isn't longer than the pool.'

Once he was out of earshot, she went on. 'What happened?'

'It's the cycle of life, Dells,' said Noleen. 'Someone died here last night and someone was born. It's the way of the world, and you mustn't upset yourself.'

'Who died?' said Della. 'A guest or one of us?'

'Oh a guest, a guest,' Noleen said. 'An old guy. Poor old guy. Gotta go sometime, right?'

'What time *did* he go?' said Della.

'Why?' said Kathi.

'No one knows,' I said.

'What difference does it make?' said Noleen.

'Ages before . . . I mean hours after . . .' said Taylor, which was such imbecility, I could have kicked him.

Della stared at each of us in turn. 'Are you telling me, that an old man died here while my daughter was being born?'

'Now, Della,' said Dylan. 'I know you've got your beliefs and all that malarkey, but I'm going to have to put my foot down and stamp on this before it takes hold.'

'Malarkey?' Della said, pulling her brows down until her eyes went dark. It seemed to me that Hiro's little wispy brow feathers lowered too. The pitch of her squealing definitely went up.

All in all, I was glad to skip out to the cop shop for my formal interview. It didn't start formal. Molly was saucer-eyed above her mask when she slid into the interview room. And she shuddered lavishly as she sat down on the other side of the table from me. 'I know she doesn't really believe it,' she said.

'Well,' I said. 'There's believe and *believe*, isn't there?' She quirked a look and I told her about the coins on the pillow and how my hands were itching earlier.

'Eugh,' she said. 'Dirty coins from people's pockets? In a baby carriage? Don't tell Kathi.'

I smiled, because she was right, of course. But it's lonely being away from your own people sometimes. It was that and that alone that had made me break into a sprint, a few days back, when I'd seen someone cross the Lode car park with a Tesco Bag for Life slung over her shoulder. I hadn't hesitated.

'Hey!' I'd said when I caught up with her.

Of course, she could have been a Californian who'd picked up a Tesco bag on a trip, but then she would have looked round with that polite and friendly American smile. This woman scowled at me and drew her neck in as if I smelled bad. A Brit, and no mistake. 'Did I drop something?' she'd said. Bingo! English!

I'd rubbed my nose, embarrassed suddenly. Maybe California was rubbing off on me and I didn't see how weird I was being. 'No, sorry,' I'd said. 'I saw the bag and . . . I'm not from here as you can probably tell and I get homesick.'

'Especially this year,' she'd said, nodding. I'd nodded too and let her think I made frequent trips home in normal times and was champing to get back to it.

'You look guilty,' said Molly, across the table in the stuffy little interview room.

'I'm just thinking about home. Della probably wouldn't think of . . . are we calling it reincarnation? Soul-sharing? . . . if she still lived in Mexico, but you cling on harder than ever once you've moved away.'

'Is that why you don't sound any more normal as the months roll by?'

'No,' I said. 'That's because the world is a globe. Not a cone with America at the top and everyone else scrabbling to reach the summit. I was thinking more about how I ended up having a cup of tea in the Lode doorway with a random English bint I've got nothing in common with just because we're both stuck over here. An English bint by the way who stuck me with the bill for a foot-long sub and an individual cheesecake, even though it's supposed to be me who's the tightwad.'

'In Della's defence though,' Molly said, 'you gotta admit it's a hell of a coincidence. The timing. I mean how often does someone die in the Ditch?'

'This is the third,' I reminded her.

'Well, yeah,' she said. 'But then there's the . . .' She waved her hand in front of her forehead.

'But that's bonkers,' I said. 'That's like saying if a bear scares you when you're pregnant your baby will have a snout and fur.'

'Still, no one's going to tell Della where the bullet hole was, right?'

It was my turn to shiver. 'Right,' I said.

Then Molly leaned in and switched on the recording machine. She said the date and time and gave our full names – it's a bit of a facer that I've been in her interview room so many times that she can spell my name without a hitch. She named another cop, waved at the two-way mirror on the short wall facing me, from where the officer was apparently watching, and then sat back and laced her hands behind her head.

'In your own words, and in your own time, Lexy,' she said. 'Tell me everything you know about Menzies Lassiter.'

'How's the overtime budget?' I asked her. 'He was my first love, Molly, so I could talk about him for quite a while. What exactly is it you want to know?'

'Background, family, criminal connections, convictions,' Molly said. 'Enemies, motive, psychiatric history. Financial trouble. The usual stuff.'

'Oh, just the usual stuff?' I said. 'Jail time and mob ties. Gotcha.'

'And then we can move on to why you broke up, recent contact, anything in your life that's hinky and might be connected. Other associates we should be talking to.'

'Uh-huh, uh-huh,' I said.

'And finally we're going to need you to talk us through yesterday evening, overnight, and this morning in more detail.'

'Right,' I said. 'I should have stopped at Swiss Sisters for a bucket of joe.'

'I can give you coffee,' said Molly, with a smirk. The Cuento PD coffee machine was the best evidence for life after death I had ever come across. It was clearly haunted by a very pissed-off poltergeist with poor personal hygiene. Even the thought of putting a cup of Brown Liquid 3 (coffee) to my lips made my stomach roll. Not that Brown Liquid 2 (tea) was any better. And as for Brown Liquid 1 (hot chocolate), I had never tasted it but from the smell I reckoned it was squeezed from the impacted anal glands of Beelzebub himself.

'So,' Molly said, when we had both stopped gagging, 'first boyfriend. Go.'

'First *love*,' I said. 'My first boyfriend was a skinny kid called Brian who dumped me because my friend dumped his friend and it made things awkward.'

'First love,' Molly said.

'I was seventeen. He was eighteen—'

'Is that statutory rape over there too?'

'Jesus, Molly!'

'Goes to motive.'

'We met at a birthday party. He went to school in Edinburgh.'

'College?'

'High school.'

'Why'd he go to high school in another city? Continuation, was it? He get kicked out of the school district where he lived?'

'Oh my God!' I said, and I couldn't help giggling. 'Please phone Fettes College and ask if they're a second-chance saloon for troubled teens. Only if I can listen though.'

'You told me it wasn't a college.'

'It's a public – meaning private – school called a college. And he went there because he lived there. He was only in Dundee for the party where I met him.'

'And you dated for how long?'

'Nine months.'

'Is that significant?'

'Ew, no! Jesus. If we'd had a secret love-child I'd have mentioned it by now. Bloody hell, Moll. Anyway, I was rounding up. Call it eight and a half.'

'And why'd you break up?'

'Because we went to the same university,' I said. 'Edinburgh.'

'Stay-at-home kinda guy, huh?'

'It's a good school,' I said, speaking American for her. 'It's like living in Boston and going to . . . whichever one's in Boston.'

'Harvard,' said Molly. 'OK. Why'd you break up?'

'Because we didn't actually go to the same university. Edinburgh is two different places in one. It's a good institute of learning for bright Scottish kids. Plus it's a party school for posh kids who couldn't get into Oxbridge. In other words, Menzies. And before the end of the first term he had turned into a textbook pillock. His friends were obnoxious, his flat was a bio-hazard, and he was mean. Suddenly.'

'Good for you,' Molly said. 'You dumped his elitist ass and didn't look back, huh?'

I wanted to agree. If I hadn't been on the tape and wasn't giving evidence in a murder inquiry, I would have found a sneaky way to let that comforting truth enter the record. However . . .

'No,' I said. 'His elitist ass dumped me.'

'Why?'

'Why does any boy dump—'

'Talk me through it.'

'It was Christmastime and we'd been invited to a party at one of his friends' houses.' I heaved a big breath, remembering. Or rather, trying not to. 'Now, I hated these people, Molly. Drawling chinless toffs, thick as pig-shit and rich as Croesus.'

'Rich as who?'

'What? Croesus. King of Lydia.'

'King of what?'

'Lydia.'

'Who the hell's Lydia? Are you yanking me?'

'It's in the Bible. Look, it doesn't matter. They were having a Christmas party. Menzies asked me to go with him, and made me promise that I wouldn't show him up.'

'Scumbag,' said Molly.

'Nah, it was a fair point,' I said. 'I'd been trolling these losers all term. With one hand tied behind my back usually. I wanted him to see through them instead of being one.'

The memory swept in and I was back there.

'We're the balls boys,' he had told me.

'Ball boys?' I said. 'Wimbledon?'

'Balls boys,' he told me again.

'Because it takes balls to be such knobs?'

Give him his due, he laughed. Then said, 'BOLS. B-O-L-S. it stands for . . .' but he paused to give me time to object.

So I objected. '. . . something I'm pretty sure I don't want to know.'

'This is all such ancient history,' I told Molly, as I shook it off and got myself back to the here and now. 'Why does it matter?'

'You're right,' Molly said. 'There's absolutely no evidence to suggest that Mr Lassiter's murder has anything to do with your shared past. Don't say any more. I'll scrub the tape. You're free to go.'

The officer on the other side of the two-way mirror banged so hard on its back that the whole thing grated in the frame.

'I'm kidding!' said Molly, scowling at her own reflection. 'Google "sarcasm" on your lunch break, why don't ya?'

'So I decided not to show him up,' I said. 'I bought a party dress. Well, first I bought a magazine. You know those December issues of women's magazines that clue you in to that year's trends for party dresses?'

'No. Seriously? Sheesh.'

I envied Molly in some ways.

'Then I bought a dress. Low, short, sequins, the whole bit. And these ridiculous shoes. Taxi shoes, they call them, because you can't walk in the damn things.'

'Hangover from foot binding if you ask me.'

'I'm not going to argue, but I was really trying, is my point. I did my hair. Did my face. I even did my toenails. And this was Christmastime, remember? Frostbite beckoned. But I'd said I would and so I did.'

'And?' said Molly, after I'd been quiet for a while.

'Turns out I'd watched too many adaptations of Brideshead and Gatsby. Nobody else was dressed up. None of the other girls had heels on. Hardly any of them had make-up on and certainly not as much as me. The boys were all in their pink cords and smelly jumpers same as ever. I looked like the fairy on the top of the Christmas tree they didn't have because they were too cool for that too.'

'And he dumped you for that? For a dress-code violation? Ass-wipe.'

'No,' I said. 'Thanks, by the way. No, he didn't say anything. Nothing. He especially didn't say anything when one of his buddies asked another of his buddies who had paid for the brass flute.'

Molly shrugged. Of course she did. I hadn't known what it meant either back then.

'And then a bit later they were talking about a brass door. And cracking up badly.'

'What the hell's a brass door? Like on a safe? That doesn't even make any sense.'

'And I heard someone mention a brass dart. And a brass nail. And again they all fell about laughing.'

'I can see a nail,' Molly said. 'But a dart? Same again. What use would a brass dart be?'

'Suddenly it was like the whole party was in on the joke except me. They were all laughing like hyenas. And I decided it was some kind of drug reference. So I asked Menzies what it was they were taking and if he had taken any. And he started laughing so hard I thought he was going to puke.

'Then finally one of them went too far, and asked who had brought the tom tit. And the penny dropped. Brass dart, brass door, brass nail, brass flute. It was Cockney rhyming slang.'

'For?'

'Tart, whore, tail. Prostitute.'

'Those fuckers!'

'Yeah,' I said.

'And he thought it was funny?'

'Yeah,' I said.

'No wonder you . . . wait. You said he dumped you?'

'Yeah.' She waited. 'Because I *didn't* think it was funny. Because I got upset and spoiled the fun.'

'Sounds like fun that was overdue for a good spoiling,' Molly said.

I thought about saying more. But there's something so irresistible about blind sisterly loyalty. It would have taken more of a woman than me to reject it and keep explaining.

'So off I stumbled, into the night, half-cut and freezing cold, on account of I was near the door when he dumped me and I

had no clue where my coat was so I left it. And then I stepped
in a puddle and ruined my shoes. Then I sat in sick in the bus
shelter and ruined my dress. It was a hard night on the wardrobe
all round.'

'You were lucky you got home in one piece,' Molly said.
'Crying and coatless in the city at night, all dressed in sequins.'

I stared hard at her before I answered. Was she slut-shaming
me? Or was she stating a plain fact, no matter how hard we all
try to forget that it's true. I shook my head. 'Nah,' I said. 'There
aren't many upsides to sitting in sick, but it keeps the creeps
away something lovely. If I had been a prostitute, it would have
been a disaster for my night's business.'

'And that's that?' Molly said. I hesitated. What exactly was
she asking me? 'I mean, you never saw him again?'

'I might have,' I said. 'I probably did. We were at the same
university for another three and a half years, after all. And we
weren't in very distant departments, physically speaking. Although
in every other way . . .'

'You did psychology?'

I nodded. 'And he did parapsychology.'

Molly snorted. 'I thought you said it was a good school? They
got a department of Ghostbusting? I bet you ten bucks Harvard
doesn't.'

I gave her a grateful smile. 'But I was lucky. Guys like Menzies
are so identikit – tall, blond, big teeth, big jumper, cords, brogues
– that as long as I didn't wear my distance glasses, I could have
passed him in the hallways every day and not known it.'

'You don't wear distance glasses,' said Molly. 'Unless you
had Lasik between then and now.'

'OK,' I said. 'Jeez, you're like a truffle pig. I kept my head
down. OK?'

'For three and a half years? You must have resented the hell
out of that.'

'It was only in the hallways,' I said. 'We didn't frequent the
same pubs and we didn't belong to the same clubs. So it was no
big deal. I had nothing to resent him for. I didn't kill him, Molly.
You have to believe me. I've got an alibi.'

She nodded. She did believe me. I was free to go. But then
came a knock at the door.

SEVEN

It was my old friend Soft Cop. (I could never remember his real name.) A giant marshmallow of a man with a slow lumbering gait and a voice like treacle dropping off a spoon, he was nevertheless as sharp as a tack in the brains department, a marked contrast to his beat partner Mills of God, who was wiry to look at and nimble in his movements, but whose mental acuity suggested a lot of strong weed in his past, or some very recent hypnosis.

'Sarge,' said Soft Cop. 'Preliminary report.' He wasn't meeting my eye so I knew it was this case that was being reported upon.

Molly took the folder from his sausage fingers and turned away from me so that – I imagine – even if I could read upside down, I wouldn't get any inside info.

'I can't read upside down,' I said. 'So you could unwind that twist before you get a crick in your neck there.'

But Molly had evidently seen whatever it was that made Soft Cop interrupt us. She snapped the folder shut and laid it on the table between us, keeping one hand on top, presumably to stop me snatching it.

'And after graduation?' she said, as if nothing had happened.

'Never clapped eyes on him again until today in his motel room.'

'But he obviously kept tabs on you.'

'What? Because he went to my parents' house? That wouldn't have needed a private detective. They still live in the same place.'

'And you hadn't contacted him?'

'Eh?'

'You're sure he didn't visit your parents to find out where you were so he could ask you to leave him alone?'

'*Eh?* Where's this coming from?'

'Because travelling all this way, especially given current restrictions, looks a hell of a lot like he had unfinished business with you.'

'Agreed,' I said. I was trying not to think about the unfinished business. 'Only me not leaving him alone would be *me* having it with *him*.'

'And did you?'

I really tried. I shut my brain down and attempted to turn my face into a mask. Evidently, I failed.

'Tell me,' Molly said. 'I'll get it out of you in the end anyway, so you might as well save our time and tell me now.'

I nodded. 'That's right. That's what I've learned from watching cop shows. No harm ever comes from telling any cop every irrelevant thing they'd like to know. Anyway, there's nothing to tell. Boyfriend dumped me. Years pass. Midlife crisis begins, probably, and he decides to track me down and catch up for old times' sake.'

'I'll get it out of your mother,' Molly said.

'You can't,' I said. 'She doesn't—'

'Know?' said Molly. 'Your mother doesn't know the thing that doesn't exist to be known? Because you never told her, what with it not existing and all?'

'What I meant was that my mother doesn't know any more than I've told you, because there's nothing more *to* know. We were ill-matched. He was a dick to me at a party. I called him out on it. He broke up with me.'

'But what makes you so sure your mother doesn't know things, if you don't?' Molly said. 'Since she had a recent visit from the guy and you haven't seen him for years? If it was me, I'd assume he told her stuff. I'd be interested to hear it, actually.'

Dammit. Molly was better at this than I had given her credit for. 'What I meant was,' I said, painfully aware that it was the second time I'd said it, 'my mum and dad aren't going to be able to tell you anything that sheds light on why he was here. Except they might, I suppose. If he told them. Hey! What if he was twelve-stepping? Tracking down the people he'd wronged to say sorry?'

'Did he have a drinking problem when he wronged you?'

'When he dumped me?' I said. 'Hard to say.' I cast my mind back. 'I mean, he was hammered that night. He was hammered most nights. But he was Scottish and drinking is our national pastime. And plus he was a student as well, so that adds a few more daily units.'

'If he's twelve-stepping he'd definitely have told your parents so . . .' said Molly. 'Openness comes before fifteen-hour apology flights.'

It sounded as if she knew what she was talking about and I couldn't help but be interested. It's an occupational hazard. She saw me noticing and scowled. Molly doesn't take well to intrusion. It's what makes being a cop such a perfect job for her: it's so one-sided. It's a literal crime to do anything that pisses her off. Oh they call it 'obstructing a law enforcement professional in pursuance of duty', but it's a total racket. Despots and divas dream of the kind of puckering-up cops take as their due, while they in the meantime tell you nothing.

'What I mean is,' I said, ringing the changes, 'whatever they can tell you about Menzies's state of mind or purpose in coming to California – and I admit it seems daft to deny it might be to do with me – they won't be able to tell you anything that connects me to what happened to him after he got here.'

'Got it,' said Molly. 'You meant A. that your mother doesn't know why you broke up and B. that she might know why he came to see you and C. that she can't know why he died. You meant all three things. And you indicated those three meanings by saying "she doesn't" then clamming up, Lexy?'

Double dammit. She was wiping the floor with me. 'It's moot,' I said. 'It's all moot. Because of my solid alibi.'

'Oh yeah,' said Molly. 'That.' She did it quite subtly but it was unmistakable; she definitely glanced at the folder on the table. The one Soft Cop thought important enough to bring in here.

'What?' I said.

'That,' said Molly, 'is the preliminary report of findings from the coroner.'

'Uh-huh,' I said. 'And?'

'It's pretty clear about the time of death. Not pinpoint. But the frame, you know. The band. The earliest possible and latest possible time Mr Lassiter might have died.'

I frowned at her. 'But we know when he died. We know "pinpoint". He died at three a.m.'

Molly pushed out her lips and nodded as if she was giving it due consideration. 'The coroner has set the time of death as between ten p.m. at the earliest and one a.m. at the latest.'

'That's not possible,' I said. 'What?'

'So turning to the question of an alibi,' said Molly. 'Ten o'clock to one in the morning, Lexy. Where were you?'

'We heard the shot,' I said. 'There must be something off about the temperature of the room or the coroner made a mistake or – how about this? – Menzies had some kind of disease or condition that screwed with his body heat. Or he'd just had a hot shower.'

'That wouldn't—'

'Or a cold one, I mean. We heard the shot, Molly.'

'I don't doubt it,' she said. 'And, best-case scenario, you sat there for hours wondering what to do about the fact that someone you knew intimately from a shared troubled past was dead in the next room. You talked it over, discussed your options. And then you heard the baby cry and you knew the quiet part of the night was finished and you'd better get ready to say he was dead already by the time people started getting up and going visiting.'

'That's insane,' I said. 'Why would we admit to hearing anything? Or if we knew it was earlier, why wouldn't we say we heard a funny noise at midnight but we didn't think anything of it.'

'Exactly,' Molly said. 'Best-case scenario, remember? But if you *killed* the guy at midnight . . .'

'We woke up at three,' I said. 'We both heard a funny noise we didn't recognize but now realize was a gun going off with a silencer attached. Then the baby cried. We got up. We didn't hear anyone leaving the room next door. We didn't see anyone leaving the room next door. And I went in in the morning. Twice! If one of us—'

'Who said "one of you"?' Molly asked. 'Taylor is nothing to do with this guy.'

'He would be if Menzies came to get me back and Taylor found out and flew into a rage and . . . yeah, you're right.'

I had never seen Taylor in a rage and was finding it hard to visualize. It was even harder to picture him going out on to the mean streets of Cuento late on Thanksgiving to score a handgun and silencer to deal with his rival.

'But why wouldn't we have said we heard the door? Or saw

a shadowy figure flit across the forecourt and slip away into the night?'

'Because this isn't Lifetime?' said Molly.

'And you know another thing that's bothering me?'

'I couldn't care less about anything that's bothering you. I care about why this dude was here in my town, and who killed him. And I care about the anomalies between your story and the coroner's report. That's it for me. I'll work the case methodically and I'll get to the answer and then nothing will be bothering me.'

'But why is what's bothering me not of interest when you're constructing hypotheses?'

'I'm not. Physical evidence is more important than navelgazing. I already got a search warrant for the motel. Now I need one for the boat too.'

'What bothers me is why did we hear the silencer at all?' I said, ignoring her. 'What's the use of a silencer that wakes someone up in the room through the wall? Or, if silencers are actually so crap, why didn't he use a pillow or something as well?'

'But if you really want to help me,' she said, ignoring me right back, 'you won't make me wait for some judge to emerge from his turkey coma.'

I had a dilemma. I wanted to ignore her again, but I had a way to score a point off her if I acknowledged what she was saying. 'Della had her baby on that boat,' I plumped for at last. 'You seriously think Kathi hasn't scrubbed it from top to bottom with double-strength bleach between then and now?'

She clearly wanted to ignore me too. But she also clearly thought she could score a point off me if she went the other way. 'Maybe he or she didn't know silencers should really be called quieteners,' said Molly. 'Maybe it was the first time she or he had ever fired a gun that was fitted with one. Must have been a tense moment when she found out, huh?'

'Or he.'

Molly inclined her head to acknowledge the point.

'You know what?' I said. 'I've had about enough of this now. I think I'll go. I've told you everything I know and—'

'I wouldn't say that.'

I took a deep breath and filled her in as rapidly as I could get the words out of my mouth: Menzies's friends from back then, his parents' names, their address – I hadn't forgotten it because I didn't know a lot of people who lived at 'olds'. The Old Manse, The Old Post Office, The Old Mill, The Old Barn were places I only knew from stories, until I met the Lassiters who lived, with a self-conscious brand of gaiety, in The Old Slaughterhouse. It was a beautiful building, full of Victorian tiles and soaring skylights, but oh how they loved themselves for not changing the name. Oh how I loved them for it too, in those days.

'Break it to them gently,' I said, as I was leaving the interview room. 'They're good people, despite everything.'

Back at the Ditch, it was full-on Babytown. Roger had gone to work (poor sod, after zero sleep) but the rest of them were set up at the long trestle table, feasting on leftovers and passing Hiro around like a party parcel, trying to comfort her and toasting her health with all the opened bottles of booze we hadn't managed to put away the night before on account of Della's contractions breaking up the party.

Todd, if you can believe it, was already on to the getting back of the figure. 'You can rub as much anti-stretchmark cream as you want into the pouch,' he said as I slid in beside him, 'but offing it completely is the only way to return to your former glory.'

'Pouch?' I said. 'Todd, are you talking about Della's mid-section? Where she had . . . however many pounds of baby until less than twenty-four hours ago? Pouch? Seriously?'

'Seven three,' said Diego. 'Seven pounds and three ounces. Eighteen inches long. How much did I weigh, Mama?'

'Eight pounds and five ounces,' said Della. 'Don't remind me.'

'And how long was I?'

'Twenty inches.'

'I win,' said Diego. He leaned in close and whispered gently into Hiro's tiny ear. 'I won. Two nil to me.' Hiro stopped crying briefly, as she considered this new experience of someone's breath in her ear then, deciding she didn't care for it, started again.

'How'd it go?' Noleen said. To me, I guessed, although her eyes were trained on the baby. 'Anything to report?'

'Enh,' I said. Then to change the subject, 'Speaking of reporting, is there anything in the *Voyager*?' With business still so sluggish, news of a murder in one of the rooms seemed unlikely to help.

'Kathi's there now,' Noleen said. 'Giving them our press release. Trying to control the story.'

'Good luck with that,' I replied. 'But good for Kathi. Out and about, mixing and mingling. How hard do you think it's going to hit you?'

'On the plus side, and for right now, I got his credit card when he checked in,' Noleen said. 'I didn't run it obviously or I'd have noticed the two different names. *C.B. Klatshovk? K.C.?* Bullshit! But I've put two nights and special cleaning on it now. His heirs can sue me if they like.' I nodded in acknowledgment of her practicality. It was either that or let my jaw hit the table in horror at her callousness. 'Also,' she went on, 'we were thinking of remodelling one of the rooms and couldn't decide which. Guess we know which one's getting the makeover now.'

'Remodelling one room?' I said. It struck me as odd.

'I'll tell you all about it when Kathi gets back. It was Todd's idea.'

'That's not usually a recommendation,' I said. I had just finished my plate of cherry pie and ice-cream, confirming what I'd argued the day before: if you hadn't eaten a bite of anything else all day, a slice of American pie was actually pretty tasty.

'And there's no rush,' Noleen said. 'We've got three weeks to finish it.'

'Huh?' I said. 'Only three weeks? How come? Are you fully booked for Christmas?'

'In a way,' said Noleen, giving Todd a significant look. 'Will we tell her now or wait for Kathi like we said?'

'Let's wait,' Todd said, in a voice he no doubt thought was innocence personified. It would have worked on me this time last year. All it told me tonight was that this idea concerned me and I wasn't going to like it.

'OK!' Della said, putting her hands on the arms of her chair and pulling herself upright in it. 'Ahhhhh. Ooooh. Owwwiiieeee.'

Everyone around the table winced in sympathy, except Hiro who was yelling at her own fists as they waved in front of her face. And also except Diego, who was motoring through a towering bowlful of pie and ice-cream as if he was being paid by the slice. 'What's wrong, Mama?' he said, pausing with a spoon halfway to his mouth. 'Brain freeze?'

'My vulva tore a little when I was pushing Hiro out,' said Della. 'It's tender today.'

A huge thought bubble formed above everyone's heads overshadowing the accompanying silence.

'Things are so much better than they used to be,' I said, eventually. 'As a therapist, a woman, and a buttoned-up Brit, I thoroughly approve of no-nonsense openness.'

'Speak for yourself,' said Noleen. 'That's just weird. *Vulva?* No way Diego knows what a vulva is.'

'It's the folds of skin around the—' Diego got out, before Noleen managed to stop him.

'Mommy was right on the edge of needing stitches,' Todd said, as if Diego – or any of us – needed more detail. 'But Uncle Roger said she could give it a day and then take another look. What do you think, Dell?'

'The ice-pack helped,' Della said. 'Oh, Lexy. I need to replace your ice-pack. Remind me if you remember.'

Like I'd forget.

'Anyway,' Della said, 'I want to talk to you about three things. We need to have a memorial for that guy who died.'

'We do?' said Noleen.

'I do,' said Della.

'Someone died?' Diego said, with his eyes like saucers.

'This'll be good,' said Noleen. 'What's the vulva equivalent when it comes to sudden death?'

'He did,' Della said. 'He went to Heaven to live with Jesus, and we need to honour his memory so that his spirit is at rest.'

'Phew,' said Noleen. 'No death vulva. Fine by me.'

'Hey, Mama!' Diego said. 'Maybe that's why Chihiro looks like a little old man when she yawns. Like you said when she woke up this morning, remember?'

Now, Diego isn't spoiled. But he does live with five doting spares as well as two actual parents and so it's unusual for one of his remarks not to meet with a few words of praise and wonder along the 'Smart kid!', 'Good job!' continuum. This particular little gem, however, was greeted by a forecourt-wide silence of greater length and deeper stoniness than Diego had ever faced in his puff. He gave us all an exhibition of his best puzzled frown.

'There's no need for you to think about any of that,' said Dylan. 'There is absolutely no connection between that guy dying and Hiro being born.'

I wished I could back him up by revealing that Menzies died at midnight, but I was still sure that had to be wrong. So I kept quiet. Unfortunately, I wasn't the only one.

'What is it?' Della said. 'You all have very sketchy looks on your faces. What are you not saying?'

'I know what *I'm* not saying,' said Dylan. 'And I'm not saying it in case I get panned for mansplaining motherhood to you.'

'Say it,' said Della.

'OK. Forget the dead guy, honey. This is a time to curl up and bond.'

'She's feeding off me every ninety minutes, *honey*,' Della said. 'And, in between times, I'm mostly scraping poop off her. We've bonded.'

'Did you scrape poop off me?' said Diego.

'Second,' said Della, 'is Trinity going to find out who killed him?'

'No,' I said, 'Molly is going to find out who killed him.'

'Trinity could help,' said Della.

'How?' I asked.

'Same as all the other times.' Which was a point.

'But all the other times we had a client,' I reminded her.

'We could take up a collection,' said Della. 'Or, since that means the three of you would be paying yourselves, you could comp this one.'

'Yeah but why?' I said.

'Why?' said Della. She held Hiro up to give me a better view of her tonsils while she screamed with her tiny little mouth as wide as it would go. 'So his spirit can leave the motel and be at rest,' she said.

'His spirit has been Cloroxed into oblivion,' said Noleen.

'What's the third thing?' I asked.

'Ah. Yes,' said Della, putting Hiro back against her shoulder. 'We need to pick our first book.' I groaned and I wasn't the only one. 'And everyone owes me twenty bucks,' she added. 'Including you, Dill.'

'It's a joint account,' Dylan said. 'It's the same money.'

'Not what you said when I spent it on a pedicure.' Postpartum Della was different from regular Della, I was beginning to see. It was like she had the opposite of Baby Blues. She was rocking a case of the Baby Hot Pinks and I liked it. Even if it meant I'd lost the bet that her plan to start a Last Ditch book club to stop her succumbing to brain fog would wash away with the last of the labour sweat. She was evidently sticking with it at least until she had got the cash.

'And I had another idea,' she said. 'Since we can't be laying around drinking wine—'

'Who can't?' said Todd.

'I can't,' said Della. 'I think we should make it a walking book club.'

'Oh, *what*?' I said. I had beef with book clubs generally. It was when I got home from the only one I'd ever attended that I burst in on my then husband and his ex-wife. They, unlike me, were not debating *The Goldfinch*, if you catch my drift. This looked set to be even worse than that, if we were going to have to do it without snacks, without stem glasses, and while trudging along on one of the very few and very pitiful so-called walking trails around Cuento, which were always packed solid with other people on account of no one having anywhere else to go. Nothing made me more homesick than trying to go for a walk in a country without the concept of public rights-of-way. On the one hand, there were parks – with arrows, litter bins, and educational boards – and on the other hand there were notices posted on trees and fences telling you to keep out or be shot. But meandering paths that had grown up on the routes where medieval peasants drove geese to market? Nada. I had shown Todd an Ordnance Survey map of the Lake District one night when I was drunk. He refused to believe me about what all the dotted lines meant.

'Power cables?' he had said.

'They're footpaths!' I slurred.

'They can't be,' he said. 'They're everywhere.'

'Exactly!'

'And they cross rivers and field boundaries.'

'On stepping stones and stiles,' I said. 'I wanna go hooooome!'

'Excellent idea,' said Noleen, causing me to swivel right round in my seat and stare at her. 'Walking book club. Count me in.'

'What are you up to?' I said.

'I'm supporting Della in her great idea,' said Noleen. 'Walking around outside with a purpose is the future of social interactions, for a while at least. I think all of us should be willing to support any new venture that puts walking at its heart.'

I swivelled back. 'What's she up to?' I said to Todd. 'Is this related to *your* thing?'

'My lips are sealed,' he said. 'How do we choose a book?'

'I've chosen one,' said Della. '*Don Quixote.*'

'Oh *what*?' I said. 'No way! Come on, Della. I thought you meant Liane Moriarty and a bottle of pink Zin. *Don Quixote* while we trail about? Come on!'

'Have you read it?' said Dylan. 'It's pretty cool.' But Dylan only ever curled up with a book when he was smoking weed and so he wasn't a reliable guide.

'You can read it in translation,' Della said.

'But you might wanna check your micro-aggressions there,' said Todd. 'It's a classic of Spanish literature being recommended by your friend who is Latinx, as am I, and—'

'Oh sod off!' I said. 'Noleen?'

'I'm on chapter nine,' she said. What the hell was she up to?

'*Don Quixote*,' I said again. 'Sheesh. Why not *The Pilgrim's Progress*? Why not *Paradise Lost*?'

'Duh,' said Diego. 'Because they don't have donkeys. Good choice, Mom.'

'I could babysit,' I said, telling myself the poor wee scrap would have to stop crying sometime.

'Hiro will be coming with us in her sling,' said Dylan. 'Diego can come along too.'

'I'm not reading *Don Quixote*,' I said. 'It's ten thousand pages long.'

'Don't be such an old woman,' said Todd.

I coughed 'micro-aggression!' under my breath but he ignored me.

'Yeah, Lexy,' said Noleen. 'Embrace the future. Be flexible. Meet adventure head on.'

I would crack her in the end; she was definitely up to something. 'In fact, now I come to think of it,' she said, in a voice so bogus that even Diego screwed his face up and waited to hear what baloney she had ready to serve, 'walking might be the answer for you too, Lex.'

'What was the question?' I said.

'When to go back to in-person therapy,' said Noleen. 'What to do if the HMOs stop covering Zoom before you're ready to have clients back on the boat, snivelling about their childhood. In an enclosed space. Where you live.'

I opened my mouth to argue – it was the Last Ditch way – but actually this was a brilliant idea. I couldn't ask my clients to keep a mask on during counselling sessions. And we couldn't sit on my porch in earshot of the entire motel. But when the special insurance coverage shut down again – and it would – half my business would be gone with it unless I changed something. The more I thought about it, the better the idea became. Fresh air and exercise isn't a substitute for honest exploration of your issues but it's the perfect accompaniment, like pink Zin and nachos for discussing books. Even *Don Quixote*. Before I had to climb down and admit any of that, however, the chain-link gate started to open.

'Here's Kathi!' Diego said.

'Gramma Kathi,' said Della. I didn't know if she was trying to make up for missing family, trying to make sure Diego's manners survived his stoner stepdad, or just trying to prove that she was all over everything hours after giving birth, but Diego wasn't having it.

'She lets me call her Kathi,' he said.

'OK,' said Della. 'She can be Hiro's gramma. She doesn't have to be yours.'

'Gramma Kathi!' Diego screamed at the top of his lungs. He went to meet the pick-up truck.

Kathi stepped out of the cab and climbed into the truck bed where something large and lumpy was covered in a tarpaulin. 'They let you go then, Lexy?' she said. 'Cool. Check this out.'

She tried to sweep the tarp off like a magician but the lumpy thing underneath was spiky too and in the end it took a bit of tugging and flapping to get it clear.

'Woweee,' said Noleen, going over.

I couldn't see what they were looking at from where I sat with the sun in my eyes, so I wriggled my way out of the bench seat and headed that way too.

'How much?' said Noleen. 'I mean worth it at any price, darlin'. But how much?'

I could see into the truck by now and it was a good question. It wasn't the only one. Kathi was standing on top of a snot-green atomic-age sofa resting upside down with its little spike legs up in the air. There was a pair of kidney-shaped side-tables with egg-yolk-yellow tops of finest melamine tucked in there too.

'Free!' said Kathi. 'It was all in the *Voyager* offices, used to be in Reception way back when. Did you know they're moving to smaller premises?'

Noleen sucked her teeth and shrugged. 'Not surprising,' she said. 'There were twelve full-time journos in there the first time I stormed the place to complain about bad publicity, and what is it down to now?'

'Three,' Kathi said. 'And two of *them* are still working from home.'

'Why did you agree to store furniture for the *Voyager*?' I said.

'Not store,' said Kathi. 'Use. It's perfect. We can use it in the room or in the office. It's ideal. I know we thought we could get Victorian stuff for the boat dirt-cheap but I was afraid this mid-century gear would break us.'

'Boat?' I said. 'My boat?'

Noleen was waving both her hands frantically at hip height with her arms straight down. Either she was doing the top half of a Charleston or she was telling Kathi to shut up because no one had told me.

'This is for the walking thing?' I said. 'The other walking thing, I mean. That's not the book club and not the counselling sessions?'

'Isn't it great?' said Kathi. 'I knew you wouldn't be an asshole about it.'

'And *I* knew,' I said to Noleen, 'that no way did you want to read *Don Quixote*.'

EIGHT

I was sitting on the edge of my box bed staring into space when Taylor arrived home that night. He'd pulled the late shift in the phone shop on the busiest day of the year, Black Friday, and there wasn't much left of him. He trailed in like a zombie, sank down beside me and let himself fall back with a huge huffed-out breath that didn't even have the energy to be a groan.

'I hate everyone,' he said.

'I'll make a Scot of you yet,' I said.

'Except you.'

'Ach, still a mushy Californian.'

'Don't ever buy me a phone as a gift.'

'Deal.'

'So how did the rest of your day go?' he said, after a bit of a pause. He reached out his nearest hand and rubbed the small of my back with his knuckles. 'Are you OK?'

'I thought it would feel different in here today, after Hiro was born on board,' I said. 'But then when you think about the people who must have been born and died on anything this age, what's one more?'

'And conceived,' Taylor said. The circles he was knuckling in my back were getting wider, almost far enough round my sides to tickle me.

'I thought you were knackered,' I said.

'Or maybe Hiro's the first person ever to be born on . . . Why doesn't this boat have a name, Lexy? That never occurred to me before.'

'It does,' I said. 'When I inherited it, it was called *Creek House* but I thought that was pretentious so I let it fade. Before it was called *Creek House* it was called the *Meadow Maria*.'

'That's better,' said Taylor. 'Wyntcha use that?'

'Because I only found out today. Kathi told me.'

'How did Kathi know?'

'Huh. Yes. Well. Exactly. Kathi knew because she's been researching it.'

'Why would Kathi do research on your boat?'

I breathed in and out a few times. Deep and slow, like they're always telling us. She had made it sound so reasonable, standing up in her truck bed with the couch and the boomerang tables.

'We're never going to fill this place over the holidays,' she'd said. 'No one's travelling. No one's going to Tahoe. No one's going to Napa.'

'They'd be taking a weird route if they went to Napa this way,' I pointed out.

'No one's going to the redwoods. No one's going to the mountains. And you wouldn't want the Ditch to go down, would you?'

'Of course not,' I said. 'But show me your working, eh?'

'So we're branching out,' said Noleen. 'Diversifying our business.'

'Go on.'

'One thing that *is* going ahead as usual is the walking tours of historic homes,' Kathi said. 'Starts the week before Christmas and runs through New Year's. Masked and distanced, windows open, all the mulled wine served outside. But it's going ahead. And so we're getting in on it.'

'Are you kidding?' I said. 'You've volunteered my boat to be filled with gawping strangers right over the holidays? How is that *you* diversifying *your* business?'

'Of course not!' said Kathi. 'Duh. Look at this stuff, Lexy. This furniture isn't suitable at all for a hundred-year-old houseboat. No, what we're doing is sacrificing a letting room – which would be lying empty anyway – and remodelling it in keeping with the motel's heyday. Space-age prints, hanging basket chairs, sunburst clock if we can find one.'

'Bakelite accessories up the wazoo,' Noleen said. 'Only the uptight dickwad gatekeepers on the Historic Residence Tour – and seriously, Lexy, you wanna see these dames; they should all move east and join the DAR or move south and join the Ladies of the whatever they got going on down there.'

'What's the DAR?' I said. 'Same as the NRA?'

Noleen withered me with a look.

'So we said how about if we do the office too?' said Kathi.

'Because what's to do, right?' Noleen added. 'I never updated anything in there anyway. Just need a little wood-effect panelling and some orange pillows and we're good to go.'

'Picture of a sad clown,' said Kathi.

'Put Todd in the corner in a pimp suit,' said Noleen.

'Right,' I said.

'And if we offer free parking to anyone with a vintage automobile, the lot could look great too.'

'Right,' I said again.

'Well, wrong,' said Kathi. 'The Sisters of the Daughters of the Garden Club of Old Stuff said one room and Reception wasn't enough to get us on the tour. It would have to be the whole motel.'

'Right,' I said a third time.

'So,' said Kathi. 'We kicked in a genuine turn-of-the-century houseboat in its original style and refreshments on deck every afternoon.'

'And where am I supposed to wor—?' I said. 'Oh! *This* is why you're shoving me and my clients out to tramp the streets? Nothing to *do* with walking therapy?'

'I'm gonna go ahead and let Todd explain that part,' Kathi said. 'But you agree in principle. Cool.'

I didn't remember agreeing to one iota, in principle or otherwise, and that's what I told Taylor, sitting side by side on my bed together, touching on how sneaky they were, how outrageous it was, how no way was I going to agree, and how unwise it seemed to have people tromping about my home given how things were.

'It's all very well for Kathi and Noleen,' I said. 'An empty motel room and the Reception office. Meanwhile they're holed up in the owners' flat. It's hardly the same for me; people poking around where I live.'

'But not while you're there, Lexy,' said Taylor. 'The walking therapy part is a great idea.'

Not at all the blind favouritism I deserved from my boyfriend.

Before I could summon a reply, we both felt the deck shift as someone else climbed aboard. I cocked an ear for the footsteps and identified it as Todd. It was something I loved about living here. Who needs a security camera when you can tell friend from foe just by their gait?

'You poor thing,' he said, breezing into my bedroom without so much as a tap on the doorframe.

'I know!' I said. 'Thank you! I was just telling Taylor!'

'I *meant* Taylor,' said Todd. 'Working the late shift on Black Friday. Would you like a back rub? A foot rub? Scalp massage?'

Taylor waved him off and Todd sat down in the little armchair I use when I'm doing my make-up. There wasn't really room for it in my bedroom. But there wasn't anywhere to keep make-up in my bathroom.

'This chair is fine,' Todd said. 'It's Edwardian. Super-uncomfortable for someone as fat-free as I am but exactly the right style. And we can switch out these drapes easily enough. I've got a collection of early bark cloth you could use. And Kathi's willing to do the sewing.'

'What the hell is bark cloth?' I said. Then I interrupted Todd as he started to reply. 'Stop. No. That's not the point.'

'You're right,' said Todd. 'We've got a whole week before the committee comes for a definitive walk-through. For now we should be concentrating on the case.'

'The case?' I said.

'The case,' said Todd. 'The murder? The dead guy? Your ex?'

'Sheesh,' Taylor said, sitting up and shuffling backwards until he was propped up against the panelled wall at the inside of the bed. It was still the original toffee-apple varnish, never painted. Same with the floorboards. I could see why Kathi thought her idea could fly. 'I forgot, Lexy. Sorry. How did you get on at the cop shop?'

'Fine,' I said. 'I mean, weird. Obviously. But fine. The new theory is that Menzies was twelve-stepping and came to apologize to me.'

'And just happened to get himself murdered by the invisible man while he was at it?' said Todd. 'Apologize for what anyway?'

'Bad break-up.'

'Nah,' said Todd. 'You were college students, weren't you? That's not what they mean in AA by past wrongs. My God, if everyone had to apologize to college boyfriends!'

'You've never been in AA,' I said. 'Have you?'

'Well, no,' said Todd. 'I may have had the odd contact high from Barb being my mother but alcoholism is not one of my worries. Back me up though, Taylor.'

'How would I know?' Taylor said. 'Anytime I drink I fall asleep before I can get myself properly hammered. The closest I ever came to AA was when they used the basement of the First Baptist right before the PETA meeting and we sometimes got to finish up their pastries.'

'PETA?' I said. 'Really?'

'I was young,' said Taylor. 'And I had the hots for a girl on the antivivisection task force.'

'So what did Molly ask you?' said Todd. 'Did you tell her everything? Please say you held something back that could give us an edge in the investigation.'

'There's nothing to tell,' I said. 'We went out, we broke up. Fast forward nearly twenty years. He died in the next room.'

'Why'd you break up?' said Todd. 'What AA non-compliant thing did he do to make you dump him?'

I should be grateful, I suppose, that everyone assumed it was that way.

'Let's do that, by all means,' I said. 'But don't start with me. Taylor, what went wrong with the bunny hugger? Todd, why'd your first love offload you? Why should I be in the hot seat?'

'Uhhhhh,' said Todd, 'you're in the hot seat because the bunny hugger – although PETA doesn't fully approve of keeping captive animals just to hug them, you know – didn't die feet from Taylor last night. And Alessandro is married to a nice Catholic girl in Madding, living in a duplex with a basketball hoop in the drive, and riding around in a Subaru. When he finally cracks and comes out, the poor wife might hunt me down and slit my throat for me and *then* it'll be the Todd and Alessandro show all day but for now . . . spill, Lexy.'

So I told them what I had told Molly about the party, the dress, the shoes, the friends, the jokes, the argument, the puddle, the bus shelter, and keeping my head down for the next three years.

There was a long silence when I had finished.

'And she bought this?' said Todd eventually.

'What? Of course she did.'

'Hm. Taylor, what do you reckon?'

'I reckon there was no way you didn't know the dress code at your own college when you'd been there for a term,' Taylor said. 'What gives?'

'Of course I knew the dress codes for *my* crowd,' I said. 'But it's like jocks and geeks and Goths and frats over here. It was tribal.'

'And you'd been going out with this kid since when?' said Todd. 'And you didn't know how any of his friends behaved? That makes no sense.'

I tried to distract them. 'You think *that* makes no sense?' I said. 'Try this. They got the preliminary report back from the coroner and the time of death doesn't match the shot we heard, Taylor and me.'

It didn't work. Todd flapped a hand. 'Prelim reports are blunt instruments. Molly was only trying to shake you up telling you that. Back to the party. What really happened, Lexy?'

'Lovely,' I said. 'Charming. It's one thing to sit in an interview room at the PD and have a woman you shared a lockdown with not believe you. It's something else to have your fiancé and your best friend on this side of the Atlantic not believe you. Thanks a bunch.'

'Who's your better friend on the other side of the Atlantic?' said Todd. 'Alison? She's maybe your *oldest* friend but come on. Have you even phoned her since Menzies Lassiter turned up dead?'

'She's the last pers—' came out of my mouth before I managed to stop myself.

'Right,' said Taylor. 'Because who among us would want to talk to our best friend and kick up the memory of dressing wrong for a party? D'you think I zip up the back, Lexy?'

'Don't talk Scottish,' I said. 'You sound like a wanker. My God, I went through all that with this lot last year. And now I've got to do it again!'

'OK,' said Taylor. 'Sorry. D'you think I came up the Clyde on a biscuit?'

'Stop it.'

'I have stopped it,' he said, with a bland smile. 'I've stopped co-opting your ancestral language like you've told us what really happened at that party. If there even was a party.'

'Oh, there was a party,' I said. 'That much is true.'

Todd was nodding sagely, the foot of his crossed leg wagging in time with his head. 'And what happened at it?'

'It was a fancy-dress party,' I began.

'We already said we don't believe that,' said Taylor.

'She means costume party,' said Todd.

'Thanks,' said Taylor. 'I'm still learning.'

'But what a quick study,' said Todd. 'The Clyde on a biscuit is advanced level.'

'Do you two need some time alone?' I said. God knows why. They had stopped bugging me about something I really wanted them to stop bugging me about. What was wrong with me? 'But it wasn't a free-choice fancy dress,' I went on. 'It was tarts and vicars. Actresses and bishops. The guys dressed as clergy and us dressed as slags.'

'Tut-tut,' said Todd. 'You mean, all the straight women and gays dressed as sex workers and all the straight men and lesbians dressed as pastors?'

'You've obviously spent no time with British public school-boys, Todd,' I said. 'They run to drag like it's free beer. I was going for speed over accuracy. All the girls and boys were dressed as tarts and vicars? Happy now?'

'I'd say women and men but let's move on.'

'My God, you're annoying,' I said, and swivelled to look at Taylor. 'And you're trying to catch up and be this annoying too? Lucky me. OK. Tarts and vicars. Only I didn't know that and I just got dressed up for a party and went along. And Menzies's horrible friends thought it would be hilarious to give me the prize for tartiest tart when I was wearing my own clothes. I didn't think it was funny. Menzies did. I got upset. He dumped me for being a bore. Puddle, bus shelter, the end.'

'Gotcha,' said Todd. 'I believe this version absolutely. Probably because I came down the Tay on a Forfar bridie.'

Taylor whistled in appreciation and Todd inclined his head, accepting the accolade.

'What the hell have you been watching?' I said. BritBox has a lot to answer for. 'And I swear on all that's holy, I'm telling the truth.'

'High stakes for a total atheist,' Taylor said. 'Don't insult us, Lexy. That's a sitcom staple. It's never happened in real life.'

'It bloody well *has* happened in real life,' I said. 'It happened to Alison when she was in her *Spare Rib* phase – anti-adornment to disrupt the male gaze kind of thing. She went to a tarts and vicars barbecue and no one knew she was boycotting the concept because she looked like a lay preacher. Or a fundamentalist, or a guitar-playing nun. She looked like a big honking Christian basically. She went straight home and shaved her legs.'

'And what happened at the party where Menzies dumped you?'

'He bagged off with a girl he knew from tennis,' I said. 'I caught them in the coat cupboard sucking the faces off each other.'

'And *he* dumped *you*?'

Shit.

'Yes,' I said. 'For not seeing the funny side. For not agreeing that anything goes at a tarts and vicars.'

'Oh, the tarts and vicars thing is carrying on into this version?' said Taylor.

Shit. He was right. There was no need for that element now, but it had taken on a life of its own.

'Lexy,' said Todd, 'do you really believe that both Taylor and I took the Union Canal from coast to coast on a caramel wafer and a teacake respectively, breaking off at Falkirk to use the wheel because a section of Hadrian's Wall prevents the two ends of the waterway from joining up directly?'

'Seriously, what the hell have you been watching?' I said. 'Look, I know it seems hard to believe when you look at me now, but I was a prissy little git when I was eighteen. I took a total huff and ruined the party, laying into Menzies and the bint. These days—'

'What was her name?' said Taylor.

I blinked. Then I opened my mouth. Then I shut it again. I managed not to say 'Toddette' or 'Taylorina', but apart from that I couldn't have been less convincing if I'd tried.

'And of course it's not hard to believe,' Todd said. 'You caught Brandon with an ex and flounced right off to Reno to start proceedings. It's absolutely in character for you to overreact to a little infidelity.'

'Right,' I said. 'A little infidelity. What would you do if you caught Roger cheating?'

'Why would Roger cheat?' said Todd. He spread his arms. 'Look at me.'

'Yeah, yeah,' I said. 'But you agree that I'm not saying anything unlikely.'

'Oh absolutely,' said Todd. 'I'm guessing that's why you selected it as your latest cover story. But it's not true. There's no way Menzies Lassiter would have got the chance to dump you for sulking if you caught him having a rummage in the coatcheck at a Christmas party. You'd have slung his ass nine ways to New Year's before he got the chance.'

Shit. Why did I say he dumped me? Well, because he did. But why did I say it when I was lying about everything else from that night? Who knows?

'So you still don't believe me?' I asked them.

'No,' said Todd. 'I'm pretty much going to take "Things that didn't happen" for fifty.'

'What does that mean when people say that?' I said. 'I've always wondered. Taylor, do *you* believe me?'

'I do,' said Taylor. 'Of course I do. But only because I came up . . .'

'. . . the Moray Firth,' said Todd.

'On a . . .' said Taylor.

'Selkirk bannock,' said Todd. '*Escape to the Country*, by the way.'

'But it doesn't matter whether we believe you or not,' said Taylor. 'It doesn't actually matter why you're lying. Because we both heard the shot. And it was three o'clock in the morning and we were in bed asleep, with Diego between us. And when the full autopsy report comes in, Molly will know that too.'

'That's one way we could do it,' Todd said. 'Wait for reports. Wait for Molly. Sure, sure, sure. Or we get on it ourselves.'

'I've talked Della out of that,' I said, which was putting it a bit strongly but they weren't to know.

'What's Della got to do with it?' said Todd. 'And who put you in charge anyway. Trinity, Lexy. Clue in the name.'

I breathed in and out. Not normally an activity deserving of a mention, but when Todd gets onto Trinity, breathing in through my nose to a count of four and out through my mouth to a count of five is about the only thing that stops me from beating him about the head with the nearest thing I can lift and swing.

I should have known. When he barged into my counselling practice – name of Lexy Campbell, Counsellor – and inserted himself as makeover queen (his word; don't blame me) and Kathi as decluttering guru, reimagining the business as a threesome, I thought that was it: Trinity for You, Trinity in the Mirror, Trinity at Home. I thought if I accepted that, life would be peaceful. Shows what I know. I should have put my foot down hard right then. Because the wholesale takeover of my professional life was just the beginning. Soon, Kathi started racking up hours as a trainee PI and, without so much as a courtesy email, Todd added Trinity for Trouble, aka Trinity Investigations. I had another foot I could have put down then. But I thought *that* was the end of it. I didn't foresee any problems. The licensing of a private investigator is just about as beset with paperwork as the licensing of a family, relationship and personal counsellor and there was no way the licensing board would be subject to any of Todd's . . . excesses.

What I didn't factor in was Todd's way of drumming up business. He didn't just work away at people's wardrobes, leaving Kathi to field queries about cheating spouses and missing dogs and me to counsel clients who'd asked me to. Oh no. He went out on the trawl, scooping up anyone he deemed had a problem and offering incentives to let us solve them. The first time he got clients for me it was a couple he overheard arguing in IKEA.

'Everyone argues in IKEA, Todd!' I remembered saying. 'They don't validate your parking if you're still on speaking terms at the check-out, for God's sake!'

'They don't validate parking at IKEA, Lexy,' Todd had told me. 'I know you're proud of learning what it means, but you need to learn its proper usage too.'

This time, though, I was sure I had him on the ropes. 'Who, pray, would be our client?' I said.

'Who, pray, do you think?' said Todd.

'The only one I can think of is me,' I said. 'I'm the one the cops are breathing down the neck of. I'm the obvious suspect out of everyone in the vicinity. But since I draw my salary from Trinity, there doesn't seem much point in me taking a chunk of it and paying it back.' That had been Della's point, but she'd never know I stole it.

It was true even though it still bugged me. I didn't fully understand the accounting procedures Todd used to turn four disparate enterprises into a pot of money to split three ways, but my income had increased steadily since he started doing whatever it was he did, so I wasn't grumbling.

'If I didn't know better I'd suspect a guilty conscience,' Todd said. 'But it's not all about you, Lexy. So guess again, our client is . . .? Or rather our clients are . . .?'

'Was he married?' I asked.

'Not to more than one person. And not any more. Divorced five years ago. One more guess.'

'How do you know he's divorced?' I said. 'How do you know when it happened?'

'Do you give up?' I nodded. 'Perdita and Anselm, of course. The grieving parents.'

'Menzies's mum and dad have employed Trinity to find out what happened to him?' I said. 'How did they . . .? Oh Todd, you didn't! That's one step up from ambulance chaser.'

'They're grateful,' Todd said. 'And they've got nothing but nice things to say about you, by the way.'

'Oh God,' I said.

'I don't know why you're having such an over-reaction,' said Todd.

'Me neither,' said Taylor, the treacherous scumbag. 'Think about it, Lexy. They're so far away and they've had this terrible news. They've only got phone calls from the cops to go on and you know how tight-lipped Molly can be.'

'Well,' said Todd. 'Hm. As to that. Far away. I wouldn't exactly . . .'

'They're coming here, aren't they?' I said. Todd's guilty look was all the admission I needed. 'That is a terrible idea,' I said. 'They need to stay at home, surrounded by the comfort of loved ones, while they process this tragedy. The last thing they need to do is travel thousands of miles and strand themselves here, all alone in a strange place, with God knows what changing rules for ever getting back again. I can't drop everything to comfort them. And neither can you, if you're serious about tricking out half the motel and my entire boat in time for this other mad scheme. And Kathi can't act as grief counsellor if she's investigating them. They need support at such a terrible time.'

'Well,' said Todd. 'Hm. Support. As to that. I wouldn't exactly—'

'No,' I said. 'You can't be serious. You cannot mean what I think you mean.'

'They volunteered,' said Todd. 'And you just made a good case for the Lassiters not being stranded here all alone.'

'I hate you,' I said. 'I've always hated you. I was being polite when I ever hinted that I didn't hate you. But I hate you so much more now that the earlier hate barely registers.'

'What are you talking about?' said Taylor.

'It's over, Taylor,' I said. 'Peace, freedom, sanctuary. California crumbles to dust today.'

'Because the *Lassiters* are coming?'

'No,' I said, 'because they're bringing my mum and dad along too.'

NINE

And that's why, despite everything, Taylor and I were pals again by the time we went to bed.

'It's good in a way,' he said, maybe convincing himself but definitely not convincing me. 'It lowers the stakes if I meet them when they're not laser-focused on rating me as a son-in-law. Right? Lexy?'

'I tell you what's good in a way. Me being out of here to let the NRA tour in—'

'The N—?'

'—then at least my mum and dad won't be across a very narrow passageway from us for however long they're staying. At least I'll be in a motel room with a lock on the door.'

'But they wouldn't be staying on the boat!' said Taylor. He was in bed already while I scrubbed off my make-up and he clutched the blankets to his chest at the very idea.

'Oh yes they would,' I said. 'That's an American thing, relatives visiting and staying at a hotel. That would only happen at home for a wedding or a funeral when the whole family descended en masse, down to the second cousins. And only then once all the airbeds and fold-out couches were spoken for.'

'Seriously?'

'Seriously. The first year here I thought every family I met was in the middle of a gigantic feud. Or a restraining order. I know it seems normal to you, but it's not normal to me and if I suggested it to my mum there'd be ructions.'

Taylor considered this for a while then moved on to the rest of what I'd said. 'So the House Tour is a go then?' I nodded. 'But double-check with Noleen, Lexy, because I'm pretty sure it's not the NRA doing it. It can't be.'

I climbed in beside him. 'What a day,' I said. 'Hiro. Menzies. Molly. And now my parents.'

'We won't be moving into the crime scene, will we?' Taylor said.

'Nope. That's the one Kathi and Nolly are planning to trick out like *Mad Men*. Whenever SOCO's finished.'

'CSI,' said Taylor.

'Yeah, them.'

So it's no surprise that I had a nightmare. I was in an Edinburgh flat full of people, lit by candles, all very Gothic. Except that the music was big band swing, for some reason. I was searching for him, for Menzies, who was sometimes Taylor, and for one truly nightmarish moment became Brandon. I kept opening doors trying to deliver a breakfast tray, but in every room there was a naked couple going at it hammer and tongs. The man was either Menzies, Taylor or Brandon and the woman was someone I didn't recognize. Does that mean she was me? 'Have you forgotten something?' she asked me in a haughty voice, glaring at me over Menzies', Taylor's or even Brandon's shoulder. I let the door swing shut, mumbling apologies, and ploughed on, wading through toffee to the next door, while the band grew loud enough to deafen me.

It was a relief to be startled awake. I lay in a sweaty mess of tangled sheets with my heart hammering.

'What the fuck?' said Taylor's groggy voice.

'Sorry,' I said. 'I had a bad dream.'

'It wasn't a dream. I heard it too.'

I lifted my head and looked at him in the light from my phone. 'What?' I blinked. 'Hey, why's my phone lit up?'

'Didn't you hear that?' said Taylor. 'It's happened again, Lexy. There's just been another shot. Another silenced gunshot. That's what woke me.'

I struggled free of the blankets and lifted my phone just as it went dark again. 'It's three o'clock,' I said. 'Oh Jesus, Taylor. It's three o'clock! Oh my God, there's a serial killer! Oh God, oh God, oh God, oh . . .' I was up, grabbing clothes and dragging them on, hopping about while I jammed my feet into my shoes, bouncing off the corridor walls as I made my way to the front of the boat. 'He's not getting away with it twice!' I shouted.

'Wait for me!'

But I wasn't waiting for anyone if there was a chance to catch this monster. Because, rough as it had been to see an old boyfriend from twenty years ago with a bullet hole in him, the available targets tonight were my best friends in the world: brave Kathi who never stopped trying; Noleen who loved her with a heart like a bear; Todd who hid a world of fear under the fabulousness; Roger the baby saver; Della who'd made a rich life for herself while the world kicked her for daring; Dylan who loved her with a heart like a golden retriever; and Diego. If that guy had shot Diego . . .

As I rounded the corner of the motel, my whole body seemed to shrivel. There was one light on. In Della and Dylan's room. I held on to the wall as I dragged myself towards the door, refusing to faint, refusing to cry. I needed to be strong for them. For whoever was left in there.

It wasn't locked. I turned the handle and let the door swing open. Della looked up from where she was feeding Hiro in the low rocking chair. Hiro looked up too, and growled at me. But hunger won out over rage and Della managed to get her latched on again. Over on the bed, two humps, one Dylan-sized and one Diego-sized, lay gently rising and falling.

'Thank God,' I said, and let myself slide down the wall before my legs gave way. 'Did you hear that? Why's your door open? Didn't you hear that?'

'Ssshhh,' said Della. 'No. So I can open it one-handed to go for a stroll with her when she . . . I mean *if* she starts crying. And still no. What's wrong, Lexy?'

'Did you seriously not *hear* that?'

'Hear what?' she asked me. Then she gasped. 'Dios, is he walking?'

'What? Is who—?'

'Menzies. Is he restless tonight? Because Hiro hasn't slept a wink. I've been feeding her for hours.'

'God's sake, Della!' I said. 'Hiro is not . . . I give up. And no, it wasn't a ghost that woke me. It was another gunshot.'

Della sat up so sharply that Hiro startled and, after a couple of smacking noises to get herself going, set to on a low-level grizzle. 'I didn't hear anything,' Della said. 'How did *you* hear it?'

'Eh?' I said. 'Look, lock your door, for God's sake.'

'Of course, once she's settled. I only unlock it when I get up to feed her. Are you sure it wasn't an owl?'

That didn't deserve a response and I couldn't spare any more time anyway. There were four more souls in this motel who meant more . . . Then I stopped. There were four more souls but they slept in twos. And I'd only heard one shot. Why wasn't there light and shouting in the owners' flat or in Todd and Roger's room? It didn't make any sense, I thought, as I hared off to check on them.

'This better be good!' came Noleen's voice as she unbolted the flat door and put the chain on.

'Are you OK?' I hissed into the six-inch gap.

'Fine, thank you for asking. Drop by anytime,' said Noleen. 'What the good god damn, Lexy?'

'Is Kathi OK?'

'Will I wake her and ask? What the actual fuck?'

'I thought I heard . . . No! Bugger it. I *heard* a shot.'

'Where?'

'I was on the boat.'

'So someone's hunting across the slough. Get a grip, will you?' Then she gasped. 'Look out.' She took the chain off, grabbed a handful of my sweatshirt and pulled me in beside her. She slammed the door and started re-locking it, swearing furiously.

'Noll?' came Kathi's sleepy voice from deeper inside.

'There's someone there,' Noleen whispered in my ear. 'I just saw him coming round the side of the office. He's heading this way. I'm sorry I doubted you, Lexy. Phone 911 and I'll let the others know.'

'I've left my ph—' I got out before a soft knock sounded from the other side of the door. The other side of a fairly flimsy hollow door of board and air and a few coats of paint. I dragged Noleen away from it.

'What's going on?' said Kathi, appearing in the passageway behind us in a striped nightshirt.

'There's a prowler,' said Noleen. 'He's right outside the door.'

'I'm not a prowler,' said Taylor. 'Why did you lock me out?'

'Oh for God's sake,' I said, setting to undo the locks and bolts again. Out on the forecourt, Della was standing in her doorway, Hiro over her shoulder and bellowing backwards into the room. Taylor made space for Noleen, Kathi and me to file out.

'We heard a shot,' I said, for what felt like the tenth time since I'd woken. 'It wasn't on the boat and it's not the Ds. Obviously it's not you two either.' One by one all of us raised our eyes to the upper level where 205, Todd and Roger's room, sat in silent darkness.

'I'll go,' I said.

'No one's going,' said Noleen. 'We need to get the cops.'

Taylor stuck his hand out to give me my phone. I took it, stared at it lying there in my palm, then stared at him, then again at my phone.

'What?' he said. 'Do you want me to call them?'

I shook my head. It was password protected and we weren't married yet, so it wasn't that. Truth to tell, I didn't know *what* it was, only that something was bothering me.

'Look,' said Noleen, nudging me hard in the ribs and pointing upwards.

'What?' I said, clutching her. I raked my gaze along the walkway from horseshoe end to horseshoe end but there was nothing to see; no bulky shadow creeping along hugging the wall, no dark shape slipping out of a propped window, no glint from the nose of a gun pointed our way. Nothing disturbed the inky darkness above the forecourt lights, which pointed down with shades like handmaid bonnets. Nothing except a faint bluish glow behind Todd and Roger's drawn curtains.

As we watched, the door inched open and Roger – we could tell it was Roger, because what murderer would go out on a rampage in SpongeBob scrubs? – edged around it. He closed the door softly with his hand flat on the wood to stop any click and then turned our way.

'What's going on?' he said.

'Why? What's going on with *you*?' said Noleen, three notches too belligerent for the situation, which is always the way sudden relief takes her. She resents the hell out of caring for anyone except Kathi. Maybe Diego. And probably Hiro soon, if not already after one day.

'I've been called in,' said Roger, trotting down the stairs to meet us. The squeak of his crocs on the metal steps set my teeth on edge.

'Did you hear it?' I said. 'What woke you?'

'Hear what?' said Roger. 'What do you mean what woke me? What do you think woke me? My phone.'

'Jesus *Christ*!' The door of Roger's room banged open and bounced off the wall. Todd stamped out, naked except for silk boxers, and leaned over the balcony. 'First you put it on Eurovision rejects instead of vibrate!' he said. Snarled, really. 'Then you make more noise creeping around trying to be quiet than you could ever make if you just did things normally. And *then* you stand about outside for a round of chitchat! Why the hell is everyone yakking their beaks off under my room at fuck it's early o'clock?'

'Todd,' Noleen said. 'You know how you feel right now?'

'What?'

'Focus on it,' Kathi added. 'That's how everyone else feels when you burst in at six with coffee we never asked for.'

'Pfft,' said Todd. 'Get real. This is the middle of the night. And you said yourself I don't ever disturb you till gone six in the morning.' He took a breath and frowned. 'What are you all doing up anyway?'

'Eurovision rejects,' I said. 'Vibrate. Phone.'

Roger gave me that look, one eyebrow up and one down. 'You know who you sound like?' he said. 'Man, woman, person, camera, TV.' Then he shrugged. 'Whatever it is, Lexy, tell Todd. I gotta go.'

'What is it, Lexy?' said Taylor.

'Yeah, what is it?' said Noleen. 'Todd accidentally said something sensible right there. Why *are* we all standing around at three o'clock in the morning?'

'I need to sit down,' I said. 'Maybe.'

'Come up,' said Todd. 'I'm too cold to come down.' He disappeared back inside his room and I headed for the stairs. He meant it about the cold. If it was summer he'd quite happily traipse around the motel in just those slinky boxers. And he had the nerve to judge his mother for her frequent bouts of public nudity.

'Do you need me for this?' Della said, nodding at the bundle in her arms. 'Because she's sound asleep at long last and I need to take my chances where I can.'

I shook my head.

'You need us?' said Noleen.

I didn't know what to say and so I said nothing, but my face betrayed me.

'She needs us,' said Kathi and followed.

Todd had a tray of drinks ready as we all crowded into his room. 'It's too late for martinis and too early for coffee,' he said. 'So have a coffee martini.'

That made no kind of sense, but I needed Dutch courage and I helped myself to what looked like the biggest glassful.

'Last night we woke up and looked at each other,' I said to Taylor. 'Right?'

'In the light from your phone.'

'So annoying,' said Todd. 'If we ever break up it's that damned phone plugged in at the bedside that's gonna do it.'

'But what woke us was the sound of the silenced shot,' I said. I had my home page up and was clicking through apps.

'Right.'

'In the motel room next to us, through a flimsy connecting door.'

'Hey!' said Noleen. 'No need to be rude. Our doors are to code.'

'Then tonight we heard it again. Just as loud, just as close.' I was still scrolling. I was on page three now, away way back in the cardio bursts and diet plans that I'd never used after downloading them. 'Even though we were on the far side of a boat, across the slough from the back of the motel, with an exterior wall and a closed bathroom door between us and the bedrooms.'

'You say that, Lexy,' Kathi chipped in. 'But you would not believe the number of people who sleep with the bathroom door standing wide open. Flush with the lid up. Don't flush at all if it's only a pee. They claim they're saving water but really they're just filthy skanky garbage heads.'

'Clarty besoms,' I said. Agreeing with Kathi is second nature now. 'But, as I was saying: tonight, when I woke up, I looked around in the light from my phone. Aha!'

'Aha?' said Taylor.

'Aha,' I said and I hit the button.

I still thought it sounded like a fist puncturing the skin on a bowlful of risen dough, but I could hear the airbag/lifeboat thing too. I played it again. And then a third time.

'Does that mean what I think it means?' Todd said.

'Yup,' I answered. 'Bang goes my alibi.'

'Dooft goes your alibi,' said Noleen. 'How the hell did that get on your phone?'

TEN

Saturday 28 November

I think – I mean if I had to put money on it, I would maybe risk a fiver – I *think* Molly believed me. Not at first. At first her eyes flashed above her mask and her brows did a quick selection of the Sergeant Rankinson top ten brow moves. But I talked her round.

'Why the hell wouldn't I have deleted it?' was first.

'Because there was a new baby and you forgot.'

'Why the hell wouldn't I have deleted it when it went off the second night?' I tried next.

'Because Taylor heard it too.'

I had said to him that I could handle this alone, but now I wished we were both packed into this horrible little interview room. Or, even better, I wish I had asked Molly to come to the boat.

'Exactly,' I said. 'Why the hell would I let Taylor hear it too?'

'Loyalty test,' Molly said.

'Loyalt . . .' I said. 'This isn't some prank, Molly. This isn't shits and giggles.'

'So you admit that it's usually both?'

'This is murder. Of course I wouldn't be so stupid as to leave an app on my phone!'

'*Someone* left it there,' Molly said.

I thought about that for a minute. 'Could you trace the purchase?' I said. 'Surely whoever downloaded it must have used PayPal or a card number. Could you tell?' I put my phone on the table and we both stared at it.

'We could,' she said. 'Prints too.'

'Fingerprints?' I said. 'Forget it. We're not all bleaching our fruit and boiling our door handles any more, but don't tell me none of Kathi's hygiene regime wore off on you during lockdown.'

Molly sighed. 'Yeah, I clean my phone with a Clorox wipe twice a day,' she said. 'And there isn't a bathroom door in the state I can't open with a knee or elbow. I'll never actually touch one again. I don't even like handling paper now. Some people lick to turn pages, you know.' She grimaced at the buff-coloured folder that was looking much fatter than this time yesterday.

'I still don't have a motive,' I said. 'Have you considered that?'

'We're still exploring the question of motive,' said Molly. 'His mother has been very helpful – well, of course she has – in the matter of mutual friends from way back when.'

'Mutual friends of mine and Menzies's?' I said. 'That's a reach.'

'Struan, Findlay, and something I can't pronounce that would be bleeped out of a broadcast,' Molly said. 'Do you remember them?'

Farquhar. I managed not to say it. Did I remember them? Sort of. I remembered them en masse. I would never have been able to say which was which, then or now. If I hadn't gone out with Menzies, I wouldn't have been able to pick him out of a line-up either.

'They sound like bagpipe parts, you ask me,' said Molly. 'But Mrs Lassiter assured me those are names parents chose for their baby boys.'

There was one called Strathpeffer too. Strathpeffer Loaning – poor bugger; destined for a life of taxi dispatchers asking, 'What number on Strathpeffer Loaning, sir? And what's the customer's name?'

Another memory came swinging in. I was answering the door at Menzies's flat one Saturday night. The kid on the step introduced himself as Nicky and I said he must have the wrong address, then I cackled like a blackbird and waved him in, floppy fringe, pink cords and all.

'You OK?' said Molly.

'Fine,' I said. Well, lied. The truth was these memories were interfering with the after-effects of another pie-based breakfast, which was already worse than the first, since the fruit ones were finished and the creamy ones needed to be used up. I'd been served a wedge of coconut concoction with my morning coffee and it wasn't lying still inside me.

'You want to tell me what you just thought?' Molly said.

I blanked her.

'Or go right ahead and tell me what Struan, Findlay and Gargling-with-pumice-stones are going to tell me anyway, before they get the chance to.'

Farquhar, I thought again. And, although it's true that I never could tell the BOLS Boys apart properly, I remembered a big sweaty face split into a grin and big horsy teeth stained dark with red wine, the same red wine I'd throw up into the bathroom sink before I went stumbling off to ruin my sandals.

'I tell you what I *will* tell you, once I've had a chance to sit and think it through,' I said. 'And that's the list of people who might have got their hands on my phone. Because someone did. I just need to retrace my steps and think who it could be.'

'A client?'

'We're still on Zoom.'

'You been in the Skweek? On the desk?'

I shook my head. It was all hands on deck for a while earlier in the year and any of us might have put in hours anywhere, but Kathi was back in the launderette now, Noleen in Reception.

'So just the Ditchers,' Molly said.

'None of whom has a motive to kill Menzies Lassiter and none of whom would dob me in for it even if they did.'

'And Taylor, of course,' Molly said.

I opened my mouth to protest, then remembered Taylor this morning, holding my phone out to me. Why had he brought it, instead of his own?

'Taylor Aaronovitch, the current boyfriend of the victim's ex. Who works in a phone store.'

'And so definitely knows better than to leave an app installed when its job is done.'

'Unless its job wasn't done till you found it,' said Molly. 'Unless this is part of the plan.'

'What plan?' I said. 'You sound like one of those conspiracy theory nutters – the absence of any sense makes it all the more likely. Wooooooooo!' I waggled my hands at her and – give her due – she did blush. 'So can we agree that if I had put the app on my phone to go off at three and give me an alibi, I'd have deleted it. And if I had been a big enough idiot to set it on repeat instead of once only *and* forgot to delete it, I wouldn't have woken up the whole motel to let them in on my blunder. At least I'd have taken it with me and deleted it while I was on my way round to wake them. *Right?*'

'That's one possible theory,' said Molly. It wasn't gracious but I knew I'd have to settle for it.

'Right,' I said. 'I think that's all the blood I'm going to squeeze from this particular stone. What's next? I give you my phone and you see if you can trace the source of the download? And I—'

'No and hell no,' Molly said. 'I said we *could* check. I didn't say we were going to. Lexy, we don't have the budget in the Cuento PD to do that kind of forensic tech. You read the *Voyager*. You know that.'

'What about Interpol?' I said. 'Since he's a foreign national.'

'Interpol. Right.' She puffed out a huge breath making her mask fill up like a balloon. 'I'll give you this. Don't remove anything or update anything in case there's a development and we ever *do* want to. OK?'

'OK. But I want the record to show that I offered to surrender my phone today and you refused. I don't want this coming back to bite me.'

'Deal.'

'And what was the hell no?' I said. 'You said no and hell no.'

'Because you said "And I". The hell no is to you doing anything. Any of you doing anything. You keep out of this. You leave this to me. I shouldn't have to keep saying that to you.'

'Got it. *You* don't follow the evidence of my phone and the mysterious app because you haven't got the budget. And *I* agree to do absolutely nothing, even though it's my phone and I've got a right to do anything I want with it. That does sound like me.'

'OK,' said Molly, reaching her hand out. 'Gimme your phone.'

'Nope,' I said. I put it in the pouch pocket of my hoodie and stared her down. 'Because you've just admitted that you can't do anything with it so, if I hand it over, you're going to tag and bag it and put it in the evidence room to moulder until the sun burns the earth and we all die.'

'So you're rescinding your offer to comply with the investigation by handing over your phone?'

'You betcha.'

'How about allowing us to search your boat without making us wait for a warrant?'

'Take a guess,' I said, standing and sweeping out before she could think up some sneaky cop way to stop me.

'How'd it go?' Noleen said, as I let myself into the office. I'd stopped at the Swiss Sisters for a midday pick-me-up of quadruple-shot latte, feeling the effects of two nights' broken sleep and knowing I had to have my wits about me for the afternoon's work. Of course, there's no such thing as going to the drive-thru for a coffee, as in one coffee, because there's no way to get home without being seen by at least three friends, all of whom love a cup of joe, and one of whom regularly brings it right to my bedside. Although, in contrast, Kathi and Noleen had never spontaneously bought me any kind of hot beverage, Kathi because she can only drink Swiss Sisters if she doesn't see the grubbiness of the kiosk, and Noleen partly because she makes a lot of margaritas by the jugful and reckons that covers her. And partly because she's banned from all the coffee purveyors in Cuento on account of her habit of asking for 'coffee' and staring stonily and silently at the barista throughout all the follow-up questions.

'Your coffee, madam,' I said, plonking her medium black on the desk. She shrieked and lifted it off again, sliding a coaster underneath it in a slick move that reminded me of close magic. 'What gives?'

'Coffee beans and water?' said Noleen, unnecessarily in my view. We'd met.

'Of course,' I said, 'but what gives?'

'I've decided there's to be no more hot cups or wet glasses or bunches of sharp keys or anything harsher than a duster on the original fittings,' Noleen said.

'They've survived this long.'

'And irony is not going to get its fangs into me now,' Noleen said. 'Imagine how dumb I'd feel if I wrecked this finish days before the final walk-through, just in time to get kicked off the tour.'

Finish, I thought, looking at the counter properly for the first time. I couldn't name the industrial process that had resulted in the mid-century marvel of the Last Ditch check-in desk – and I would put money on it now being illegal and the people who'd made it living out their days on lavish workers' comp – but I reckoned it would take a bandsaw to tarnish it. A chainsaw to demolish it. Still, if Noleen was in the coaster business suddenly, who was I to argue.

The rest of the office was looking pretty spiffy. The green couch and end tables had replaced a sectional of spectacular ugliness, which made up for that by also being deeply uncomfortable. Noleen kept it deliberately to dissuade guests from lingering. The white cast-iron cafe chairs – also no joke on the bum if you sat there for any length of time – were gone too, along with their matching table; one of those knobbly ones that tip cups of hot liquid onto your knees through the decorative holes.

'Is breakfast off then?' I said but, even as I spoke, Todd was backing into the room dragging the replacement dinette with him.

'Wowzeroni!' I said. 'That's fabulous.'

It was a white Formica table straight out of the Sixties, with a ruby-red leaf design at two corners, and chrome legs. 'Where are you getting this stuff?'

'This was in my mom's garage,' said Todd. 'I remember it from when I was a kid and I was embarrassed for my friends to see it because everyone else had black ash.'

'You need to lose the gum before Kathi sees it,' Noleen said, pointing to where a half-ring of grey blobs was stuck on the underside.

'Or before I commit a crime and they trace my DNA,' said Todd. 'I can't believe it's still stuck there after all these years. You chip it off, Lexy, and I'll go for the chairs.'

'I'm not . . .' I said, but he was gone. 'I'm not chipping ancient gum off a vintage table,' I said to Noleen.

'In case you damage it?'

'Let's go with that. Speaking of crime instead of furniture for a moment, why does no one seem to care that a man was killed here yesterday? I mean I know I was always going to care a bit more than the rest of you because I knew him, but how can you even think about the NRA thing?'

'I asked you how it went,' said Noleen. 'You didn't answer. I don't want to bug you.'

'It went terribly,' I said. 'If we're thinking about Menzies's killer being caught, that is. Very well, if we're thinking about Trinity getting to work a case because the cops haven't got a clue. They won't commit to . . . what did she call it? . . . "forensic tech" to trace the source of the app. So I got to keep my phone and I'm going to set Taylor on it. Meanwhile I need to concentrate hard and compile a list of anyone who could have got their mitts on it long enough to set it up.'

'Good luck with that!' said Noleen.

'What's that supposed to mean?'

'Aw gimme a break! I've seen you leave it in a bathroom stall, on the hand-drier outside, in your car in full view of passing skeeves. You leave it behind here, you leave it in the laundromat. You go out for hours and leave it lying around wherever you put it last. You left it on the boat last night when you thought there was a murder going down!'

'Well make your mind up!' I said. 'I've heard you nagging Dylan till he's curled in a ball about how he never lets his phone out of his sight. Ripping the living piss out of him for having a waterproof case to use in the shower. You told him to get a paternity test because no way was he fertile after keeping his phone in his front jeans pocket all these years.'

'You never heard of a happy medium?' Noleen said. 'Grab the other end of this before I put my back out.'

Together we manhandled the table into position in the far corner of Reception. It was a solid piece of workmanship and we were both puffing by the time she was happy with its placement. I was roasting hot too, and also still stewing. 'I've never left my phone in a toilet cubicle, by the way,' I said, 'because Kathi has trained me too well and there's no way I'd ever put it down in there. Ew. And the time I put it on the hand-drier was to record how noisy it was and complain to the manager. I left it here once, but only because I was hammered thank you very much. And once in the Skweek, again because I was drunk out of my skull. And once in Todd's car because I was choosing a pumpkin and didn't want it to fall out of my pocket into the mud. Passing skeeves! Right, because that's job number one for any self-respecting skeef, isn't it? Choosing pumpkins from a grow-your-own patch.'

'You think skeef is the singular of skeeves?' said Noleen. 'Who are you, Chaucer?'

'Why are you being so aggressive?' I asked her.

She stuck out her hand. 'Noleen Muntz,' she said, shaking mine. 'Who are you?'

That made me laugh and then Todd was back, carrying a stack of four matching chrome-and-vinyl chairs, and the moment passed. We arranged the chairs around the table and sat down, coffees in hand.

It was the weirdest sitting experience I'd ever had. The seat cushions, plump and shiny, settled gradually under our weight, letting out long, slow, *very* loud farting noises along with a strong whiff of Barb's garage – mouse, oil, and old booze.

'Oh, shame,' I said, thinking what a bummer it was that they looked so cool but weren't usable.

'Oh my God!' said Noleen, putting one hand over her mouth. 'That takes me right back to double-dating at the milk bar.'

'I had forgotten!' said Todd. There were tears shining in his eyes. 'Oh, I'm so glad it's not too late to mention it on the flyers.'

'Wait, what?' I said. 'You think those fart sounds are OK?'

'OK?' said Todd. 'They're iconic. People are going to be lining up for the ride.'

'Nostalgia,' said Noleen. 'That's what we've got that the rest of these fancy schmancy Victorians ain't. The Ditch's gonna be the jewel in the crown.'

'Maybe you won't need the boat after all,' I said.

'Oh they definitely want the boat,' said Todd. 'They were very clear about how much they wanted the boat.'

'Anyway,' said Noleen, with a calamitous attempt at nonchalance, 'let's not forget we've a murder to talk about, Todd.'

'Huh?'

'Huh, indeed,' I said. 'What's going on, Noleen? Why are you being so weird?'

'What *is* going on?' Todd asked her. Then he turned to me. 'Weird how?'

'Nothing,' said Noleen, staring very hard at him. 'Nothing is going on. And I'm not being weird, *Todd*. I just don't think there's any reason to doubt that the ladies on the committee will want the boat, once they've seen it.'

'Oh!' said Todd. 'Right. Well no, of course you're not being weird. And of course they'll want the boat. Once they've seen it. Why are you asking dumb questions, Lexy?'

'Seriously,' I said. 'What is it?' I looked from one of them to the other. They were being monumentally bogus. And they weren't going to give it up easily. Still, for sheer self-respect, I had to try.

'Did you . . .' I said, thinking hard, '. . . oversell the place and you think I'll be offended when they turn up their noses? Because I won't. I don't care what some random women from the NRA think of my home.'

'You mean DAR,' said Todd.

'No she doesn't,' said Noleen. 'It's the Historic Residence Tour. HRT.'

'They've got a way with subliminal marketing,' I said. 'I'll give them that.'

'Yup,' said Todd. 'They know their demographic. And they're not going to pass on the houseboat, Lexy. They'll love it.'

'Do I need to have a tidy round or anything?'

'Oh. Um. Well,' said Todd. 'You were out, you see.'

'You've been in there today?' I said. 'You've been meddling?'

'I've been staging,' said Todd.

'Oh!' I said, turning to Noleen. 'And you knew about this? Is that why you were being so aggressive?'

'Best form of defence,' said Noleen. 'Pre-emptive attack.' She gave me an unrepentant grin.

'Exactly!' said Todd. 'Noleen reckoned I should run it past you before I piled in. I ignored her. That's why she got weird. Right, Nolly?'

Noleen rolled her eyes and shook her head. 'You suck,' she said. 'Lexy believed it until you made it all fake again. You suck so bad sometimes.'

'Look, never mind all that,' I said. 'I want to see my boat tricked out HRT-style. Let's go.'

ELEVEN

'But really,' I said, 'where did you get all this?' I was standing in the living-room doorway of the boat, gazing around. Gone were my serviceable armchairs and midget sofa and in their place was a two-seater from early in the twentieth century, upholstered in what looked like sealskin and with dark tartan seat cushions. It wasn't pretty, but it was certainly authentic. The IKEA lamps were gone; the new ones had horses as bases and tassels hanging from their silk shades. The flexes were brown twists and I decided not to ask about fire safety. (There's plenty of water around a houseboat if an ancient electrical cord ever starts smoking.) Even my books had been changed, for leather-bound sets of classics, and my modern prints had been replaced by a watercolour of a gypsy caravan and an embroidered Home Sweet Home.

'Some of it is Amaranth's,' Todd said, bustling round plumping up velvet throw cushions and smoothing the nap of the sealskin. 'Some of it is my mom's. A lot of it came from the storeroom at the retirement community. They're overflowing since they didn't get to hold the Fall Frenzy. So I borrowed it and said I'd sell what I could and only take back what no one wanted.'

That made sense. The UC Cuento Retirement Community Fall Frenzy was a highlight of the calendar year for vintage fans, bargain hunters and lovers of curios. I hated the sound of it when Todd first floated the notion of a visit: those well-travelled professors downsizing out of their houses into supported flats and having to get shot of their libraries and artworks? It sounded sad. And then, as the years passed, they had to downsize again to the residential home and the furniture went too – appliances and antiques the same. Finally, of course, they downsized one last time into a box and even their jewellery and wedding china, the very last of the treasures, had to go. All in all, I'd done a fair impression of a dog en route to the vet when Todd dragged me along last year.

But that was before I saw the operation in full swing. My God, those old people were motivated sellers! All dressed in blinding neon sweatshirts, with change aprons like market traders, they put timeshare peddlers to shame: throwing in unwanted extras to secure the price; starting scratch bidding wars when two customers glanced at the same item; flat-out lying about provenance if they thought you were gullible enough to fall for it. Not a single one of them looked sorry to be seeing their clobber go.

'Hated it since my wedding day,' said a wild-haired old lady, poking a rolled-up rug with her walking stick. 'I wrote a thank-you letter but it nearly killed me.'

'My husband wore every single one of these damn fool hats,' said another. 'Even the fez. Wore them to class and gave out extra papers to students for laughing at him. The man was an asshole. Who the hell wears a pith helmet to the grocery store?'

'Assholes?' I hazarded.

'Assholes,' she said, nodding. 'Same assholes who wear deerstalkers to the movies.'

'You're selling a deerstalker?' I said, thinking it would make a good joke present for Kathi as she completed her PI training hours. Not that she'd let a second-hand hat touch her head.

'Nah,' said the widow. 'The kid in the seat behind snatched it and filled it with Cola. Asshole had it coming.'

'So you like it,' Todd said, as I surveyed my living room. He was hovering near the brass Benares side table, fussing with an ashtray he'd set there. 'You're smiling at least.'

'Happy memories,' I said. 'How can you sell the stuff to the visitors, by the way? Have you got back-ups?'

'Red dots,' said Todd. 'Like a show at an art gallery? We'll take their names and deliver when the tour is finished. Come see the dining room.'

It gave me a pang. I spent more time in here than anywhere else on the boat, seeing clients and doing the endless HMO paperwork, and it was the nicest office I'd ever had. Now, all that was gone and in its place sat a heavy old walnut table and six heavy old walnut chairs, a heavy old walnut sideboard squeezed in too. The table was set with ornate china and crystal and looked completely full even without any food.

'You'll be lucky to get a red dot on this lot,' I said. 'Where are my files?'

'Room 105,' Todd said. 'I didn't peek.'

I threw him a look as old-fashioned as the lacy tablecloth. 'Fair enough. And now I've got to go. I need to compile a list of people who might have got their hands on my phone. What?'

Todd was staring at me out of wide-open eyes, working his jaw a little and shuffling his feet a bit too. 'Nothing,' he said.

'Have *you* had it?'

'Are you asking me whether I murdered a complete stranger and framed you for it with a gun-noise app?'

'No,' I said. 'What about Noleen though? She was very weird just there.'

'Did Noleen do her best to tank her already struggling business by murdering a complete stranger and top that off by framing her friend?'

'Don't be soft. I mean, did Noleen mess with my phone?'

'No,' said Todd. 'I mean, how would I know?'

'In all your years of self-improvement,' I said, 'with the peels and the personal trainers and everything, you never took a single acting class?'

I didn't need one. I knew enough to recognize a scene-capping line. I swept out without another word.

Every kneejerk defence I'd just lobbed at Noleen aside, the truth was I had my work cut out for me trying to narrow down the list of people who could have put that app on my phone. I *did* leave it behind when I went on morning walks and coffee-runs, otherwise people phoned me and ruined the whole mindful meditation vibe. Except OK, it was really because if I took it I checked my socials and watched videos of baby pandas falling down. And, OK, when I say baby pandas falling down, I mean red carpets and real house-wives. And yes, OK, I was going to have to stop telling myself I only watched the real housewives to be able to communicate with my clients on their own terms, because any time I name-dropped Teresa, Aviva, Ramona and Nene, none of my clients ever had a clue what I was on about. And OK – finally – when I didn't delib-erately leave it behind on the boat, I did occasionally leave it behind by accident wherever I'd taken it. I could think of three places right off the bat: the Lode, Cuento's premier supermarket; the Casual Browser, Cuento's premier bookshop; and Odie's Ovens, Cuento's premier pizza joint. Or my three favourites anyway.

By the time I arrived at the Lode, I had composed a story which, while it might not work, at least wouldn't raise suspicions. I hoped.

There was no one else ahead of me at the customer service desk. Of course there wasn't. At the Lode, the pyramids of fruit were polished and symmetrical; the fish was fresh enough to swim away if you dropped it back in the sea; the cheese counter – no smell of cheese somehow – was decorated with grapes so shiny and so uniform I had always assumed they were plastic until I ate one one time to make Todd laugh and he didn't think it was funny. (Which, to be fair, was an accurate response: eating a real grape isn't the prime slapstick eating a plastic grape would be.) In short, the Lode is so unsettlingly perfect that no customer has ever had a complaint.

Still, they keep an assistant smiling like a lunatic behind the counter, calling out cheery greetings to everyone.

'Good morning!' sang today's example, doing a perfect eye-smile above her mask. She put her head on one side. 'How are you today?'

'I'm OK,' I said, 'but I've got a bit of a problem.'

I watched to see if she would short out and start sparking at such unprecedented news, but she only knitted her brows together in a deep frown and leaned towards me. 'I'm so sorry to hear that? How can I fix it for you?'

'Well,' I said. 'I left my phone here last week—'

'Lost and Found?' she said, bursting into action.

'No! No, I got it back. Thank you,' I waggled it at her. 'But I didn't get the name of the person who handed it in. And I wanted to give her or him a little thank-you gift.'

She clapped her hands together and – I swear – levitated. 'What a beautiful idea. That's so sweet of you.'

'So you're OK with that?' This was too easy.

'I can't imagine anything more randomly kind and reciprocal!'

I blinked. The programmer really needed to work on the plausible human language software with this one. 'OK, well, cool,' I said.

'If you would like to choose a gift and bring it here, I'll run your card and wrap it for you, then we can contact your Good Samaritan on your behalf.'

'Ah,' I said. 'You couldn't just tell me . . . So I can just . . .'

She gazed at me with bottomless solemnity. She couldn't actually say the word 'no' to a customer, but I got the message anyway.

'Right. Great. Got it,' I said. 'I'll do that.' Because I could give permission to the phone snatcher to contact me and then either break them or cross them off my list. 'I'll be in the scented candle and lotion aisle then.'

She did a huge eye-grin and I made my escape.

I got about ten paces before someone squared up in front of me and stopped me dead with her six-foot force-field. It was another Lode assistant. Had the one on Customer Service paged an emergency candle consultant? I wouldn't put it past them.

'Did your friend find you?' she said.

Now, this was a puzzler. In the supermarkets and corner shops of home, that would mean: had someone I knew from life outside the shop, and who was looking for me – and had asked a shelf-stacker where I was for some reason – been successful in their quest.

But this was the Lode, where everyone was your buddy, and she might easily mean that the customer service assistant was on the hunt for me to share a wider eye-grin or be even more helpful. Or . . .

'Ack,' I said. 'Don't tell me I left my phone again!'

The eyes of the candle consultant flared briefly in panic.

'Phone?' she said. 'Where? What?'

Seriously, the programmers needed to build in more flexibility. I had completely freaked her out with an off-script response.

'Sorry,' I said.

'Please don't apologize,' she said, with an uneasy look behind her. 'I didn't mean to suggest that you had done something wrong!'

'Sorry,' I said again. 'I didn't mean to suggest you'd suggested.'

'You can suggest anything!'

'Sorry.'

'Please, please, please stop apologizing!' Her voice lifted into real distress.

'I'm not apologizing,' I said. 'I'm just British.'

Then we both took a breather.

'Can I ask you a question?' she said, after a while.

'As long as it's not "Are you sorry?"' I said. 'Sorry.'

She ignored me and ploughed on. 'How long did you live in Australia?'

'What?'

'Your accent?'

'I'm Scottish.'

'But your friend is British, right?'

I considered doing it all again. I used to do it. Many's the time I launched into my whole Scottish/British/European routine, stopping in on England and Wales too, with a nod to Northern Ireland and the Republic. I was very proud of it. I used Canada for Ireland, Alaska for Ulster, Mexico as France, etc. and the lower forty-eight as England, Scotland and Wales, with Hawaii coming on as Gibraltar. It was perfect. And you know what? It never worked. Not one single time. People who managed to understand that they were both American and Californian still couldn't wrap their heads round the bombshell that I was British and Scottish too. These days I tended to accept that people here thought British and English were synonyms and that I was probably Scandinavian. Or indeed Australian. Life's short. Besides, today I had bigger fish to fry.

'My friend?' I said. Had I somehow tracked down the phone thief already?

'Your friend that was looking for you?' she said. 'But wasn't sure where you lived?'

I stared at her, hoping she'd think the ingredients of a normal expression were hidden under my mask and not realize that actually my eyes had died as my heart sank.

'A friend from home?' she said. 'Hoping to surprise you? Did you hook up?'

Did we? If bringing eggs and coffee to his corpse counted as hooking up, then yes.

'Is everything OK?' she said.

Almost nothing, was the honest answer, but I couldn't tell her that. It would be like stamping on a baby bird. Like pulling the wings off a flower fairy. I missed the shop assistants of home more than ever, those disaffected, laid-off miners who filled shelves and drilled you with cold stares, those divorced mums and strapped grannies who judged your basket and told you to make your own soup instead of buying the overpriced muck they were running through the till. You could have a proper set-to with people like that. The Lode assistants were all UCC students, full of hope and optimism. A harsh word could crush them.

Even a harsh silence had done for the current specimen. With tears shining in her eyes she said, 'Do you want to speak to my manager?'

'*Eh?*' I said. 'Fu . . . I mean, sod off. No way. What do you take me for?'

'What?'

She looked sincere. On the mean streets of Cuento, or the mean aisles of its premier grocery emporium anyway, that still meant what it used to.

'We didn't give out your address or anything,' she said. 'We would never do that.'

'Oh I know!' I said. Or I would be en route to the phone busybody to see if they were also an app-uploading murderer.

'We just said that you did live here. And you do. And you're kind of famous, from that case with the body and all the blood and everything? And you run a public-facing business with a website and so it's like all to the good to let as many people as possible know where you are, isn't it? And we didn't tell her anything she didn't know anyway.'

'Who didn't—' I tried to break in, but she was unstoppable.

'Because she wanted to double-check that we were both talking about the same person and she asked if you were the MFT except she called it something else, from being British. I want to say meditation guide . . .'

'Guidance counsellor?'

'Is that what they're called in Australia too?'

'Scotland,' I reminded her. 'And who are we talking about now?'

'Your friend? Who was looking for you? And asked in here where she could find you?'

'She?' I said. '*She?*'

'Oh no!' said the assistant. 'Oh my gosh, I'm so sorry. I didn't ask their pronouns.'

'No, no, no,' I said. 'I mean, the friend I was thinking about is a he.'

'I am so deeply sorry,' the assistant said. 'I assumed, because your friend was wearing make-up and a mini-skirt – a beautiful black pleather mini, as I recall – that they – he, sorry! – was woman-presenting.'

I smiled at her. There's a lot wrong in this world but some things are headed upwards like they're strapped to a rocket. 'Don't fret,' I said. 'We're talking about two different people. My man friend – he/his – found me . . . sort of.' I took a beat and decided not to tell her the details. She was upset enough already. 'I wonder who my woman friend is. She hasn't tracked me down yet. Something to look forward to.'

Then I made my escape. Ten minutes later, I had a micro-wavable seaweed eye-mask in a gift bag lodged at Customer Services along with one of my business cards, ready to be passed on to whoever had handed in my phone. Then, if they got in touch, I could work out how to bump them into confirming whether they'd downloaded an app, set as it was to go off at three in the morning, and – oh yeah – killed my ex-boyfriend.

Or maybe, given that detail, I'd better hand their name over to Molly to pursue.

Because that detail was kind of the point. And kind of the thing I was willing myself not to think about, twatting around after my phone, obsessing about a list of places I'd left it. Buying gel masks, for God's sake!

Menzies Lassiter was dead. He had gone to my parents' house to try to get in touch with me and, before he quite managed it, he was dead. And I was lying my lips off to the cops about—

I stopped. My brain stopped spinning and my feet stopped walking. It took the honking of a harried Black Friday Boxing Day bargain hunter to jolt me back to life again. (I was standing in the way of a coveted empty parking space near both the trolley corral and the front door.) I raised a hand in apology and moved out of the way. Why the hell, I suddenly had the wit to ask myself, did Menzies set about finding me by going and bugging my mum and dad? Who does that? What person under the age of eighty would *ever* do that? It's like needing a plumber – or a pizza – and padding out to the hall to get the Yellow Pages from the drawer in the telephone table. If Menzies wanted to track me down, he'd google me. And he'd find me when he did. Surely. How many Leagsaidh Campbells could there be?

I whipped out my phone and did something I had never done before. I searched my own name. There were fourteen thousand hits but, as I discovered by scrolling and scrolling (and scrolling), they were all me. There were professional listings from my past in Dundee, and current listings from here in Cuento. There were news reports of our first case, and our second, and our third, although not anything on this fourth one yet. There were alumnus lists from Edinburgh, social media posts from long-ago weddings. And of course there was the Todd effect: the relentless promotion of Trinity all day every day anywhere clicks could be clicked.

I opened the door of my car and sat sideways on the driver's seat with my feet still on the tarmac, reflecting on the utter lack of any kind of privacy surrounding any bit of my life, except for the precise map coordinates of my houseboat. Which was about to change as soon as the HRT got underway.

So if – and it was a big if – Menzies had gone to my parents instead of Google for the only good reason I could imagine, and if – an even bigger if – he needed to find me urgently to warn me about something bad coming my way, and if – a *huge* if – he was killed because of that, then I was in a lot of trouble and I was about to be in a lot more.

But those were three family-sized – nay, party-pack – ifs and I should walk them back right now before I freaked myself out for nothing. Fi, Fi, Fi, I murmured. Take it logically. For what reason had Menzies got to me through my parents instead of Google? And for what separate reason had he come? And for what third unrelated reason had someone killed him?

The person from the next car over was back with his shopping. He glared at me for sitting with my door open, six inches from touching his. Because that's a real thing when your car is new and shiny and you've mistaken it for a personality. I tucked my feet in and slammed my door closed, catching sight of myself in the wing mirror as I did so.

My face looked bloody awful. Some of it was down to lack of sleep, an excess of pie-based carbs, shock, grief and talking to my mother. But at least a bit of it was the strain of kidding myself that anything else had happened here except this: Menzies tried to find me without leaving any digital trace of his search; then he came to warn me about the bad juju he was avoiding; and finally he'd been killed before he got the chance. Plus one more thing. I was next.

TWELVE

I ran it past the rest of the Ditchers at the Last (pies excepted) Great Leftovers Challenge that night on the forecourt. Not all the Ditchers, mind you. Diego was worn out with the excitement of his baby sister. Dylan was almost more flattened by the wash of emotions that had come along with a baby daughter. And Della had, you know, actually done everything. So they weren't there and the talk didn't need to be PG.

Although I could have done with it being PG13 instead of the X-rated surmisings and general ghoulishness that started up as soon as I floated my theory. Maybe it was the food and the talk combined. Nothing about dried-up, gelatinous, warmed-over Thanksgiving dinner was particularly calming to a digestion already wrecked by worry.

'Maybe I'd believe he came to woo me if he'd come the usual way,' I said.

'The usual way?' said Todd. 'You mean in your bedroom window with a lute in his hand and a rose in his teeth?'

'You don't climb in windows with a lute,' said Taylor. 'You stand under them.'

'He'd drown,' said Kathi.

'I mean,' I said, 'tracking me down on social media and messaging me. Who the hell goes to a person's parents?'

'A suitor?' said Noleen. 'Going to ask your dad for your hand?'

'No way,' I said. 'No!' This was in response to Kathi trying to pass me a platter of cornbread stuffing. Not the casserole dish of extra stuffing, crisp on top and burnt underneath – the stuffing that had been up the turkey so it was glazed with a layer of melted and recongealed fat. I shuddered. 'He didn't ask for my hand. My dad would definitely have told me. We had a deal. Ever since the first time a loser boyfriend had the bloody nerve to go behind my back and ask for my hand, my dad promised me he would always tip me the wink if it happened again.'

'Does it happen often?' Roger said, stopping with a big revolting spoonful of the ex-turkey-innard stuffing halfway between the serving platter and his mounded dinner plate.

'If Taylor does it, it'll be four,' I told him. 'Did you do it for Todd?'

Roger started so violently that a big fatty blob splatted on to the tablecloth beside his plate. 'Did I go all alone into the lion's den and open a discussion with Barb Truman about my private life? Take a guess, Lexy. My God, I'd have been lucky to get away without her doing a cough test.'

'*I* did it,' Todd said. 'It would have been weird if we'd both done it and I got in first. I still remember the way your mom looked at me.'

This was interesting. To the best of my knowledge none of us had ever met Roger's mum.

'She told me,' Roger said. 'At length. She was sorry she didn't film it.'

I was sorry she didn't film it too. I didn't need the details to know that Todd would have put on quite a show. 'But to get back to the point,' I said. 'I think Menzies stayed on the down-low because he wanted to reach me without anyone knowing about it or being able to find out about it by hacking. And he nearly made it. But he failed.'

'To be fair to the guy,' Noleen said, 'he didn't exactly bust a gut. He checked in and went to beddy-byes with you right outside his window. If he had urgent business with you, he sure set it aside to comply with the principle of federal holidays. Nah, Lexy. He came to get you back. Then he saw you making goo-goo eyes at Taylor all night and knew he was wasting his time.'

'And then what?' I said. 'Killed himself with an invisible gun? At least my thing hangs together. He knew I was in danger. He found out where I was. He covered his tracks – because you don't get much lower down the down-low than Keith and Judith Campbell – and he came to warn me. The bad guy got to him before he made it.'

'I prefer the invisible gun,' Taylor said.

'Veritas,' said Kathi. 'Do they do anything this fancy?'

'Why the hell would Veritas be involved?' I said. 'You think Menzies was a spy? You think this was a hit job?'

'Wut?' said Kathi. 'I mean assisted suicide.'

'Gravitas, you idiot,' said Noleen.

'Do you mean Dignitas?' I said.

'What's Gravitas?' said Todd.

'What's Dignitas?' said Roger.

'I have no idea what Gravitas is,' I said. 'Dignitas is a very well-organized and ethical Swiss charity that advises on end-of-life decisions and offers accompaniment in the final moments. For fuck's sake. It doesn't do destination deaths overseas. It doesn't do theme-night – frame your ex while you croak! And it certainly doesn't send guys with silencers to shoot the dying smack in the middle of their beans. What is wrong with you?'

'Jeez, calm down Lexy,' said Kathi. 'I only asked.'

'Do you know you sound like P.G. Wodehouse when you're angry?' said Noleen.

It was news to me she knew what P.G. Wodehouse sounded like. But that was by the by. 'Can you even . . .?' I said. I lifted an imaginary phone. '"Hey, hi? Is that Switzerland? Yeah, I want to die but I want to have some fun along the way. Tell me what you think of this for a wheeze, why don't you?"'

'But you said they do musical accompaniment?' said Todd. 'That's pretty freaky all on its own.'

'Oh my GOD!' I said. 'Not musical accompaniment! They provide *companionship*. You thought I meant a lounge singer with a grand piano? You're all such freaks.'

'I'd like bongos,' said Noleen. 'You'd be relieved to die to get away from the damn things.'

'I was making a serious point, actually,' Kathi said. 'Would Veri-Gravi-Dignitas step in to remove a gun and dispose of it? Save it falling into the wrong hands? Or maybe to pass it on to the person's heirs as a part of their estate?'

I snorted. The leftover yams, extra-burnt now, didn't taste any better for hitting me in the back of the nose. 'Why not check?' I said. 'Phone up Switzerland and ask Dignitas if they traffic weapons as part of the deal. Call them Very Gravy Dignitas while you're at it. See how it goes.'

'There's no need to be rude, Lexy,' Noleen said. Noleen is the rudest person most other people have ever met unless they once ran into Princess Margaret at a beach party, but she's also fiercely protective of Kathi. It's right on the line between sweet and sickening.

'I'm obviously wasting my time with you all,' I said. 'I'll save it and tell Molly instead.' I was lying. I had no intention of going anywhere near Molly again if I could help it. I'd sit with Perdita and Anselm if they needed support while they spoke to her but, as the main attraction, no way.

THIRTEEN

nstead, I carried on with my phone quest. Where had I left it and who had interfered with it when I did? I knew for a fact I had put it down on top of a row of books in the Casual Browser. It was still there forty minutes later when I went back, but I reckoned it was worth asking if any of the staff had seen someone fiddling with it. It would be one more potential clue ticked off the list.

Getting into the shop was the challenge. I wasn't moving all that nimbly; the cream pies were finished and breakfast today had been pumpkin, which wasn't resting lightly inside me even though I'd tried to think of the filling as a healthy vegetarian mousse (and tried even harder to ignore the fact that it was exactly the same colour as what we'd all seen inside Hiro's first nappies. 'Ewwwwwww,' Diego had said. 'What's *that*? Is she *OK*?'). But all my efforts were in vain when the rest of them started sharing family recipes and I found out that there were two tins of Carnation milk, four eggs, enough spice to open a really bad candle shop, and the merest smidge of actual pumpkin.

So I was lumbering along like a stoned elk, rather than slipping in and out of the crowds unseen, and the thing is that the Browser still had the pick-up table across the open door like in lockdown, encouraging customers to call in their orders and shop without actually entering. The ability to nip round tight corners would have been handy. On the other hand, the assistants who worked there were too mellow to actually wrestle anyone determined to get past them and so, elk or no elk, I squeezed through the gap and into the body of the kirk without too much pleading. The owner was behind the counter, frowning at the computer. She was a bookshop owner of the traditional type: loved books, hated people. The pandemic was basically her dream come true. I'd be surprised if she ever took the table away.

'Ahem,' I said.

She looked up and scowled at me. 'How did you get in here?'

'I asked.'

She looked past me and scowled at the staff member in the doorway.

'Well, don't cough on my books,' she said. 'And use the sanitizer before you touch anything.'

I pinged my mask elastic to draw her attention to it and pumped two lavish blobs of sanitizer into my palms.

'So,' I began, 'I was here a week ago and I left my phone, then I came back and I found it again.'

'Good story,' the owner said. 'Are you published?'

'I wondered if you had seen anyone tampering with it while it was unattended?'

'Is there a problem?'

'Yes. Someone downloaded something extremely troubling on to it and I'm trying to work out who.'

She considered me for a long moment before she answered me. 'Are you going to sue me?'

'What for? I mean, no.'

'And when was this?'

I cast my mind back and managed to pin it down to within a half-hour.

'I wasn't here,' she said.

'Can you ask the staff?'

'You can ask them yourself,' she said.

'Can you tell me the rota?' I said. 'Tell me who was on then?'

'I can't hand out—'

I waved away the rest of the answer. 'Yeah, yeah. OK. I'll tell Sergeant Rankinson and she can take it up.'

Her eyes flashed. 'It's a police matter?'

'Murder?' I said. 'Yes usually.'

She would rather die dancing the can-can than look surprised, but it took her a minute to organize a reply. 'This is the latest outrage at that dreadful motel, is it?'

That was putting it a bit strongly, in my opinion. It was only the second murder at the motel. Plus that time a body was found there, but had died somewhere else. And the other thing wasn't murder after all.

'Was your phone used to send texts between co-conspirators?' she said.

'No, it—'

'To issue a threat?'

'No, it—'

'Was this murder part of a spree?'

'No, it—'

'Then I'm at a loss to understand how a phone foolishly left behind in my store for a mere forty minutes days before the crime was committed can be implicated.'

'I'm trying to—'

'But in the interests of civic duty, you can talk to Pat.'

'Thank you.'

'Or look at the security feed, if you prefer.'

'Wait, what?' I said. 'I didn't know you had cameras on in here.' I tried feverishly to remember what angle I'd been holding the latest T.L. Swan at, as I thumbed through it for the mucky bits.

'They don't cover the whole store.'

'Do they cover Romance?' I said.

'Hardly,' she said. 'Those trashy paperbacks?' Did I mention that she was a humongous book snob as well as a misanthrope. 'No, front door, back door and overpriced – I mean oversized – Art.'

That made sense. Those glossy artbooks *were* expensive. 'That would be very helpful,' I said.

'Because I don't like the idea of that sort of person frequenting my business,' she said. She put her head back and looked down her nose at me as if squinting through reading spectacles. In fact, she had had Lasik surgery about a year ago and could have looked at me from any angle at all, but some habits are hard to break, I suppose. 'Although, as I say, I'm struggling to believe that a phone briefly on a shelf in my store a week ago can have anything to do with a murder in a rundown flophouse on Thursday.'

'It was a red herring,' I said. 'A misdirect. An attempt to frame an innocent person.'

'That seems highly unlikely in real life,' she said. 'That's the sort of thing that happens in those ludicrous mystery novels.'

'What books *do* you read?' I said. 'Not Romance, Crime or Art, and I'm guessing not Westerns. Fantasy? Self-help?' I was winding her up. It was impossible not to.

'I read the biographies of great men,' she said.

'Just men?'

'When a woman rises to sufficient prominence, I will certainly read her biography too.'

Which left me kind of speechless. When I had gathered my wits again, I said only, 'I'd appreciate a gander at the security feed. Thank you. Do I need to come round the other side?'

'Gander,' she said. 'British for perusal? You would need to come into the office. Perhaps tomorrow?'

'Tomorrow is good,' I said. 'I'm free all day.'

'You've certainly taken to California life with gusto,' she said primly. Then she hesitated, 'Can I ask a question without you flying off in a huff or bursting into tears like a child?'

'I'd have thought so.'

'Good,' she said. 'Because it's by no means guaranteed these days. People reach for grievance and indulge emotion far too readily, I find.'

I wondered if she had ever considered that if people burst into tears and blew their stacks around her all the time, the reason might be very close to home. I didn't wonder long, mind you.

'Are you sure it wasn't a prank?' she said.

'Am I sure that a murder wasn't a prank?'

'I'm not talking about murder. I'm talking about whatever occurred during an unrelated brief mislaying of a cell phone. Are you quite sure it wasn't simply a tasteless prank? You know your friends better than I.'

I was so bugged by that 'I' I nearly missed the rest of it. It's not something I'm proud of: the way proper American grammar strikes me as prissy. Why shouldn't they say 'whom' if they want to? Why shouldn't they say, as I *had* in fact heard someone say once, 'I am he' instead of 'This is him' when they answer a phone? Well, 'So they don't sound like they're in a Henry James adaptation' in that particular case, but the general point stands and I shouldn't have been distracted enough to nearly miss – nearly to miss, as Americans would have it – the only bit that ought to have struck me.

'Friends?' I asked her. 'What have my friends got to do with it?'

'What *do* your friends *have* to do with it?' she said, actually correcting me now, which was irritating on a whole new level. 'I assumed it was the same day.'

'As what?'

'As the day one of your little friends was looking for you.'

'Why would one of my friends be looking for me in here?' I said. 'And when you say "little", what do you mean exactly?'

Because Menzies was a pretty commanding presence the last time I saw him. The second to last time, I should say, since the last time he'd been flat on his back in a Last Ditch bed with a bullet hole in him. The second to last time, he was sweeping up on to the stage at graduation to be bopped on the head with John Knox's knickers. Not that I looked closely. I was pretending he was one of the other large, posh, golden lads who, along with the golden lasses, were taking away middling degrees and a lifetime of contacts. Unfortunately, my mum and dad were there too and my mum hardly touched on how proud she was of my splendid achievement in between sighing about Menzies and asking me for the eleven thousandth time if we couldn't work on it and sort things out.

But if not Menzies, then who? Todd and Roger were big guys. Della was always coltish and had been nine months pregnant the last time she was out and about. Dylan was little front to back and side to side but he was a good six foot if he ever stood up straight. Noleen and Kathi were Munchkins right enough, but Noleen had the physique of Fred Flintstone – even she admitted that her spirit animal was the capybara – and Kathi's default expression would stop anyone, even the owner of the Casual Browser, from calling her 'little'.

That was pretty much it for me and friends. None of them was little and I lived with them, so if they wanted to see me they would catch me at home. There was Taylor, I suppose, but he was also not notably small, and Diego – little, right enough; too little to go trolling about town after me under his own steam. Barb was short, but if she needed me she'd get to me through Todd. Amaranth, Taylor's mum, was tiny but she was blind and didn't make a lot of solo flights as a result. Also, she'd get to me through Taylor.

'Did you get a name?' I asked. I was hoping it was Menzies and he'd written it down for her so I could correct her pronunciation.

'I didn't mean literally stunted,' she said.

I smiled. I get a lot of passive-aggressives through my office, usually as one half of a warring couple (of whom the other half is going quietly out of his or her mind), so I recognized the impetus here. She wouldn't answer any question unless it was a way of avoiding answering another even less welcome question.

'I see,' I said. I did. 'You meant "negligible" in some other sense? What, like a library user? Kindle fan? Grammar not up to snuff?'

She didn't follow and she didn't like that. 'I simply mean that one would expect a woman of your years to have a private life, even a social life, somewhat less disorderly.'

I blinked. *I* would expect a woman who owned a successful book business to have the means of getting that stick removed from her arse. Life is full of surprises. I managed not to share these thoughts, but other thoughts slipped out. 'You disapprove of one of your customers asking after one of your other customers?' I said. 'That's too disorderly for you?'

'This is not a dead letter drop,' she said. 'It's a bookstore. She wasn't a customer.'

My shoulders dropped. I hadn't noticed them rising but they must have been grazing my ears because they fell far enough fast enough for the strap of my shoulder bag to drop off one of them.

'*She?*' I repeated. Was it the same mysterious stranger from the Lode? 'Was she British?'

'Yes, she,' the Browser boss said, once again answering the less useful of two questions. 'And I wouldn't go so far as to call you a customer either.'

'What?' I said. 'I bought a book here last week. When I left my phone.'

'A Marian Keyes paperback,' she said.

That's when I got really angry. Scoff at Nick Hornby if you must; sneer at Liane Moriarty if your heart is a stone in your chest. But leave my Marian out of it or prepare to hurt.

'You read spy thrillers,' I snapped at her. 'Or why else would you say "dead letter drop" that way?'

'I do *not*!' she said.

'Oh yeah, I forgot. Biographies of great men. OK, so you binge-watch them on Netflix. Have it your own way.'

Sweeping out felt so great that even having to stop and wiggle my way round the end of the kerbside pick-up table didn't bother me.

FOURTEEN

B ut I had probably blown it as far as looking at the security footage went and, if Pat was a loyal employee to the boss from hell, I had to get to her before her next shift too. That shouldn't be a problem: she also worked at Odie's Ovens on weekend evenings, I happened to know (because when you've got a foot-high rainbow mohawk, customers remember you, especially if you have to wear the world's bumphliest hairnet over it when you're cooking), and she volunteered at the Beteo County SPCA sometimes, where she was one of many rainbow dye-jobs and the smaller of the two mohawks, actually. One way or another, I'd find her.

Of course I started at the Ovens. For one thing, I had definitely left my phone there fairly recently. Also, they sell by the slice and I had hardly eaten any dinner last night on account of the twice-burnt marshmallow and nodules of fat theme. I took my paper plate outside to the pedestrianized, table-strewn street that was one of the few silver linings to come out of 2020 and waited for a busboy, trying to look as if I wasn't eavesdropping on the next table along.

I didn't actually try not to eavesdrop. It's good continuing professional development for me to listen into private conversations. And this one was a doozy.

'He's a complete fantasist,' said the woman facing me. She had a plate from the sushi bar next door and she was picking individual balls of roe out of a California roll with the tips of her chopsticks.

'I think he's a romantic,' said her friend. She was facing the other way, but I could tell from her elbow movements that she was eating a taco with a lot of enthusiasm. 'An idealist.'

'And as for that friend of his? Either the poor schmuck is a total masochist or he's suffering from coercive control and he doesn't know it.'

'He seems happy enough.'

'Wow,' said the sushi-picker. 'Deep analysis.'

The taco-guzzler laughed and took a big drink of beer, ending up with a fizzy burp.

I was agog. Usually I can tell which one of a pair of women is moaning about her partner and which one is being a good friend, whether that friend is agreeing and sympathizing or cajoling and countering. This pair was different though. They were both just pitching in, no walking on eggshells, no umbrage about the no walking on eggshells. Maybe, I thought, they were talking about the boyfriend of a third pal who wasn't there. But why hadn't either of them mentioned her? And shouldn't a trained therapist like me be able to tell? Shouldn't a fellow woman be able to? Was this how women younger than me talked these days? Maybe it was a problem that I lived with all my friends and never saw anyone else. Maybe it was an even bigger problem that, if I tried to think of small friends, I went straight to Amaranth in her eighties and Barb, a very hard sixty-five.

The busboy distracted me before I could glean any more or worry any harder.

'Finished?' he asked. Somehow, I had gulped down a whole searing-hot slice of pepperoni and jalapeño with extra cheese and there was nothing left on my plate but some red grease. I pushed it towards him. 'Is Pat coming in tonight?' I said. 'She usually does Sundays, right?'

To my astonishment, his eyes flared and he took a step backward. 'You're Lexy Campbell, aren't you?' he said.

'Um, I am,' I agreed, 'but it normally takes more than my name to strike dread in people. What's up?'

'Patti needs these shifts,' he said. 'Foot traffic is way low at the Browser and she won't make her rent without this job too. So if you could straighten it out with her instead of going to Bill, that'd be way cool.'

'I have no idea who Bill is,' I said. 'Or what it is that needs to be straightened out. Or basically, what you're on about.'

'Good,' said the busboy. 'Let's keep it that way. She'll be here in half an hour. You want another slice to keep you going? Beer?' He was scanning my face pretty avidly and he could see that more pizza and beer to wash it down with wasn't cutting it. He dug deep. 'Tea?' he said.

'Odie's serves tea?'

'I could go to Starbucks on my break and get you some.'

'Tempting,' I said. 'It is the most reliable cup of tea in the whole of North America, but I'd rather have information. Why are you freaking out? What is it that Pat thinks she's done to upset me?'

'She lied about you. But wait though! Hear me out!' Because of course I had started expostulating. Who wouldn't?

'Lied to the police?'

'Huh?'

'Lied when?'

'What diff—?'

'How did they know to ask?'

'What?'

And then both of us in perfect unison, like we'd been practising for days said: 'What are you talking about?' And then, 'You go.' And then we both pressed our lips together to signal that we were waiting to hear what the other had to say. It was quite the double-act we had going, that busboy and me.

'Patti did the right thing,' was his opener when he ended the silence at last. 'First do no harm, right?'

'That's doctors,' I said. 'And explorers maybe. It could be *Star Trek*.'

'Because she wouldn't take no for answer, this chick.' My face registered something, obviously. He guessed wrong what it was, mind you. 'Sorry. Woman. Person. Fellow human.'

I shook my head. 'So a woman was asking for me?'

'She was.'

'Did you recognize her?'

'Nope. Should I have?'

'Do you know Molly Rankinson?'

'Again with the cops. Of course, I know Rankinson. I work at a pizza joint that stays open till two. It wasn't her.'

'Good. And you're saying Pat lied about me to this mysterious woman?'

'She said you had moved to Idaho.'

'That was resourceful of her,' I said. 'I'm grateful. I'll tell her that when she gets here.'

'Don't be too grateful,' he said. 'She didn't lie for you. She lied because she was getting a hinky vibe. But the ch—'

'—ick is fine,' I said. 'I don't care what you call her.'

'OK, so she never said she was a cop. Makes sense. Pat doesn't love cops so a hinky vibe is no surprise really. But if this ch—'

'I really don't care.'

'—ick had showed her badge . . .'

'I don't think she *was* a cop,' I said. 'I think she was a . . .' I kept the 'a' going as long as I had breath, waiting for inspiration to strike and get me to the end of the sentence, but I had to inhale again before anything had come to me. Who *did* I think she was? This woman pursuing me all around the town. Not a dragged-up Menzies, not someone who wanted to hand over my left-behind phone in person at the Lode, and – going out on a limb – not a friend.

'Because if she *was* a cop,' the busboy said, 'Patti would have lied to her about a lot of stuff but maybe not for you, no offence.'

I shrugged it off. I liked Pat – she was a good source of book recommendations and she volunteered to help animals – but we weren't bosom buddies by any means.

'I'd still like to thank her,' I said.

The busboy held out a hand like a maître d' and gestured behind me. 'Tell her yourself.'

I twisted round in my seat and once again I had the unpleasant experience of the very sight of me stopping someone like a bullet. Pat half-turned away and cast her eyes around for an escape route.

'Peace!' I said, holding up my two hands. 'I think I owe you a drink. Have you got time to sit and talk to me?'

She came forward like some kind of wild animal, interested in the food on offer but wary of a trap. 'Lexy Campbell, right?'

'Still right here in Cuento, CA. Idaho is having to get by without me.'

'Oh, he told you about that, did he?' she said with a look over her shoulder to where the busboy was bussing a table as if he was an exhibitor at a bussing expo. 'Nice work, Deon! Good job!'

'And as I said,' I told her, 'I'm very grateful.'

'Oh you are?' she said. 'OK, then. Who *was* that dude who was looking for you anyway?' I think I preferred 'chick'.

'I have no idea,' I said. 'Thanks for not sending her my way.'

'Anytime,' Pat said. 'Unless you like killed someone or something. But Deon said all those murders at your place were other people, right?'

'Right,' I agreed, wishing there was a way to take issue with it – all those murders at your place! – but knowing I didn't have a leg to stand on. 'Can I ask you a few questions about her?'

She sidled into the other side of the picnic table and half-shrugged off her jacket. As soon as the Odie's logo appeared though, one of the arguing women at the next table called over, 'Server? Could we have a couple of Fat Tyres, please?'

Pat shrugged her jacket back on and ignored them.

'They're not even eating pizza,' I told her.

'My shift doesn't start for twenty minutes,' she said. 'Whether they're eating pizza or not, I came in early to grab a bite.'

Indeed the busboy was already headed our way with two plates and two drinks.

'So describe this person,' I said, when I had taken a big bite out of the narrow end of my pizza and washed it down with a slug of beer. Who was I kidding that I couldn't deal with a second slice and impromptu alcohol?

'Woman,' she said. 'Standard-issue.'

'What did she want?'

Pat shook her head. 'Looking for you, she said. To surprise you with a visit, she said. But she had lost your street address and she didn't want to blow the effect by texting you, after coming so far.'

'Street address,' I echoed.

'Exactly,' said Pat. 'Weird way to describe a boat on a slough, right? That's what I thought. So I told her you had moved to Idaho.'

'And she believed you?'

'I don't know. She didn't argue or ask for proof.'

I took a more measured sip of my beer, trying to think my

way through this. *Was* it the same person as was asking for me in the Lode? Were *either* of them the same person who was asking for me in the Browser? Had to be. But why did she keep asking? I wasn't exactly anonymous in this town.

'Where would you say she was from?' I asked Pat. This would clinch it.

'Not here. Definitely overseas. Ireland? Iceland? South Africa?'

In other words, Scottish. I'd been accused of coming from all three places and many more. 'And what exactly does standard-issue look like?'

'Princess Diana?' said Pat. 'Or you know, Julia Roberts. Or Anne Hathaway or someone.'

'So big eyes and skinny?'

'And dressed kind of Jackie O,' Pat said.

'Formal?' I said.

'Or Victoria Beckham.'

I was losing faith in Pat's powers of observation, frankly. Or maybe from a rainbow mohawk and biker jacket point of view, Jackie O and Julia Roberts were twins.

'And did you see her anywhere else besides here?' I said.

Pat shrugged.

'Did you maybe see her in . . .?' I said, then I bit my lip. I shouldn't lead her. 'Actually, can I change the subject?' I said. 'You were in the Browser when I left my phone behind, I think.'

Pat shrugged. 'When was this? Pre-lockdown?'

'Last week sometime.'

She shrugged again. 'It should be in Lost and Found,' she said.

'I got it back,' I told her.

'So no loose ends,' she said. 'What's your beef?'

I didn't know what to say. The silenced gunshot app was a major clue in the case and it would be stupid to leak it. If I told Pat, she would tell Deon and he would probably tell everyone. He hadn't been close-lipped with me.

'Someone put something on it,' I said. 'For me to find.'

'Fucking dick pics!' said Pat, so loud that the two friends, one of whom had the coercive controlling boyfriend but I couldn't tell which, turned and raised their glasses.

'Hallelujah, sister!' one of them called over. 'They ain't even pretty in professional photoshoots, with good lighting and a filter. No one wants one. Ever.'

'Is it AirDropped?' her friend said. And then she shouted so loud that it rang out even with the baffling effect of the gazebo roofs dotted around the block. 'Did someone AirDrop a dick pic? Because I've just been in Deuce Hardware and picked up a nice new set of secateurs in their small-business-Sunday sale and I am good to go!'

There were some laughs and cheers from the rest of the diners and drinkers sprinkled about, but no deep blush and sudden slink away. Although I supposed that AirDroppers of dick pics and people who know what secateurs were probably didn't have a big overlap. And also there was no dick pic. That too.

But, I reasoned to myself, where was the harm in letting Pat think that *was* what had happened to me and my phone?

'Could you check the feed?' I said. 'Next time you're in the Browser?'

'Tell me the times and I'll find him,' she assured me.

There was the harm. If this 'friend from home' who was tailing me all over hell and creation was the same person who eventually found me, installed the app, and killed Menzies, dick pics weren't a good cover story.

'Her,' I said.

'Ew,' said Pat. 'I mean, I'm all for equality.'

'But ew,' I agreed. 'Thank you.'

'Hey, is it the same person?' she asked me. 'The friend who wasn't who'd lost your address but didn't? And this twisted bitch with her dickless pic?'

So much for not leading her. 'I don't know,' I said. 'You'd be the best person to say if you saw the same woman twice.'

Pat stared at me. 'You're right,' she said. 'And you know what? I *did* see her twice. Only the other time wasn't at the Browser. It was in the Thrift. I came round the corner with an armful of Halloween costumes we hadn't sold, and she couldn't get out of the place quick enough. She went into reverse like a remote-controlled kiddy car. It was kind of weird. You don't see people walking backwards that often, do you?'

'So you think she saw you and ran off.'

'Backwards, like I said. And I thought she was a regular,

because I recognized her. Big eyes, good shoes, weird clothes, like I said.'

'Jackie Kennedy weird,' I chipped in.

'Right. Ann Taylor weird. J.Crew weird.'

As opposed to zodiac spandex and tour T-shirts normal, I thought but didn't say. I love Cuento but Halloween is dicey. You can't congratulate anyone on their costume in case they're not in a costume. It's worse than tarts and vicars. Except it's true.

'I mean, I didn't make too much of it,' Pat was saying, 'because a lot of our customers are pretty socially awkward, you know? On account of how cheap our prices are and how strongly poor mental health correlates with poverty.'

I really did love Cuento, or maybe just California generally. All of that came tripping right off Pat's tongue and it was a lot kinder than the way I'd have put it back home: you don't half get a lot of nutters in Oxfam.

'But then one of my co-workers saw me staring and said something that didn't hit me till right now.'

'Go on,' I said.

'She told me the dude came in the same way.'

I couldn't make much of that. I tried. 'You mean she came in the out-door?' The Thrift was one of many places who'd put in a one-way system along with the six-foot rule. The whole world had turned into IKEA.

'No, I mean she came in backwards and only turned round when she was through the door. Then she went out backwards too and didn't turn round till she was clear of the rugs in the outdoor area.'

'That *is* weird,' I said. 'Would that be like a . . . superstition maybe?'

'A what?' said Pat. 'You mean like an ancestral belief? Do you really call cultural practices superstitions? Wow. How old are you?'

God, I hated California sometimes. I wasn't talking to the person who actually did the bloody door thing, was I?

'I know my people think it's bad luck to come into a new house by the back door,' I said. 'And worse luck to enter by one door and leave by another.'

'Or sleep with your feet facing the bedroom door,' said Pat.

'My Irish granny believed that totally. Because that's how your corpse goes out, feet first, yeah?'

'And there is something knocking about my brain somewhere,' I said. 'You enter in the footsteps of the person before you and you . . . Ach, what is it?'

'Roundhouse practice,' said Pat. She drew breath to explain some more, but I swooped in. I needed to raise my stock a little.

'That's it!' I said. 'The Patwin people at Big Time. They walk in the footsteps of the person who's first in the roundhouse and they walk out backwards in the same footsteps.'

'How d'you know that?' Pat said, suitably impressed.

'I asked them,' I said. 'How else d'you ever know anything?'

'You disturbed indigenous people at Big Time with dumb colonial questions?'

'No,' I said. 'I asked a guy setting up a barbecue in a park why everyone was coming out of a huttie in reverse. He coped. Like I'd cope if you were in Dundee on New Year's Eve and asked me what all the coal was for.'

'That's different,' she said.

'Why?'

She glared. She'd gone right off me and it was mutual.

'I think I'll go and talk to the person who saw her coming in,' I said. 'In case I can get more details. Are they on duty today?'

She kept glaring and had started scowling too, by which I deduced that the answer was yes and she begrudged giving it to me.

'Well maybe I'll pop in on the off-chance.'

'Pop in?' she said.

'Shoot along there real quick,' I translated. 'What was the name? Of your colleague?'

'Colleague?'

'Co-worker,' I translated. I smiled at her. 'Sorry. Would you like me to assimilate faster and more thoroughly? Do you resent immigrants holding on to their mother tongue?'

'Oh fuck off,' she advised me.

And, bingo, I liked her again. She maybe had one Irish granny but I was sure there was some Scottish blood in there too.

So I had a spring in my step as I took the couple of blocks to the corner where the Beteo County SPCA Thrift Store spilled its budget wares out into the sunshine. And I was proud of myself for thinking 'couple of blocks' and 'thrift store' instead of 'round the corner' and 'charity shop'. I was assimilating just fine. In my own opinion, which was the only one that mattered.

Still, I rehearsed a spiel for the volunteer on duty and was wondering how to lead into it as I approached the door and saw the answer to the puzzle staring right at me.

Literally, staring right at me. As in with a lens and a red light to show that it was working. There was a camera above the side entrance where the rugs were heaped up. The mysterious stranger pretending to be my friend, the California equivalent of an Oxfam nutter, wasn't honouring her ancestors, *or* outwitting the devil, by going in and out backwards. No, she was keeping her face off the security feed.

You know, like murderers do.

FIFTEEN

I walked on by, swinging my arms and smiling, as if the Thrift was a graveyard and I was on a dare at midnight. Daft, really; there was no reason to think the woman was on my tail, watching me catch on to what she was up to. Except, of course, that she had been on my tail for at least a week now, shadowing me from Lode to Browser to Odie's to home to killing my first love feet from my bed.

I wasn't strolling now. I wasn't running either, thinking that would be conspicuous. Rather, I was doing that speed-walking that looks like threatened diarrhoea, much more conspicuous than a flat-out sprint. And I was going the wrong way. Plus, I realized as I patted my pockets, I'd left my bloody phone somewhere.

And now the very peace and shade of the peaceful shady streets at the start of Cuento's residential neighbourhood started to freak me out. There was absolutely no one around in any of these picket-fenced front gardens, nor swinging on the swing-seats on any of the deep porches, nor sitting by an open window in any of the downstairs parlours. The very leaves of autumn were getting to fall and settle on the grass in a highly un-American way.

It was small-business Sunday, after all. And the conscientious citizens of old east central Cuento were out making sure that the downtown shops had a good day and survived the year.

If that woman was on my tail right now she could probably have her way with me and there wouldn't be a single witness to tell the tale. Behind me, a car was driving along slower than Roger Bannister on the beach and my hackles rose along with my certainty that it was her and she was kerb-crawling me, picking her moment to pounce.

The relief as the car passed by and I saw the DoorDash decal clinging to the side! I had to stop and hang on to the fleur-de-lis on top of the nearest picket fence while the adrenaline left. Just my luck that I had picked the fancy fence of the only house for blocks around that wasn't lying empty. A woman in an apron, bustling about on the porch, stopped and shaded her eyes to stare my way.

'Can I help you?' she said. It made a change from 'Did your friend find you?', at least.

'I'm fine,' I said.

'You sure?'

I had no idea what to say now. Never in the history of 'keeping your head down until you've made miles more trouble than you ever could, if you just spoke up' – aka British life – had anyone kept pushing after an 'I'm fine'.

'I'm just . . . I was . . . But I'll . . .' I said, which was amazingly articulate of me in such an unprecedented situation. Then I cast my eyes around for something to distract her, while I ran away. I was hoping for a squirrel but I saw something much better. Driven into one corner of the velvet lawn that reached, pillowy as moss but without any actual moss of course, from the clipped shrubs around the base of the porch to the raked bark chips around the base of the fence, was a wooden sign, with black lettering so fancy it was well-nigh illegible.

WELCOME TO BETEO COUNTY 2020 HRT

it said. Or at least it should have. But the first two letters of the acronym were exactly the same so it either said:

WELCOME TO BETEO COUNTY 2020 HHT

or it said:

WELCOME TO BETEO COUNTY 2020 RRT

But in either case, it gave me an out. That is, it gave me an in. 'Ah,' I said. 'I found you! I've been looking so long I've got light-headed from hunger. You're on the Christmas Tour?'

'Holiday Tour,' the woman said. She had put her broom under her arm like the . . . what even was it that high-up soldiers put under their arms during troop inspections? Was it a riding crop? A shepherd's crook? A multi-purpose baton? A specific-purpose stick with a military name I had never heard?

'Right,' I said. 'Romantic Residences of Cuento. Or Historic Homes.' I was hoping she'd pick one and solve the font. But no such luck.

'We don't open for another week,' she said. 'And then by appointment.'

'Oh, no, I'm not a customer,' I said. 'I'm on it. The tour. My house is. My home. We just joined this year.'

That was open sesame, clearly. She laid her broom aside and came down the path to the gate, beaming. 'Welcome, welcome, welcome,' she said. 'My co-decorator. I'm Eleanor Brewster, by the way. And you are so right. We are both historic *and* romantic. *My* home is. And I guess yours is too.' Which was no help at all in deciphering anything. She opened the gate and ushered me in. 'Obviously I haven't started on the yard but the interior is ready. Come and see. Feast your eyes. And perhaps later I'll come and see yours. Who is doing your catering? We've got Solstice and Equinox in the back yard offering sliders and soup cups.'

'Um,' I said. Solstice and Equinox, despite sounding like a yoga studio, was actually one of the swankiest of Cuento's eateries, with napkins the size of tablecloths and tablecloths the size of bedsheets. They had led the great plate exodus sweeping the town, Todd had told me, shifting to chunks of wood and bits of slate when even the high-end tapas bars of San Francisco were still insulting their patrons with actual round pieces of glazed china.

'You caught me,' I said. 'I'm not as hands on as you seem to be. I'll ask my staff when I get back home.' Noleen hadn't said a word about catering as far as I could recall. (If it had been left up to me, I might have put out a bowl of Twiglets and a big bottle of something fizzy.)

'But you'll be there for some of the tours, won't you?' she said. 'The patrons do so appreciate the personal touch. I bake in the kitchen all the livelong day for the whole two weeks. I put on my Victorian garb and my ruffled pinafore. I pin my hair up and cover it with a cap. And I just bake and bake and bake.'

'I hadn't planned anything specific,' I said, wondering what would tie in best with a houseboat. Me in raggedy dungarees fishing off the side with a sapling rod? Me on the porch in a Depression-era shirt-waister, shucking peas into a bucket? No way was I baking. My kitchen's too small, even without gawping tourists. 'So,' I asked, hoping to distract from my obvious short-comings, 'are you staying during the two weeks? Do you retreat to a couple of bedrooms with a camp stove?'

'Oh no no no no no no,' she said. We were on the porch now, and she stopped moving. Maybe I'd blotted my copybook and blown my chance of getting a neb inside. False alarm. She had only paused to put on a mask she plucked from a basket of individually wrapped disposables by the door. Once it was fitted on her face, she added a pair of paper bootees from a second basket and took a pair of gloves from a third.

Hurriedly I did the same.

'Thank you, dear,' she said. 'I hope you don't mind. I've always asked visitors to cover their feet, in case they damage the parquet. And I do insist on the gloves, because it's impossible to stop them touching the banisters as they walk upstairs. I would have brought in masks years ago if I'd thought of it. I'm very pleased that now I can.'

I had put my own mask on by this time, so I didn't need to raise a smile in response to the idea that COVID might be a bit of a bummer, but at least it stopped any breath getting on her furniture. I squeezed up my eyes so she'd think I was smiling, but behind my mask I stuck my tongue out at her. The mask tasted like cinnamon.

'Welcome to the historic Brewster Mansion!' she said, sweeping open the front door.

I rolled my eyes. It wasn't a new build by any means, but it was lucky if it was older than the average red pillar box back home. And mansion? It was a nice house, but it was a house on a street in a town, and you could probably gift-wrap the whole place without having to special order the red ribbon.

My eyes stuck mid-roll and left me gazing up the stairwell to the cupola soaring above me. This place was a Tardis. It was *absolutely* a mansion. It looked like flipping Southfork on the inside.

That wasn't all. It was over-the-top lush and luxy too. Parquet, like she said, and the gleaming banisters, plus royal-icing plasterwork and rococo furniture. All of that was probably year-round. The holidays had taken it into the stratosphere. The chandelier hanging just under the sparkling skylight was obviously a special one just for Christmas, a kind of upside-down Christmas-tree shape of purple and gold ribbons and baubles with animatronic humming birds fluttering all around it on invisible wires. There were purple swags down the banisters too and under the pictures, which looked like ancestral paintings from everything I've ever seen of ancestral paintings in stately homes. The actual Christmas tree, tucked into the sweep at the bottom of the stairs was lost under its load of purple and gold ornaments. I only guessed there was a tree at all because, even through the cinnamon-scented face mask, I could smell the resin.

'I'm almost finished trimming the tree,' Mrs Brewster said, pointing at a tray of gold glass icicles that lay open on the floor.

Almost finished? I boggled at her. There wasn't a spare inch of tree left to hang them from. She'd have to roll the icicles under the edge of the canopy until they clinked up against the bucket. Or nail them into the trunk like spikes. This tree was trimmed.

'I leave it until last because it's the true spirit of the holidays for me. Everything else has to be done a little early, you know. Well, of course you know. Who knows better than we?'

Us, I thought. But didn't say. I also didn't say that it was November and there was a month to go till the first day of the

holiday that was making her all misty-eyed. Or that all over
America people were deciding what kind of pie to have for
breakfast today, since they had barely scratched the leftovers. I
certainly didn't say that it was news to me that we had to decorate
the houses for Christmas as well as for history. I was too busy
trying to remember where I'd stashed the one little cardboard box
of tangled fairy lights and balding robins that I'd been planning
to strew about my rubber plant, because there was no space on
board for a tree except where the rubber plant sat and there was
no space to move the rubber plant to in the meantime.

'Come look around,' Mrs Brewster said. 'I've themed the
rooms and' – she gave a simpering little giggle and looked down
with completely false embarrassment – 'I have to admit, I do
tend to let myself go. I kept it tasteful and restrained in the foyer
here so as not to overwhelm the senses but, I cannot tell a lie, I
have let rip in the rest of my home.'

Tasteful, I would give her. There were two colours, and they
were purple and gold, not bubble-gum pink and acid yellow. And
nothing was flashing, inflated, or based on a Disney character.
The only animatronics were zoologically accurate to the region
and were smaller than life-size, or at least they were far away
up in the roof. Tasteful was fair.

But *restrained*? Only my mask elastic kept my jaw from falling
open as I scampered after her through the double pocket doors
into the first room. I had to see this. I also had to do some serious
shopping, or scrounging, or crafting, as soon as I got home. If I
was going to be anything except the source of a lot of one-star
reviews on the HRT website and maybe also a hit piece in the
Voyager, I had my work cut out for me. But I had to see this first.

The parlour was a winter wonderland in the *Frozen* castle
meets *Game of Thrones* style. Snow – OK, glitter – swirled at
our feet and ice – OK, glass – tinkled in the breeze. There was
a skating rink with a collection of fairies gliding around too. The
animatronics were getting bigger and weirder. Also, it was cold.

'Is it just me or is it chilly in here?' I said.

'I'm blowing cold air up through the floor vents,' said Mrs
Brewster. 'I can let you know the name of the engineer I use.
For next year. He's booked up already for this year, of course.'

'Of course,' I said, thinking I could do a draught but only by leaving the windows open, which also let in the smell of the slough and the fields beyond and was only practical if I was sure mosquito season was truly over.

'And so the next experience comes with a warming cup of hot cider,' said Mrs Brewster, shepherding me on through a door into what I supposed was a dining room, done out Dickensian-style with a lot of velvet and even more swags than the foyer, along with two little street carts, one set up for hot drinks and one apparently geared towards the roasting of chestnuts. In a wooden house. I wondered what the fire marshal would have to say and wished I was mean enough to report her.

'Of course, the chimneys on the carts are just for show,' Mrs Brewster assured me. 'The smoke will be dry ice and the actual chestnuts will be cooked outside and kept warm. But the carts are quite authentic, don't you think?'

'They are,' I said. 'So's the food.' Because there was a feast laid on the table that looked more life-like than anything that had ever been set down in front of me for actual eating. The pig's head still had real bristles at the snout end.

'Oh, the food's real,' she said. 'I put it out earlier for the photographer and then later I'll run it up to the homeless shelter.'

'Ah,' I said, wondering what the less fortunate of Cuento's citizens would make of a roasted pig's head. The flyers for the food pantries usually tell us to give things like sanitary protection and nice marmalade and avoid tins that need an opener. 'Wait. Photographer?'

'The official photographer for the tour, dear,' Mrs Brewster said. 'Today's the day for the interior shots. Tuesday for yards. When's he coming to you?'

'Ahhhhhhh,' I said. 'My staff will probably . . .'

She nodded. Then, doing that stagey looking over both shoulders to check that none of the nonexistent other people who weren't there could hear her, she whispered, 'A word to the wise – did you tell me your name? – don't mention your staff to the guests. Of course, *you* know and *I* know that one person alone couldn't achieve what we achieve but no one wants us to destroy the magic.'

I nodded. No one would have any doubt that one person could achieve what Todd and Noleen were going to achieve on my boat. They were more likely to wonder who I had paid to get on this tour alongside the Brewster mansion, but she didn't need to know that.

'Come and see the carousel,' she said, tucking her arm into mine. Ten minutes ago, I would have assumed she meant a miniature, or that 'carousel' meant something different here, maybe one of these spinning dishes you fill with nuts and sweeties, but now I prepared to choose my horsey and climb on.

Gloom fought doom fought pity (self) as I trailed back to the Ditch an hour later. I blamed Todd. His silver tongue had talked me and multiple others into many things before now. Trinity was the biggest of them, in my case. Moving into the Last Ditch was probably the apotheosis with Roger. Barb was hard to say; maybe that was a wash because she had taught him everything he knew about getting his own way and they cancelled each other out. Whatever. He had obviously done it again. He had charmed the board, or its chair at least, and talked the Ditch and the boat into inevitable humiliation when his hubris crashed head-on into a horde of visitors who were going to leave the Brewster mansion, full of cider and chestnuts and still slightly giddy from the carousel, and arrive here to sample the delights we had scraped together to offer them.

When I saw him, I reckoned he already knew. He and Noleen were sitting outside Reception looking just about as crestfallen as anyone as bumptious and deluded as Noleen and Todd respectively could ever be.

'What's up?' I said.

They only stared at me.

'Kathi OK?' I tried next, because maybe it was something completely different. 'Della? Baby Hiro? Is Diego finally facing what sharing his mommy means? What's wrong? And don't lie to me because something is.'

'Lexy,' said Todd. My heart unhooked itself from where it was hanging in my chest and went plummeting down, like a lift with its cables cut, to splat out around my feet. This was bad. From hoping it wasn't the HRT changing their minds I did a neat 180 and started praying that's *all* it was. I heard the Skweek door open and saw Kathi come down the stairs to join us. At least it wasn't her then.

'Oh no,' I said. 'Has the photographer been? Are we dumped? I can't say I'm surprised because you wouldn't believe what I've just seen.'

'What photographer?' said Todd.

'From HRT,' I told him. 'Aren't they coming round to do the promo shots for everyone today?'

'First I've heard,' said Noleen. 'I gotta go put a bowl of pine cones on the desk.' She clamped her hands on her knees and rose.

'I wouldn't,' I said. 'There's no point, Nolly. I've just had a sneak peek at one of the other houses on the tour and a bowl of pine cones isn't going to cut it. Todd, how exactly did you get us on to this tour? Did you flirt with the chair?'

'What makes you think it was a woman?' said Todd, for all the world as if any man who'd serve as chair of the Historic Residence Holiday Tour was ever going to be a straight one. 'And I didn't have to. They were looking to expand their reach beyond, you know, the usual crowd.'

'Deep-pocketed benefactors with good taste and time to spare?' I said. 'Why?'

That's when I noticed that Kathi was pinching the bridge of her nose between thumb and forefinger, kneading vigorously. 'Can we just not?' she said. 'For once could we just not spiral off into nonsense when there's a big fat horrible real thing to deal with? One time?'

'What's up?' I said. 'Has Molly been back? Did they find something bad in the autopsy? Did his parents phone? Are they here? Surely they can't be here already. What's happening?'

'Do you want me to tell you?' said Todd. 'Or do you want fourteen more guesses before you give in?'

'Todd, for God's sake,' Kathi said. 'How can you tell jokes? What's wrong with you?'

I frowned at her. She's got more patience with Todd than anyone else in the world, including his husband and his mother. It wasn't like her to snap at him this way. She answered my frown with a blank gaze and I turned to Todd instead. What *was* wrong with him? He had missed his cue to deliver the same answer he always delivered whenever anyone asked him what was wrong with him, which happened quite often. 'Nothing,' he'd always say. He meant it too.

He saw me noticing his silence and said it now. 'Nothing. I'm practically perfect in every way.' He paused, waiting for the others to join in, like a chorus. 'Same as Mary Poppins,' he added, still speaking solo. 'Only I,' he finished in a mournful voice, 'look better in hats.'

'What the hell is going on?' I said. 'Seriously.'

A look pinged around the three of them like a bee in a bell jar. No one spoke but I could still hear them. Who's going to tell her, they were all thinking.

'I can't bring myself to say it,' said Todd, as if one of them had spoken the words out loud. 'I'll show you and then *you* can tell *us*. I think it would be better, despite everything, if it came from you.'

We rose and trooped in single file round the side of Reception and along the path to the slough. We mounted the steps and gathered on the porch, where I was interested to see that the olde-worlde transformation of my home into a stop on the HRT trail had taken another step forward. Here was a spinning wheel set up before a three-cornered stool, and a butter churn lurking in the corner where I usually keep my chiminea.

'Nice,' I said, feeling sorry for such puny efforts as I remembered the collection of music boxes at the Brewster Mansion, all featuring different characters from *The Nutcracker* suite and all, somehow, playing the same tune in perfect time.

The living room had a sewing basket with a pile of darning spilling out. There was an actual sock with an actual half-finished darn on an actual hole, the needle twinkling in the fairy lights. 'Lot of domestic servitude going on in this decorative scheme,' I said, eyeing the little kneehole desk with its inkwell and half-written letter on creamy parchment. 'What year is this supposed to be?'

'Eighteen sixty-five,' said Todd. 'The year the boat was built.'

'Big yarn year, was it?' I asked him. 'Spin your own and mend your socks kind of a time?'

'It's authentic,' Kathi said. 'My nonna had a butter churn.'

'But did your nonna live on a boat?' I said.

'Come see the kitchen,' said Todd. I turned to look at him, trying to decipher his tone. I had only heard that voice being used to say things like 'Come view the body' or 'Help me mop up the vomit'. Or in one notable case, 'Who shat in the barbecue?'

Not much had changed in the passageway, except the pictures were now family portraits à la *The Others*, but the kitchen had moved on. The initial impression was a profusion of colour: a higgledy-piggledy heap of vintage tins and boxes, bright cloths and ribbon ties, old rolling pins and potato mashers, towers of Pyrex and pyramids of coloured drinking glasses, all in a red, green and gold theme for Christmas, to match the reindeer print curtains and the jolly Santas on the place mats set out on a minuscule table that somehow had been crammed in here. I thought briefly of Mrs Brewster's table, set for twelve, and the boar's head that was going to the homeless shelter when the photoshoot was done.

Then my brain caught up with my eyes and I looked again. How could I see tins and boxes, plates and Pyrex, glasses and mashers and, now I had a second look, sets of silver cutlery tied in gingham ribbons, not to mention copper jelly moulds, and painted enamel kettles and cooking pans? None of that should be possible because there wasn't enough workspace in here to have a pile of crap lying about. But the crap *wasn't* lying about. It was in the cupboards. And it was only visible because of another innovation.

'Um, where are my doors?' I said. The skeletons of my kitchen cabinets were still there, but they'd been turned into open shelves, complete with Christmas shelf liners and scalloped edgings.

'They're in storage and we'll replace them,' said Todd, but still in the corpse, shit, vomit voice. 'Why?'

'You better had,' I said. 'That's all. I don't want open shelves in my kitchen.'

'No?' said Kathi. 'You prefer doors you can close over all your secrets?'

'Huh?' I said. 'No, I just don't relish that layer of greasy dust you get. They don't show you that in the magazines.'

'Well, they're in storage, like Todd just told you,' Noleen said. 'Along with all the crud you had hidden behind them.'

'*Almost* all the crud,' said Kathi.

'Yeah,' said Todd. 'Almost all.'

'What did you break?' I said. 'Is that what you're getting at? Just tell me.'

'Nothing,' said Todd. 'We put everything in storage except for one thing that we kept back until you could tell us more about it.'

He stared at me. I stared back defiantly. For a while. But then paranoia got the better of me. What the hell had they found in my kitchen cupboards that I had forgotten leaving there? It wasn't drugs, because I'm on a green card and don't want to get deported for crimes of moral turpitude. Also, I don't really like drugs much; none of them taste as nice as Chardonnay. And it wasn't anything bedroomy. Not in the kitchen. And actually not in the bedroom either. Not since Taylor came along. Was there a gift from Todd I'd said I loved and stashed in the back of a cupboard because I secretly hated it? I didn't think so. Todd's great at presents and impossible to offend. The couple of times he did get it wrong, I told him and asked for the receipt to return it.

So what could it be?

'You're going to have to tell me,' I said. 'Put me out of my misery.'

'Lex,' said Noleen. 'We found it. Stop bluffing. Come clean and help us work out what to do.'

I shook my head. 'I've got no idea what you think I need to come clean about,' I said. 'Or what I might have to help you decide what to do about.'

'OK,' said Kathi. 'Play it that way.'

'Play what?'

'We found the gun, Lexy,' said Todd. 'But we haven't called the cops yet. We waited to speak to you.'

SIXTEEN

I t's a cliché worthy of a drawing-room comedy, but it came out of my mouth and I couldn't stop it. 'I have never,' I said, my voice shaking with fury, '*ever,* been so offended in all my life.' That didn't capture what I was feeling though. 'Scratch that,' I tried next. 'I'm not offended. I'm wounded to the quick.' My God, now I sounded like a reject from a Georgette Heyer novel. I tried again. 'For two pins, I would rip off my own arm and beat you all to death with it.' Now I was a cross between a pantomime villain and Al Capone. One last try. 'I am so fucking angry that you shower of morons could think this of me!' That was more like it. 'Get off my boat. Wait! First take your *Little House on the Prairie* crap off my porch and get all your Doris Day drek out of my kitchen before I hoy it into the slough and you with it, and then get off my boat.'

'Get out my pub!' said Kathi in a passable South London accent. She'd taken to *EastEnders* like a Cockney to the manner born.

'This isn't funny and I'm not joking,' I said. 'You think I killed Menzies and hid the gun on board my boat then went swanning off and let you crawl all over it?'

'That's what I said,' Noleen chipped in. 'Dumb as a brick.'

'And what about you?' I said to Todd. 'Pal o' mine. Buddy boy. Colleague and friend. You think I'm a murderer. And a really incompetent one at that?'

Todd opened his mouth to answer me but I held up my hand and cut him off.

'Don't! Don't say another word. Get off my boat. Get me off your stupid website. Keep my name out of your mouth from this day on. Goodbye.'

'Tell us how you feel, Lexy,' Todd said. He was joking. He was actually winding me up, the bastard.

'I *will* tell you how I feel,' I said. 'I hope you get an infestation of wasps in your bathroom, bedbugs in your mattress, moths in your wardrobe and ants in your fridge. I hope a spider lays eggs in your ear and intestinal parasites burrow—'

'Lexy!' Kathi said. She got in between Todd and me as he cowered in the face of my invective. And my jabbing finger.

'And I hope *you* get mould, dry rot, wet rot, mushrooms and backed-up plumbing. I hope junkies start sleeping in all your doorways. I hope all your binbags explode. I hope you get norovirus and dysentery and food poisoning all at the same time while the water's off, and have to shit in a bucket and puke on the floor, and I hope there's legionnaire's disease in the pool filter and dog mess tracked over every carpet and you don't notice till after your work-out and it's in your *hair*.'

'Of course we know you didn't kill him,' Todd said, gathering himself and standing up straight again. I could see him perfectly because Kathi was cowering now. 'Someone is framing you.'

'So what the cockroach in your cornflakes and toe-jam in your taco are you accusing me of?'

'We're accusing you of hiding whatever it is in your shared history with this guy that makes you worth framing,' said Todd. 'We'd like that to stop now.'

'Oh,' I said. 'I see. Well, in that case, sorry.'

'Aw man,' said Noleen. 'You blew it, Todd. I wanted to hear what she had in the barrel for me.'

'Next time,' I said, trying for haughty. The truth was, Noleen was Teflon. She was Kryptonite. She had no chinks in her psychological armour whatsoever. Except one. 'To be going on with, I would have hoped Kathi leaves you.'

I thought she would laugh. I certainly didn't think she would look at me with such an expression of pain, disbelief and bewilderment that I'd spontaneously spurt forward and try to hug her.

'Back off,' she said. '*I* hope Molly falls for it and you spend twenty years in a super-max eating pudding cups.'

'And they're all pumpkin spice flavour,' said Kathi. 'How could you wish me dogshit in my hair?'

'I hope your cellmate does your astrology chart,' said Todd. 'Every single goddam day. Moths, Lexy? Moths? You'd strike at the very heart of me? At my *clothes*?'

'Where is it?' I said, ignoring both of them. 'Where have you put it? You know you shouldn't have moved it?'

'We didn't,' said Noleen. She grabbed the front of the sink, finding one of the few bare patches in between the gingham tea towels and the knitted dishcloths that were draped there. Then she knelt, with a bit of groaning, leaned into the doorless bottom cupboard and lifted an aluminium double steamer out of the way. There, towards the rear of the space, sitting on a patch of bare wood, with the shelf-liner rolled up in front of it ready to spread backwards when the cops were done, sat a squat black handgun. It lay on its side with the business end pointing towards the sink pipes.

'You decorated round it?' I said. 'Are you insane? Molly's going to gut you.'

'Kathi cleaned the floor and the cabinet exterior before we opened it,' Noleen said. 'Any evidence was long gone.'

'Still going to gut you,' I muttered. 'And what exactly do you want me to tell you? If you *haven't* all lost your collective minds after all and you *don't* think I'm the most incompetent and complacent murderer ever born?'

'Duh,' said Todd. 'We want you to tell us what you keep in this cabinet and when you last opened it up?'

'Duh, yourself,' I said. 'It's the cupboard under the sink, Todd. I keep Vim, Brillos, Fairy, and binbags there, same as everyone. Oh for God's sake! Comet, SOS pads, dish soap and garbage sacks. Catch up, will you?'

'And when . . .?' Noleen began.

'Because with your cooking,' Todd said, 'you must use SOS pads every day.'

'But I haven't been eating at home,' I reminded him. 'I've been coasting along on the endless leftovers since Thursday. Where's my bin?'

'We got you this one,' Todd said, pointing to a painted enamel waste-paper basket with a pattern of trellis and roses all over it.

'Idiot,' I said. 'I meant what did you do with my real bin. Because if I rake through the liner, I'll be able to tell you if I've changed it since Thursday.'

'I haven't stored your garbage can with the bag still in it!' said Todd.

'How about the doors?' I tried next. 'Did you wipe the door handles, Kathi? No chance of the fingerprints of whoever stashed that there?'

'I didn't "wipe" anything,' Kathi said. 'I washed the surfaces with sugar soap and hot water after the birth. Then I washed them again with ordinary soap and hot water before we started the decoration. And I rinsed them with a vinegar solution and I buffed them dry. So probably not much chance of fingerprints, no.'

'Molly is going to gut both of us,' I said. 'She's trying to get a warrant to search this place since the autopsy blew my alibi and I found the app on my phone. She's going to hate getting a warrant for a boat cleaner than a surgical theatre, isn't she?'

'She knows me,' Kathi says. 'She'll know it's a red herring that I cleaned up a little.'

'I thought she knew *me*,' I said. 'Didn't stop her making some very nasty insinuations.'

'*I* thought I knew you, if it comes to that,' said Noleen. 'But turns out I don't got any more clue than these two about what it is in your past that's brought all this to my door.'

I stared at her for a minute or two. 'Where is my binbag?' I said.

'To the dumpsters!' said Noleen. 'Let's go.'

She wasn't in a chatty mood, so I had plenty of thinking time. Unfortunately. More than enough time to think about that night at the party I'd been pretending was a tarts and vicars. Time to remember the last conversation I had ever had with Menzies Lassiter, his voice drawling with an undercurrent of easy laughter, my voice taut and shrill as I tried not to cry. The fuzzy, blurred feeling that lasted until the cold-water shock when I went in up to my ankle in that freezing puddle. There was a lot I wasn't telling them. Because there was a lot I didn't let myself think about. There was a lot that was so well tamped down after all these years that I could barely remember it. It's a strategy that works pretty well sometimes.

'I never had a therapist tell me that before,' one of my clients had said once, when I'd advised her not to dwell on things she couldn't change.

'How many therapists have you had?' I asked. I was kind of kidding.

'You're the ninth,' she told me.

California.

California, where the weather in November means that a dumpster in the sun can be an unpleasant thing to have business with. Noleen opened the lid of the big grey one dedicated to landfill and let it clang back, releasing the smell of some very ripe rubbish into the air.

Unfortunately, I'm not as independent as I could be. And I don't like wasting money either. If I was in the habit of buying my own bin liners, they would look different from the motel bin liners and I would have been able to home in on the right one straightaway. As things stood, there were seven identical contenders – white bags with orange ties and noisome contents – all waiting for my attention.

'Can't you remember anything about the one you brought from the boat?' I said. 'Or where it landed?'

'I didn't kiss it like a love letter going in the mailing box,' said Noleen. 'So, no.'

'Maybe I don't have time,' I said. 'I don't want Molly to catch me halfway through the search when she gets here.'

Noleen gave me a look. 'Who do you think's gonna call her?' she said. 'That's your job. So work out when you last opened that cabinet then get on the phone and get her down here. Take responsibility, Lexy. This is on you.'

'Huh. Except for the bit where you decorated the front half of the cupboard and just left the gun lying there.'

'It's not a crime,' said Noleen.

'Oh come off it! It must be.'

'Nope. It's a crime to not report a lost gun, but it's no crime to keep shtum about a found one.'

'But I bet you don't want to be there when Molly sees it.'

Noleen gave me an uneasy smile and drifted off.

I leaned over the edge of the dumpster and waved a hand in the direction of the nearest binbag handle. Yep, just as I thought. I couldn't reach it. I was going to have to climb in.

As I dragged over one of the plastic chairs from the lounge and hopped up to clamber in beside the stinking refuse, I remembered the day that moving to California had first been floated in my hearing. 'It's sunny every day,' Brandon had said. That was a lie. It was sunny all summer then it was foggy and rainy and grey, just like home. 'And life is easy there,' he'd claimed. Another whopper. Life here was more complicated than anyone in the old country would be able to stand, or ever be sober enough to manage. 'There are beautiful beaches,' he said, waving his hand as if to sketch them. Aye right. With sea so cold you couldn't swim in it unless you wore a wet suit. 'Beautiful mountains,' he continued. They were OK, but I was Scottish; I was over mountains. Also they were ninety minutes away, which was a bit like living in London and bragging about the Cotswolds. 'The people are friendly,' he'd told me. This was true, but misleading. The people were so friendly it creeped me out and I was terrified it was catching. 'And the food is fantastic,' he'd finished. He knew me so well after only six dates. Every time I remembered *this* claim I almost got angry enough to phone him and take it up again. The food was *not* fantastic. The Thai food was fantastic; the Korean food was fantastic; the burgers and fries and the Mexican food were fantastic. The fruit was fantastic and the bread was fantastic. And the fish and the cheese and the olives. What he had not told me – what he had been very careful never to tell me – was that this is a country without pies. Worse! That this is a country that thinks pies are sweet. Creamy or fruity or spicy or whatever the hell is actually in a bear claw. This is a country that doesn't know pies should have beef in. And gravy. Or pork with jelly. Or lamb at a push. I'd even settle for cheese and potato after all this time. He hadn't told me any of it. How different my life might have been if I'd known.

But then I'd have missed California. All the glamour and excitement of living here. This was the thought drifting through my brain as I swung over the lip of the bin and used my momentum to plumph down among its contents. Lucky me.

Maybe the first bag I opened would be mine. I untied the knot in the plastic straps and peered in. Kathi and Noleen, I decided. All the rubbish had been wrapped in Ziplocs before being placed in the binbag. Some of it – food waste and what looked like dental flossers – had been encased in a double layer of Ziplocs. This was the hand of Kathi, definitely.

I tried another one. It was tied very tight in a triple knot and after picking at it a while I admitted I was going to have to claw through the bag itself to get in. By the time I opened the tiniest little gap in the plastic, I knew this hadn't come from my kitchen bin. This was the refuse of a family with a days-old baby. This was the very binbag containing her first nappies. And probably Della's postpartum pads too. I turned the bag upside down so the tear was at the bottom and considered taking up with Noleen the question of why exactly these dumpsters sat in such a sunny spot.

After a deep breath – ill-advised, I must say – I tackled a third one. Todd and Roger. It smelled lovely when I opened it, since it was full of nothing but crumpled tissues smeared with expensive cleansing products and a couple of pairs of the disposable socks Todd wears in bed to let the scented lavender and beeswax overnight foot solution soak into his heels.

So, I reckoned, this last one on the top layer must be mine. I picked at the tied handles until they loosened, then opened it up and peered inside.

I had forgotten one, of course. One more room had been occupied at the end of last week. Menzies's room. And clearly he, or someone else, had emptied his bucket between his afternoon arrival and his middle-of-the-night permanent departure. Here was a pair of boarding passes for Edinburgh to Schiphol and Schiphol to San Francisco, a long sticky luggage label, a collection of pocket Bombay-mix – mint wrappers, receipts, handi-wipe sachets – and one other thing. I stared. I even fell back out of my careful crouch so that my bum hit the sheugh behind me like I had told myself I wasn't going to let happen. I barely noticed the warm wet of nameless provenance seeping through the seat of my jeans, though. I couldn't believe what I was seeing.

On one level, it was a Kit-Kat wrapper. One of the shiny red paper-bands that went round the silver foil on a four finger Kit-Kat. Except it didn't any more, did it? Kit-Kats were wrapped in boring heat-sealed plastic just like everything else now. They hadn't been folded into silver foil and lapped up in a cummerbund for years. I didn't know when exactly it changed, but I knew they were still the old way in the very early 2000s, because Menzies had bought me a Kit-Kat on our first date. We had shared the fingers – one for him and three for me – and then I had balled up the foil and thrown it out the bus window at a pigeon (I was such a show-off when I liked a boy in those days; and these days too, I had to admit, as I remembered my first burping contest with Taylor). But the cummerbund? I had slipped it into my pocket when Menzies wasn't looking, transferred it to my wallet when I got home, and kept it there.

Not so very long after that bus journey, lying in bed in his house when his parents were out, we had one of those emetic, falling-in-love conversations we all used to have at that age. (Do other people still have them? Should I maybe start one sometime: *Taylor, what's your deepest desire?* I dismissed the idea. It would be something to do with funding habitats for migratory birds anyway.)

But that afternoon in Menzies's bed, the question on the table was what's the mushiest thing you've ever done since we met? Menzies had blushed – all the way to his belly button as I remembered; I'd never seen a naked person blush before – and admitted that when he was bored in an anthropology lecture he had made an anagram out of our two names. 'If we got married,' he said, 'We could be the Amplebec-Saltires.'

I hooted with laughter. 'What a sap!' I said. 'And what an ego! I'm not changing my name.'

'You said you wouldn't make fun of me!' he said. 'This is supposed to be a trust game.'

'You can make fun of me, if you like,' I said. 'You can rip the piss out of me with one of your mum's grapefruit spoons. I don't mind.'

'We haven't got grapefruit spoons!' he said. But the belly blush had deepened, and I knew that if I ransacked the drawers of the sideboard downstairs I'd find a full set of them, probably in a velvet box. 'What's your mushy secret?' he asked me. 'Or pay a tickle forfeit.'

I wasn't sure I could handle tickling without letting a fart fly, so I leaned over the edge of the bed and swiped up my jeans. I plucked my wallet out of the back pocket and plucked the Kit-Kat cummerbund out of my wallet. I held it up just under my eyes and batted my lashes at him. 'The first thing you ever bought me,' I said.

He didn't laugh. He got very solemn and his eyes started to glisten.

'Oh, please!' I said. 'If you ever want me to have sex with you again you need to buck up pronto.' But the wobble in my voice meant that it didn't quite come off and instead of any more banter we hugged each other and settled down in a soft silence I can still remember.

So it was all the more significant seven months later on our last night, when I riffled through my wallet, so much fatter now I was a student living away from home, with my Blockbuster card and my matriculation card and my lunch vouchers. I thought I'd lost it for a minute, but then a red glint caught my eye.

I grabbed it and shook it in his face. 'And you can have this piece of embarrassing shit back!' I screamed at him. 'A Kit-Kat! A fucking Kit-Kat! Not a red rose or a bottle of wine or a box of chocolates, Menzies. A bar of bloody chocolate from a pub vending machine. And I was such a gullible fool I treated it like a . . .'

To be fair, I'd done well to get all that out. It would have been a miracle if I'd actually thought of a way to land the line. Instead I took hold of each end to rip it up and smash the bits in his sneering stupid face.

And I couldn't do it.

And he saw that.

And the sneer got bigger and more heartbreaking.

And the stupid Kit-Kat wrapper fluttered to the ground as I turned and staggered away to my puddle and bus-stop.

And then, clearly, Menzies picked it up and kept it. All these years. Brought it to California with him. And then finally threw it away. All in all, if it wasn't for the missing gun, this would be looking more like suicide every minute.

I let the wrapper fall back into the binbag and retied the handles, wondering what to do. Should I leave the bag here and ask Molly if anyone had searched for it? Or take it and tell Molly I'd found it. Or leave it and say nothing. Or take it and say nothing. I simply couldn't decide. Although my decision probably wouldn't register anyway when it was set beside Molly finding out about the gun in my kitchen that Todd and Noleen had decorated around, and that I'd known about for an hour now.

I grabbed the bag and got my feet underneath me to stand up without having to put my hands down, slightly judging Kathi for the dreadful state of her bins. Of course I understood: there was no way for her to get the dumpsters clean enough to be bearable, so she'd decided to block their existence from her consciousness. As a result, Noleen managed them. And as a result of *that* I was sitting in a puddle of bin juice.

'What was that?' came a voice from somewhere outside, while I was still in a crouch. I didn't recognize it, beyond knowing it was female, American, and nervous-sounding.

'Ew,' said another voice much the same. 'That dumpster is open. There must be a rat inside.'

'I'll call the manager,' said voice one, 'and have her close it up.'

'She's scary,' said voice two. 'She'll bark at you. I can close it.'

Shit. I had two choices now. I could stand up and style it out. Somehow. I could crouch here and say a cheery hello when one of them came over to seal up 'the rat'. Or I could burrow into the stinking rubbish and hide, which would make me sound a lot bigger than a rat and no doubt end with one of these two women phoning animal control.

Thankfully, it didn't come to any of those unsavoury choices.

'Ew, no,' said voice one again. 'Don't touch the nasty thing. Let's just leave.'

'I had misgivings about this place from the start,' said the woman I was beginning to think of as Ew Two.

'Me too.'

Double shit. I had lost Noleen a bit of business.

'But the idea is that we walk around,' said Ew One, 'not that we sit in this glorified parking lot staring at dumpsters.'

Triple shit! They were from the HRT, come to judge us on the final walk-through. And I was blowing it.

'Glorified?' said Ew Two and then they both tittered.

'Let's go. We've done enough,' said Ew One.

'We gave it a fair attempt,' said Ew Two.

'I thought it was an odd choice from the start,' said Ew One. 'But we had to show willing.'

'Which we did,' said Ew Two. 'But there are limits.'

'What a relief!' said Ew One.

'Never to have to spend another moment of life dealing with that deluded, boundary-free do-gooder,' said Ew Two.

Oh, poor Todd!

'And his little sidekick's no picnic either,' said Ew One.

Who did she mean? Kathi? Me?

'Because let's face it,' said Ew Two, 'there's down to earth and then there's crude and obnoxious.'

Ah. Noleen.

'We're going to be accused of racism you know,' said Ew One. 'Are you ready for that?'

'What?' said Ew Two. 'They'll play the race card? Do you think so?'

'Can you doubt it?' said Ew One. 'You wait and see. We are going to be accused of anti-Hispanic bias for walking away from this.'

'It's not racism,' said Ew Two. 'It's honest elitism. There's such a thing as objective value.'

'I agree.'

'Thank you.'

'Thank *you*.'

'You're welcome.'

I heard the retreating footsteps, and slowly, slowly, I stood up to watch them as, cloaked in their own smugness like a pair of chrysalises in Lululemon cocoons, they walked away.

'Molly?' I said, into my phone when I'd speed-dialled her (and what does it say about my life that I've got a cop on speed-dial?). 'Developments. You might want to come.'

'Such gracious generosity,' she said. 'You bet your sweet little plaid ass I'm coming. I got a warrant.'

'Tartan,' I said. 'And arse. And medium at best. But I want you to make a note of the fact that I offered an invitation before I knew about the warrant. The thing is, we found the gun.'

There was a long silence. As far as speech went anyway. The sound of Molly's crepe soles on the CPD lino was actually pretty noisy.

'At least, I should say we found *a* gun,' I said. 'But since it was planted in my house a couple of days after a gun crime, I'm going out on a limb.'

'Did you touch it?'

'No. I need to make sure you know that. Because when you see it, it's going to look as if there's no way someone didn't touch it. But no.'

'I can't wait,' said Molly grimly. 'Anything else?'

I looked down to where the re-tied binbag was resting against my legs and considered my options.

'No,' I said, in the end. 'What kind of thing were you thinking?'

'That's a strange thing to say,' said Molly. I heard the change in sound as she exited the echoing police station and came out into the car park. Her breath got noisier as her steps got quieter. I heard the click of her car door.

'Everything about this is strange,' I told her.

She disappeared for a second or two while she started the engine and her phone synched. Then she was back.

'Not to me,' she said. 'It's a pretty open-and-shut case to me.

Motive, means, opportunity and evidence of guilt. The only mystery is why I didn't bring you in already. That's probably going to end today.'

'Utter bullshit,' I said. 'What motive? He's an old boyfriend I haven't seen for well over a decade. Closer to two.'

'Until he comes back into your life,' said Molly.

'So presumably *he* had a motive for *that. I've* got no motive for *anything*,' I said. 'And what "means", while we're at it? How the hell would I get my hands on a gun, Molly? "Means" would be tracing a gun to me before the shooting. Finding a gun near me, after it, is nothing.'

She didn't say anything. I heard the indicator as she took the corner out of the police station car park, headed this way.

'And as for opportunity,' I said, 'he was locked in a room to which I didn't have a key, while I was in another room with two witnesses, on a night when no one in the motel was reliably asleep. There was less opportunity to be creeping around getting up to stuff on the night of Thanksgiving than any other night since I've been there. And that's if I knew he was there. Which I didn't.'

'So you say.'

'Of course I didn't. You think I would have agreed to serve him breakfast if I'd known who he was? And actually, do you think I would have agreed to serve him breakfast if I'd been in there and killed him? That would be insane.'

'Double bluff,' Molly said. She sounded muffled. She must be in the underpass, I reckoned. Mere minutes away.

'And there's absolutely no evidence of guilt,' I said. 'You mean the app? Maybe if the app was removed and you found a trace of it. Maybe. But leaving the stupid thing on there and waking up Taylor when it went off again is evidence of innocence. So is the gun in my kitchen cupboard.'

I heard the indicator again just before Molly hove into view. 'Where are you?' she said into the phone. I saw her lips move in time. 'Are you on the boat?'

'I thought detectives were trained noticers,' I said.

She twisted about in her seat, looking for me. I waved when she spotted me.

'What is this, Samuel Beckett?' she said, slamming the car door and strolling over.

'I'm impressed,' I said. 'With your literary knowledge. Not with your detective abilities. Why didn't anyone look for Menzies's bin liner?' She frowned. 'Oh for God's sake, garbage bag then.'

'He had only just checked in,' said Molly. 'He hadn't thrown anything away.'

'That's where you're wrong,' I told her. 'Here.' I lifted the binbag and held it out. 'More evidence of innocence,' I said. 'Don't thank me now. You've got work to do.'

SEVENTEEN

'The fuck's going on in here?' Molly said, heartfelt but unprofessional, as she looked around the boat kitchen minutes later.

'It's for the HRT,' I explained.

Although, same rules for me as for Diego: it's only an explanation if it explains, In this case, Molly's frown merely deepened. 'What?' she said. 'Aren't you a little young for that? And for this kitschy crap too?'

'Holiday Residence Tour,' I said. 'We're joining in this year. One motel room plus Reception and the boat.'

'Really?' Molly said. 'The gals with the snowblowers in their living rooms and the chefs handing out amuse-bouches for twenty bucks a pop? That doesn't sound like your style. And this doesn't look like theirs.'

'Be that as it may,' I said. Ordinarily I would worry about sounding pompous but Molly had just come out with 'amuse-bouches' minutes after a nod to Samuel Beckett and so, if anything, I had some catching up to do. 'That's why Todd and Kathi were guddling in my cupboards and that's why they found this.' I lifted out the double-steamer and pointed.

Molly kneeled down and shone a pencil torch into the darkness. 'And they just left it there?'

'They decorated round it and waited until I came home so they could ask me about it,' I said. 'Then I phoned you.'

'After a stint in the dumpster,' said Molly. 'What do you usually keep in this cabinet? When did you last look in here?'

'Exactly,' I said. And then, 'Bugger. I keep my binbags in there and so I went skip-surfing to remind myself when I'd last changed it. But I got distracted by Menzies's bag. I'll need to go back while I'm still clarty and give it another shot.'

Molly sat back on her heels and stared at me. 'I see,' she said. 'Apart from bugger, binbag, skip-surf, and clarty.'

'You need to meet me halfway,' I said.

'I can do better than that,' Molly said. She smiled, which made me instantly suspicious. But it didn't seem like a sarcastic smile that was soon to be followed up with Miranda rights and the click of cuffs. 'I can try to help you find out who's framing you, Lexy.'

'Eh?' I said, sagging backwards in relief and banging into a cast-iron muffin tin full of fake muffins that was resting on my draining board as part of the general Hallmark-level frou-frou fakery. It clattered to the floor sending the muffins – knitted, now that I took a closer look – rolling into all four corners of the room. 'Why didn't you tell me that before?' I said. 'For Christ's sake, Molly! I get that you've got your professional pride but, seriously, if me finding Menzies's binbag has put me in the clear you should have told me without the time delay. You've put me through ten minutes of unnecessary hell since I shredded your theory out there.'

Molly was shaking her head. 'You're insane,' she said. 'You shredded nothing and I kept you waiting no time. The reason I now believe you're being framed is . . .' she paused in an extremely cheesy way; she even waggled her eyebrows, '. . . this is the wrong gun.'

'Wh—?' I said, then tears started pouring down my face. It was as if my plumber numbskull had opened a valve.

'This is a .38. The bullet in Lassiter's brain came out of a .45.'

'Uh-uh-hooo,' I said. 'I duh-don't think I ruh-realized how stress-fuh-full it's all buh-been.' Then I put my face in my hands and wept.

'I ain't hugging you,' said Molly. 'Get a grip.'

It took a minute or two but with a deep sniff and a slap of my own face, I got a fairly decent one. 'But you do still need to look in the binbag,' I said.

'All in good time,' said Molly. She had taken approximately a hundred pictures of the gun and she was now picking it up with a pencil through the trigger, just like on *Columbo*, and dropping it into an evidence bag.

'Why do you think the killer would put an obviously wrong gun in my cupboard?' I said. 'There's no reason for it that makes any sense.'

Molly stood up with a loud groan. 'My knees are shot,' she said. 'I can think of three reasons right off the top of my head. One, the real gun is traceable. Two, this murderer is so sketchy and deep into the dark side he can't even imagine innocence and it never occurred to him you'd call the cops and report it. Three, it's the same as the app on repeat. Double bluff. He's sowing so much confusion he thinks we'll get lost in the noise. What?'

I wasn't aware that my thoughts had shown on my face. 'A ghost walked over my grave,' I said. 'Or is it a goose? Either way it's . . . overkill. Sowing confusion, kicking up a dust storm and hiding in it . . . I don't know.'

'Goose,' said Molly. 'And now for the garbage sack. Say, you're pretty ripe already, Lexy. What do you say to opening it up and letting me take the pictures?'

I was going to protest but I could smell the bin juice on my jeans and see it in the creases of my palms and Molly was being nicer to me than she'd ever been, so together we went back out on to my porch where it lay waiting.

'Gloves,' said Molly.

'Why?'

'Aw jeez! You didn't wear *gloves*?'

'I was raking about for my own rubbish,' I said. 'Of course I didn't wear gloves.'

'You know,' said Molly, 'in polite circles ladies wear gloves in a dumpster no matter *what* they're searching for. Mostly on the east coast, admittedly.'

'Funny,' I said, snapping on the powdered latex pair she handed me. 'Should I slice it open down the side to save touching the handles again?' Molly rolled her eyes and shrugged, as if to say it was too late for caution now, so I got stuck into the knots.

'Boarding passes,' she said, clicking a picture as I lifted them. 'Luggage label. Is that a condom wrapper? Is the cond—?'

'It's the sachet that a mini-hand-wipe came in.'

'Huh. OK. Heathrow shopping concourse receipt for . . .?' She squinted.

'An *Independent* newspaper,' I said. 'Which tracks. Menzies took a lot of stick for reading that when we were all Guardianistas at university. Sort of like the *Chronicle* and the *WSJ*.'

'Starbucks receipt for . . .' she squinted again.

'A latte and a bran muffin,' I said. 'Schiphol. I don't know if that tracks. I knew him pre-Starbucks.'

'When the world was young,' said Molly.

I held up the mint sweetie papers, one in each hand, and she clicked. 'Assorted candy wrappers,' she said.

I held up the final item. 'Ditto,' she said. 'That it?'

It would have been that easy. She didn't know squat about the wrappers of British Kit-Kats. If *I* didn't say anything she never would.

'What?' she asked.

Of course. My big pregnant pause had tripped her alarm and the decision was out of my hands. So I told her.

'This has to be some major mind-fuck, Lexy,' she said when I was done.

It was hands-down the kindest word I'd ever got from her and I told her so.

'Yeah, yeah, don't push it,' said Molly, back to normal as quick as that.

'I better go. I'm riper than a Camembert that got held up at customs. You're going to catch whoever did this, aren't you? You're going to get him?'

'That was the plan,' Molly said.

'Because I've got to be honest, the frame-up has been occupying my thoughts – I'm only human, you know – but I do care about who killed him too. Scumbag that he was.'

'Was he?'

'Enh,' I said. 'I loved him and he broke my heart. If that makes him a scumbag then there aren't many non-scumbags alive, right?'

I think she believed me.

I plumped down beside Taylor in a plastic chair in the forecourt lounge after my shower. I had always spent a lot of time outside ever since I moved here. (The novelty of it not being too cold wore off eventually, but the novelty of it not raining was going strong.) So I didn't have to change much in the spring of 2020 when all of life moved en plein air. Everyone else took a while to catch up, but once they got the idea it stuck. Here we were in November and these plastic chairs were the hottest seats in the whole place. Taylor wouldn't have dreamed of waiting for me anywhere else. He was me now. Everyone was me now. Living outside in the baking heat and the occasional mild chill. Putting an umbrella up if it did start to spit.

Everyone was Kathi now too. We wiped and washed and sprayed and wiped again, like she'd been doing for years. We *all* opened doors with a tissue; we *all* summoned lifts with an elbow; we *all* worked the cash dispenser with a ballpoint pen.

Sadly, we were all Noleen too. We were grumpier and more foul-mouthed by the day. Less patient, more forthright. Easier to deal with, Noleen claimed. Everyone knew where they stood. 'In the blast range of your white-hot rage?' I said, expecting her to quibble.

'It's good for you,' she replied. 'Toughen you up so life can't break you.'

Taylor wasn't looking too tough today.

'Bad news?' I asked him, once we'd finished our hellos.

He laughed and shook his head. 'You're funny,' he said. 'I made a wee bet with myself.'

'Don't say "wee",' I told him. I had been through this with the rest of them two years ago.

'That you'd assume it was bad news,' he went on, ignoring me. 'I can't wait to visit Scotland and see a whole nation full of you, looking on the dark side, braced for tragedy, plucking misery out of merriment. It's gonna be a blast.'

'Until you get glassed,' I said.

'Drunk?'

'Good guess,' I said, with a tip of the head in recognition of how much he'd learned. 'But not in this instance. It means to be struck in the face with the jagged remains of a broken glass.'

'Why . . .?' said Taylor.

'Oh, because it usually happens in a pub where glasses are to hand,' I explained.

'Not that! Why the hell would I get hit with broken glass?'

'For laughing at strangers,' I said. 'So it's *good* news then? Did they catch the killer?'

'They did not catch the killer,' Taylor said. 'And you tell me if it's good or bad. Your parents aren't coming.'

'Are you kidding?' I said. 'That's lottery-number good news!'

'And Menzies's parents can't get here either.'

'Oh no! Are they OK?'

'No idea,' Taylor said. 'It was Noleen who spoke to them. They weighed it up and decided to stay put and liaise with the cops from home.'

'How do you not know whether that's good news?' I said. 'Did you particularly want to hang out with grieving parents, who probably think I murdered their son?'

'Well, because the thing is,' said Taylor, 'Petra and Anders—'

'Perdita and Anselm.'

'Yeah, them. Since they can't come, they asked if you would take care of the you know.'

'I really don't.'

'Repatriation of his remains.'

'Umm, lemme think,' I said. 'My answer is "No". So, good news all round.'

'Except Noleen already said yes and they faxed through a document outlining what they want done.'

'Did she,' I said. It wasn't a question. It was more of a holding utterance. Just a way of marking time until I found out whether the anger bubbling up inside me was going to emerge as a bellow that Noleen would be able to hear from where I sat, or if it would turn out to be more physical, so I'd have to go to the office and slam my hands on the counter while I hissed at her.

'Are you OK?' said Taylor, just as Molly had done.

'I'll be fine in a minute,' I said. Turned out my anger was the cold kind that conferred extra resolve. I walked over to the office with a steady step and opened the door.

'. . . can't do it,' met my ears. I stopped with the door ajar. That was Della. 'Maybe I forgot what it was like to have a tiny baby,' she was saying. 'Or maybe it's easier when there's only one. Or when your baby's soul isn't tied to the restless ghost of a murdered man. But then there was only one of *me* too and now there are two of us and Diego is a good boy.' She sniffed. 'My beautiful boy. But it's too hard and I can't do it. I was a fool to think I could make all of this work. Or maybe if it was a different . . . but he's . . .' she laughed. 'The truth is I can't stand him. We seemed like the perfect match, but he's so selfish and immature and, to be honest, when I go to bed at night I just want to sleep. To rest while Hiro is resting. To rest if Hiro ever rests. To rest in between Hiro's cries. The last thing I want is to have to go along with all his romantic mierda.'

'Of course you can't do it,' Noleen said. 'You shouldn't even try. And no sane person would call it "romantic" by the way. So . . . Fold your tent, cut your losses and don't apologize for anything.'

'I'm sorry,' said Della. 'To try so hard and fail so badly.'

'Fuck 'im,' said Noleen. 'Fuck 'im all the way to . . .'

I let the door fall softly closed. OK, I thought. So, for one thing, obviously, I couldn't go marching in and start whining about having to do a bit of admin for two grieving people stranded so far away from where they wanted to be. But for another thing, I needed to lay my hands on Dylan pretty sharpish. Literally lay my hands on him. On his upper arms, to be precise, which is the best place to hold a man if you're trying to shake some sense in.

I knocked on their door.

'Entrar!' Dylan called out. I would have said learning Spanish was in the plus column, but maybe it annoyed Della. It certainly annoyed her whenever I gave it a go.

When I got inside, the scene that met my eyes was hard to interpret as a tableau of deadbeat daddery. Hiro was grumbling and fidgeting in a rocking recliner, which was actually rocking because Dylan had a hold of the edge of it with the toes of one bare foot. He was balanced on the other while he folded clean washing. He was making pretty neat little white squares out of pop-under vests and rolling up the tiniest little pink socks into balls the size of cottonwool puffs. Meanwhile, Diego was hard at work doing sums at the round breakfast table, headphones on, Zoom showing a gallery view of his entire second-grade class with his teacher highlighted in the middle.

'Why is there school on a Sunday?' I said.

'He's rewatching it,' said Dylan. 'Señorita Moreno, you know.'

I didn't but I didn't have time to waste either. 'I need a word?' I said.

'Cattywampus,' said Dylan, with a huge grin. 'I'm practising my dad jokes.'

Curiouser and curiouser. I ploughed on. 'Can you come outside so Diego doesn't hear but keep the door open so you can still see Hiro?'

'Diego can't hear anything except Señorita Moreno,' he said. Then he mouthed, 'He loves her.'

'Still, this is not for his ears,' I said.

'He only has ears for Señorita Moreno,' said Dylan. 'What am I telling you? Shoot, Lexy.'

'Noleen is advising Della to leave you,' I said. Two birds one stone; it got the gist of the issue into play and it paid Noleen back for volunteering me as an undertaker.

'No way,' Dylan said. 'You must have misunderstood.'

'Not out of a clear blue sky,' I told him. 'She advised it after Della said she can't stay married to you. It's partly the baby and Diego needing so much attention, but it's partly because of you. This isn't me saying this. This is your wife. So can I speak plainly?'

'Evidence suggests yes,' said Dylan. 'Non-dad joke.'

'She said you were selfish and immature.'

'I was!' said Dylan. 'You know I was. I was a total waster except I was also a stoner. So I was half-stoner and half-waster, but then I got my act together like a ninja for Hiro coming. You know that, Lexy. You watched me.'

'I'm just telling you what I heard.'

'Look, she's probably upset. It's only days since she gave birth. She was venting. I don't mind.'

'But that's the thing, Dylan,' I said. 'That's the worst of it. She wasn't venting. She wasn't even upset. She was completely calm, completely objective, completely fine.'

She was in fact as cool as those two women at the pizza place. I really had lost touch with the youth of today.

'Shit,' Dylan said. Then he glanced over at Diego. He was right though; his very favourite of all sweary words hadn't penetrated the bubble of Señorita Moreno talking to him, even on catch-up. 'What can I do?'

'Leave her alone for a start,' I said. 'Like you just reminded me, she had a baby days ago. I can't believe you're pestering her about S-E-X already. I'm surprised at you. I'm shocked, actually.'

'I can spell,' said Diego suddenly, proving what a multitasker he was: doing sums on a worksheet, falling in love with his teacher, eavesdropping on the worst possible conversation he could possibly have picked to eavesdrop on . . . 'You're wrong, Lexy. Mama isn't angry with Dylan-dad. Why would she be? She's not even angry with Hiro. And Hiro poops her pants and cries all the time. Nobody warned me about *that*, by the way.'

'Sorry, man,' Dylan said. He turned to me and lowered his voice. 'Lexy, you gotta believe me, I would never "pester" Della about . . .'

'S-E-X,' Diego supplied.

'. . . ever and especially not now,' he concluded. He turned back again and spoke a bit louder. 'Diego, do you know what we're talking about, Lexy and me?'

'Sure,' said Diego, lifting one earphone away from his head to make it easier to deal with the annoyance of us. His hair was flattened into little marcel waves all over the side of his head, slightly sweaty and totally adorable. 'S-E-X. It's how they did stuff in movies before CGI. But don't worry. I never tell Mama what we watch when she isn't here.' He settled the earphone back against his head again and returned to the joys of Señorita Moreno.

'He is my favourite person,' I said.

'Mine too,' said Dylan. 'Three-way split anyway. And Della knows that. She wouldn't take him . . . I can't even say it. She couldn't take Hiro . . . I definitely can't say that. She couldn't. She mustn't. And why is she lying to Noleen about me hassling her?'

'To be fair,' I said. 'She didn't say S-E-X. She said "Romantic mierda".'

'She got that right,' said Diego. 'We hate rom-coms, don't we Papa-D?' He was obviously circling the target of calling Dylan 'Daddy'. Getting there slowly.

'Romantic?' said Dylan. 'I did write a song.' Diego blew a raspberry. 'But it was a lullaby. For Hiro. I thought she liked it.'

'I wouldn't mind a song,' said Diego.

'I've got to go,' I said. 'This is far too disruptive of Diego's schoolwork, clearly.'

'I've finished,' Diego said, waving a fully filled sheet of sums above his head.

'Still,' I said. I opened the door and slipped away. Della was crossing the parking lot. 'Hey,' I said. 'I was just stopping to gaze at your beautiful children for a minute. It's like putting your face in flowers.'

Della beamed. 'Is she asleep?'

'I wouldn't go that far,' I said. 'But man she's cute.'

'I'm blessed,' Della said. Then she frowned. 'Don't laugh. It's hormones.'

'I'm not laughing,' I assured her. 'I'm glad to hear it. If you did have any less . . . fluffy happy feelings, you know, because hormones can hand you those too . . . I hope you'd come and talk to me before you did anything major.'

'Major like what?' said Della.

'Like anything. Like . . . going straight back to work or resigning or buying a house or cutting your hair. Or anything.'

'I hardly have time to *wash* my hair,' said Della. 'Or buy the lotto ticket to get the money to buy the house. No big changes planned there.'

And so, since there was no way to dig any deeper without admitting I'd eavesdropped on her, I gave her a quick hug and went on my way.

'What happened about the gun?' Noleen said, popping out of the door of Reception like a whack-a-mole that way she does.

'I don't want to live in a country where that's even a question,' I told her. 'You're all nuts.'

'The hell did I do?'

'Volunteered me to deal with a funeral,' I said.

'Ah,' said Noleen, drawing herself up to the full five foot four. 'Yes. I indicated that if need be, and in the absence of other options, you would be the best person to oversee cremation and repatriation of the ashes. It's a fucking parcel, Lexy. It's not a flag-draped coffin coming into Dover, for God's sake.'

'Why me?'

'Because you know both ends – here and there – and you

know his parents and you come from that barbarous place where the idea of cremating a son before you've even said goodbye and then shipping him home in a can like a fucking ham is an idea a mother and father could even contemplate.'

'What?'

'What what? Didn't Todd tell you? That's what they want done, this Paloma and Aspen. Cold-hearted bastards, you ask me.'

'Perdita and Anselm,' I said. 'Why is cremation any more cold-hearted than anything else?'

'Are you kidding? Ask him.' Todd was making his way over from the Skweek staircase.

'Cremation or burial, Todd,' I said. 'It's like chocolate or vanilla ice-cream, right? Whatever floats your boat.'

Todd held up one finger and nodded with his eyes closed, as if to say he acknowledged the fairness of the question but he had other things on his mind. 'It's all gone very quiet on the HRT front,' he told us. 'I have no idea why.'

'It could be the fact that someone was murdered,' I said. 'It could be that, don't you think? It's not quite the tone a holiday house tour is usually aiming for.'

'I never thought of that,' Todd said. 'I've had my spies out to see if someone else has come up on the inside and overtaken us, but as far as I can tell none of the old-timers on the tour even know that we're joining them, much less know that an even more uppity upstart is ousting us before we get going.'

'What spies?' I said.

'OK, Kathi's spies,' said Todd. 'Miss Picky. She has a boatload of contacts in rug-cleaning and drape-steaming circles and there are no late-order rush-jobs that she knows of.' He opened his mouth like a choirboy and played a little tune on his cheek with his fingers. 'What were you asking me?'

'What's wrong with cremation?'

'Oh, Lexy,' he said. 'No one likes a prig.'

'I have no idea what you mean,' I said.

'A vault, a mausoleum, rolling green acres and shady pines,' said Todd. 'They're all fine. But not *compost*. It might be green but it's still wrong.'

'Ash,' I said. 'Not compost.'

'Worse!' said Todd. 'Mulch!'

'Weirdo,' I said.

'Psychopath,' said Todd.

We left it there, each of us self-righteous, mystified and seething.

EIGHTEEN

Monday 30 November

Funny he should use that word. My first client the next morning was Simon, who I called Simon the psychopath in my head and sometimes out loud to the other Ditchers when he really got to me. He was one of the worst liars I'd ever come across in a professional setting. Or any setting. It's usually psychiatrists who get the full-on narcissistic bullshit merchants, not therapists like me, and indeed this guy had only started coming to make his wife think he was serious about change, so that she'd get *less* serious about leaving him, because California is a community property state and he couldn't afford to buy out her share of the house.

'Which means,' he explained to me at our first session, 'I'd have nowhere to store my boat. There aren't many homes in Cuento with a garage that size.'

'Is this your main concern about your marriage ending?' I'd said, trying to lighten the mood. I thought he'd laugh and maybe blush and assure me that he loved his wife and valued her in many ways.

'Pretty much,' he'd said. So I put him down as brutally honest with extra brutality. It was three sessions later I realized he was the biggest purveyor of pork pies ever born. He didn't even *have* a boat. He was just messing with me.

Today, for the first time, it felt as if it might be mutual. As I had showered off the bin juice in the bathroom of my motel room the afternoon before, luxuriating in the endlessness – well, the free-ness – of the hot water and the sense of space behind the shower curtain of a standard bathtub, unlike the Lilliputian shower cabinet on board, and looking forward to the sumptuous fluffiness of the towel waiting at the end of it (courtesy of Todd; the actual Last Ditch towels were pitched at the precise point on the scale where no one would complain on TripAdvisor but no one would steal them either), I had struggled over how to have my usual weekly tough talk with Simon when I had just lied to Molly, and was immersed in an ongoing lie to Taylor, my parents, Noleen, Kathi, Todd, Roger, Della, Dylan, Diego, Hiro if she counted and, of course, me.

Play it by ear, I'd decided, as I turned my face up into the hot spray.

'Is this ethical?' Simon asked me when we met at the entrance to the UCC arboretum, the nearest bit of open space to our usual venue. He was exquisitely attuned to the scruples of everyone around him, even while he cheated his way through life with blank disregard for the messes he left in his wake.

'Moving off Zoom and on to face-to-face therapy?' I said. 'Of course it is. We'd been meeting face-to-face for months when we went virtual.'

'I meant having sessions in public where I might be overheard,' he said. He had a high regard for his image, unrelated to his behaviour. Of course he wouldn't want anyone passing by to hear him regale me with a week's transgressions.

'Between the masks, and the fact that everyone else is either having their own conversation or wearing earbuds,' I said, 'I think we're fine.' Although, to be fair to Simon, which is more than he deserved, I was a bit surprised by the number of people who'd been struck with the same idea as me. There were women doing manicures on park benches, seminar classes chuntering on about Melville and haplogroups, a lawyer with a Bluetooth and a laidback attitude to confidentiality talking very loudly about contract loop-holes, and of course there were couples who'd been locked down together since March having whispered rows. And not whispered rows. I should have brought some business cards with me.

'Do you *really* think we're fine?' Simon said. Yes, he checked whether I was lying to him. He did it all the time. He had a zero-tolerance policy towards incoming inaccuracies, despite being a living firehose of total arse-gravy.

'I really do,' I said.

'Are you sure you're not sticking to your plan just because it's your plan and you don't want to climb down?' He wasn't even kidding about *this*. Like all narcissists he had a bone-deep cynicism about the notion that anyone in the world was different from him, less at the mercy of their worst selves, more able to do the right thing despite not feeling like it.

'We've been over this,' I reminded him. 'This is not a two-way street, Simon. I'm here to help you. You can take the help or we can call it quits. I'm not asking for your help and I don't want it as a gift.'

'That's pretty hurtful,' he said. 'That's not helpful to me, while I work on my self-esteem.'

'We've been over this too,' I said. 'You don't need to work on your self-esteem. Your self-esteem, like your self-everything else, is stratospheric. You need to work on developing better patterns of behaviour, so that it's a genuinely good idea for your wife to stay married to you.'

'You are a tough nut to crack,' he said with a smile. He still believed one day I would re-evaluate everything I thought about him if he could only work out how to charm me. That was the only reason he kept coming back. Why did I *let* him come back? Well, I didn't expect to be able to help – I was only the latest in a long line of counsellors he'd spoken to – but he was the best kind of professional development exercise. Any session where I didn't just smack him in the face with his own case notes and scream at him to grow up was a source of pride.

We walked in silence for a while. But Simon never could resist a captive audience. 'Wait till you hear the latest,' he said at last. 'She wants me to join a book club with her.'

'I might need to sit down,' I said. 'What a bombshell.' He never minded sarcasm. It was the best thing about him, really. 'Are you going to?'

'Do you think it's a reasonable request?'

'Yes,' I said. 'Depending on how she couched it when she raised the issue. What did she say?'

'She said she had found out about a new book club and she wanted us to join it together, her and me.'

'Then definitely yes. That seems eminently reasonable. Why do you ask?'

'I don't want to join a book club!'

'And that is a reasonable position too.'

'You agree?' he said, a leap of delight in his voice. 'Cool.'

'Absolutely,' I said. 'Of course, you are currently' – I managed not to say *allegedly* – 'trying to show your wife you're serious about learning to be more generous, consider her more, pay attention to her needs and wants. I think going along to this book club with her would be a perfect way to tackle some of that.'

'You just said it was cool to say no!' he cried, again finding great injustice coming his way.

'Simon,' I said. 'Your wife offered you an olive branch. She didn't cross her arms and tap her foot and say, "Work out what I want." That's a gift. Your choices are to do this thing and do it with a glad heart, grateful to have the chance to make up for some of the other stuff you've done—'

'Or?'

I suppressed a sigh. 'Or say no and accept that your wife will have feelings about your refusal and you can't complain about them.'

'That doesn't seem fair!'

'I know it doesn't,' I said, and a small sigh might have seeped out along with the words.

'Why should I do things I don't want to do?'

'You're missing the point.'

'I don't want to join a stupid book club,' he said. 'You say I should do it anyway. What am I missing?'

'What you're missing is the fact that it's your wife's desire that matters here, not yours. She has asked you for something at a moment when you've assured her you are going to make big efforts to offset other choices from the recent past, so you wanting or not wanting what's there to be done – right there in front of your face! Dead easy! – it kind of doesn't matter.'

'Matters to me.'

'You need to ignore that.' I was getting tired. When I thought of the walking therapy as an alternative to Zoom, I hadn't considered the fact that sparring with Simon exhausted me even when I was slumped in a chair with both hands available to hold my head in.

'And you said we should both let things go, but here you are bringing up "other stuff". Again!'

'I said *you* could – not should – *could* try letting things go,' I said. 'I've never said your wife could or should let things go, because I've never met her and I'm not her therapist and that would be incredibly unethical.'

'I didn't mean me and my wife,' Simon said. 'I meant me and you.'

'That's worrying,' I said. 'I should know whether you're talking about me or your wife, Simon. Do you see that? I hope so.'

'Shouldn't you try to model good behaviour?' he asked next. Like every other weasel who'd been dragged to therapy by his wife multiple times and agreed to go with the sole aim of getting the therapist on his team and arming himself with yet more ways to mess with the poor woman's head, Simon had all the patter. He had once trailed into my office and reported – direct quote – that he had been experiencing 'suicidal ideation'. He hadn't. But even if he had, he'd have said, 'I can't go on. I want to end it.' Suicidal ideation! It was as if a baby, instead of crying, lifted its head and said, 'It's been four hours, Mother. Could I have some milk, please?'

'I'm not married,' I said. 'I can't model the appropriate behaviour for an errant husband making amends. I've described it to you, at length. And I've given you books to read and exercises to do. The ball's in your court.'

'Only,' he said, ignoring me completely, like he always did if I said something unwelcome, 'you sound kind of unhinged.'

'You wish.' He had tried this before, telling me I was upset, that I was finding it hard to be professional, that I was too flustered to be helpful to him. He was a pretty standard-issue misogynist when you got right down to it.

'Yeah,' he said. 'But I've never seen you hysterical before.'

'Hysterical,' I repeated blankly.

He gave a huge huffy sigh and said something about not being allowed to say anything any more. At least, I think he did. To be honest, he was receding into a kind of fog. Because, for once, he might be right. It probably *was* me, borne back into the past like Gatsby – or was it his upstart pal? Of course, it was the upstart pal, actually. That's what made it the only book I could remember chunks from. What with me having been one and all. A hanger-on, one of the BOLS Boys said. It might have been Struan; it might even have been poor Strathpeffer. Whoever it was, he was hanging on pretty hard to Menzies that last night, drunkenly advising him to let me go. 'A townie girlfriend,' said another one. That could have been Findlay, because he wasn't as beefed up and rugby club looking as the rest and I'd come to think of him as Spindly Findlay. Whether it was or not, I remember someone drawling, 'Townies are a stage we all go through, mate, but don't get stuck there.' I had wanted to say that I was a student at the same university they were at, and I was from a different town, Dundee, while Menzies's mum and dad lived ten minutes away, so if anyone was the townie it was him. But I couldn't stop crying. Then the crying morphed into laughing as one of the golden lasses who'd attached themselves to . . . maybe Farquhar, but God knows . . . called me a social climber. As if we were in some play in the Seventies and I was trying to get a golf-club membership. She thought she was so cool with her menthol cigarettes and her dress-over-jeans look she said she'd picked up on her gap year (this was just before we all started doing it), but no one who says the words 'social climber' is the cool kid anywhere except the ladies' auxiliary. And that's debatable.

After they'd all had their say – hanger-on, don't get stuck, social climber – Menzies made his final assessment of the situation. He lifted an eyebrow and spoke in that cool, collected, above-it-all way he had, letting the fag smoke slip out between his lips like a ribbon. It had thrilled me so deeply on the first few dates that I forgot to listen to what he was saying. (It had also fooled his tutor into thinking the confidence must come from intellect and had led to a resit of a first-year final when the initial mark should have got him an exit as swift as a trip down a coal shute.)

'No need to get hysterical, Lex,' he'd said, through the ribbon of smoke.

I showed him hysterical. I started shouting, waving my arms like a windmill, stamping my foot, wrenching off the earrings he'd given me and throwing them at him, taking my naughty Christmas knickers he'd given me out of my bag and smashing them into his face. And that's when I saw the corner of the Kit-Kat wrapper peeping out of my wallet and shied that at him too.

'Are you OK?' Simon said. It was a very long way back to the arboretum. When I got there, I gaped at him. Was the most self-centred and oblivious client I'd ever encountered expressing concern for another person? That was a breakthrough. 'Because if you're not capable of providing counselling you shouldn't really charge me for this hour.'

'I'm fine,' I said. I took one of those deep breaths with all the counting that you're supposed to take all the time. I can never remember the count, but surely it's mostly about the breathing. 'How many times did you lie this week?' I asked him. 'Just to your wife, I mean. Have you been keeping count, like we said?'

'I tried,' Simon said. 'But it was stifling.'

'Stifling what?'

'Spontaneity.'

'Spontaneous what?'

'You're quite judgemental sometimes, Lexy.'

'What neutral or benign thing, which therefore doesn't lend itself to judgement, have I judged?'

And so we beat on.

After Simon, Helen should have been welcome.

'How've you been?' I asked her.

'I don't want to bring you down,' she said. 'Best just to say I'm fine.'

I waited a bit to see if she would remember every single other conversation we'd had about her saying stuff like this, and self-correct. But the only sound was our footsteps.

'That's not anything you should be worrying about,' I said. Again.

'You always say that,' she noted. But she didn't, apparently, make the leap to the obvious conclusion.

'You're not going to bring me down,' I said. 'Any more than you'd turn a doctor's stomach by showing her a . . . lesion, or upset a cleaner with a dirty house.'

'Oh Lord,' Helen said. 'I never thought of that before. What if a doctor is hungover, or newly pregnant, and you march in there in the morning and put your feet right in those stirrups. I never thought to ask the scheduler when the best time for disgusting stuff is.'

'Helen,' I said, but while I was trying to decide where best to attack this new anxiety, she ploughed on.

'And everyone cleans for the cleaner, don't they? No one lets a cleaner clean dirt. That would be so rude.'

'I disagree,' I said. 'Have you ever weeded a garden?'

She nodded. 'At my grandma's. She had a little farm down in Marin. You don't see those itty-bitty little fifty-acre places now. It's all been gobbled up by corporations. I worry—'

I interrupted. Received wisdom is you don't interrupt a client in therapy. Hell, those early guys didn't even interrupt lengthy silences, or their clients' desperate pleas for any sign that they were listening. Money for old rope in those days. But if I didn't stop Helen adding new worries – like food sustainability, which is definitely where she was headed with this – we'd never get to the problems that had first brought her to me.

'Well, cast your mind back,' I said. 'What weeds were most fun to pull out? The titchy little ones that you had to pinch with finger and thumb? Or the big hairy ones you grabbed with both hands after you'd loosened them with a fork?'

'That is so true,' Helen said.

'I reckon a cleaner would far rather clean a filthy house than go through the motions in a clean one. The satisfaction of before and after, you know?'

'I never even spared a thought for ruining her day,' Helen said.

'And yeah, sure, doctors go into medicine to make people better,' I said. 'But I've never believed they call all the other doctors and students to a bedside because they're stumped. I reckon they just want to let everyone see the enormity so they can gossip about it on their coffee break.'

'And it's the same for you?' Helen said.

'Well,' I said, playing for time, 'I'm not a voyeur or a sadist or a trauma tourist, but I'd agree that the tiny little changes at the end of a therapeutic journey are less personally rewarding for the therapist than the first big steps that bring a person back from the brink.'

'Well, in that case,' she said, 'life couldn't be more shitty if I fell over on a pig farm.'

I laughed. 'Oh Helen,' I said. 'I know this might not help but it's awesome that you're funny even when you're feeling like this. You feel like using it to start a toolkit inventory?'

This was something she could just about stomach, whereas a blessing count made her so angry she had once walked out and banged the door behind her.

'I am funny,' she said, immediately and obediently. Too obediently, for me. 'I am self-sufficient and independent.'

'Um,' I said. 'OK.'

'You're right,' Helen said. 'Sorry.'

'No need to apol—'

'Sorry.'

'No need to—'

'Sorry!'

'No—'

'I'm finished. OK, I'm not self-sufficient and independent. I just think I should be. I'm lonely and scared. Those aren't in my toolkit.'

'But the courage to say it could be.'

'I'm brave enough to say I'm scared,' she went on. 'I am brave and funny.'

'Three tool minimum, like we said,' I added gently.

'I'm rich enough for therapy so I don't bore my friends.'

I made a parping sound like for a wrong answer on a game show.

'Sor—'

'N—'

'I stopped!'

'So you did,' I said. 'Sorry.'

'You get to say it?'

'I do. Sucks, eh?'

She laughed. 'You're funny too, Lexy.'

'But back to you?'

'I am funny and brave and confident enough to ask you to contribute the third thing.'

'You're beautiful,' I said. She'd asked me for the third thing plenty times before and I'd always said stuff like strong, kind, reflective. I didn't know how she would take this, but it was an obvious true fact about her and not saying it was starting to get weird.

'I'm seventy-one years old!' she said. 'I wasn't even beautiful when I was *twenty*-one. Why would you say that to me?'

'Bring a photo of you at twenty-one next time,' I said. 'Because I can't comment in the absence of evidence, but I am looking at you right now and I see beauty.'

'I'm too old!'

'Is Helen Mirren beautiful?'

'That's different.'

'Judi Dench?'

'She's got regal bearing.'

'Patrick Stewart.'

'It's different for men.'

'It is,' I said. 'Jammy bastards. So how many years has Annette Bening got left before *she's* ugly?'

'All right!' Helen said. 'Nag, nag, nag. I am brave and beautiful and funny. And you're weird.'

'Guilty,' I said. 'So. How've you been?'

By the end of the day, I couldn't decide whether I needed my people like I'd never needed them before, or whether all I wanted was to slink into my room without any of them seeing me. And I was sick to death of looking at trees.

When I turned in at the gate, I noticed a large and very shiny 4x4 idling nearby, clearly hoping to gain entry. I waved them through and went to tell Noleen, who I found huddled in Reception with Todd.

'Good news,' I said to her. 'Customers.'

'Oh he's here?' said Noleen. 'Well, Lexy, it's good news for you too. Remember how snotty you got about helping out Aaron and Penelope.'

'Not even close,' I said. 'What do you mean?'

'You're off the hook. They found someone else, so it's safe for you to stop complaining.'

'And are they who they look like?' I said. 'Because that car said FBI to me.'

Noleen rolled her eyes.

'Definitely not FBI,' said Todd. 'Could be CIA, I suppose.'

'How do you know that?' I said. I'd been kidding but he sounded serious.

'Because you have to be American to join the bureau,' he told me. 'The agency isn't so picky. Double agents, triple agents, foreign assets, defectors, informants. Who can say?'

'Seriously, though,' I said, 'what the hell are you on about?'

'Why don't you go see?' said Noleen.

So I slipped back outside, with Noleen and Todd in tow, just as the driver's door opened. A ghost stepped down, pushed up his sunglasses and grinned at me.

NINETEEN

'Struan?' I said. 'Findlay?'

'Ha ha, very funny,' he said.

'Wait. *Farquhar?*'

Noleen snorted. 'You poor bastard,' she said, clapping him on the back with the flat of her hand and causing him to take a stumbling step forward. 'I saw it written down and that's bad enough. But Farker? That's hilarious.'

'Farik,' said Farquhar. 'Most people call me Farik these days.'

'Isn't that an Arabic name?' said Todd.

'Isn't that a racist question?' said Farquhar. It wasn't the only strange thing about seeing him again after all these years, but it was certainly one of them. The last time I'd hung out with Farquhar . . . Oh, what was his last name? Vass! I remembered because Menzies and the rest of them used to call him Vaseline, Vas Deferens, Vasectomy. The hilarity never stopped. Anyway, the last time I hung out with him he was telling tasteless jokes about North Korea, complete with comedy pan-Asian accent and hand-assisted facial expressions. And now here he was wagging his finger about racism. And he was wearing the kind of over-priced extra-snug winter leisure wear I had only ever seen in San Francisco at the weekend, when Bay Bunnies togged up like Sherpas to take their dog round the block. Also he had one of those all-over stubble dos that made his head look like an egg that had been dipped in milk and rolled in breadcrumbs. Grey ones. I think of that as American too because it's so ubiquitous here. It was certainly a big shift from the last time I'd seen Farquhar, when he was still rocking an early Hugh Grant flop to go with his baggy jerseys and boat shoes. Of course, we should expect that people from our pasts have come up to date in the interim, but it was still astonishing to see someone as old-before-his-time as Farquhar Vass had been at twenty now getting younger with age like the rest of us.

'No,' Todd was saying when I tuned back in, 'it's not racist at all. It's an objection to you brown-washing yourself by appropriating a name, white boy.'

'Well, aren't you a dear,' said Farquhar, causing Todd to lift an eyebrow. I needed to get him on his own and explain that Farquhar might sound camper than a van with frilly curtains, but really he was just British.

'What are you doing here, Farquhar?' I said.

'Perdita and Anselm asked me to take care of things,' Farquhar said. 'And of course I jumped at the chance. So often, after a death, you say "Anything I can do?" and there's nothing. This time I can do *everything*. Take it off their shoulders, the poor things.'

'But where did you come from?' said Noleen.

'Edinburgh,' Farquhar said.

'What?' said Todd. 'If you could get here from there, why didn't . . .'

'Perdita and Anselm,' I said.

'. . . come?'

'Grief,' Farquhar said. 'They're paralysed by grief.'

'I thought it was the travel restrictions,' Noleen said. 'That's what she told me.'

'Well, yes, of course,' said Farquhar. 'Travel arrangements are a nightmare at the best of times, but when the red tape is double-strength and you're weakened by recent tragedy, it's all so much more impossible.' Todd and Noleen nodded doubtfully, but I could hear the strain in his voice. I wasn't buying it.

'No,' I said. 'It wasn't added pressure and lack of energy. It was the fact that flights from the UK aren't landing. How the hell did *you* get here?'

'What?' he said, and I was sure I could see a sheen of sweat under the stubble on the top of his head. 'I drove. From Palo Alto. I live there now. What is it you're asking me?'

'Hang on,' said Noleen. 'You just said you came from Edinburgh.'

'Right,' said Farquhar. 'I do.'

I narrowed my eyes and considered him objectively. On the one hand, he might be telling the truth. (Not everyone was Simon.) I'd lost track of the number of times someone had asked me where I'd come from and I'd said 'Cuento' and they'd laughed and then I'd laughed too. So maybe . . .

But Todd had just asked how Farquhar had got here *from there*? That was the moment to mention Palo Alto, surely. 'What do you do in Palo Alto?' I asked him, in case he was lying and I could trip him up.

'Tech.' He waved a hand. 'Fun for me, deathly dull for everyone else.'

'Lucrative, though,' Noleen said, with a nod at the four-by.

Farquhar gave a tight smile, the signature smile of a Brit when someone mentions money. Almost as if he'd rather discuss murder to spare anyone further embarrassment, he turned to me and dropped his voice. 'Do you have time for a quick chat, Lex?'

My hackles rose like the struts of an Amish barn. Lex? *Lex?* I hadn't seen the guy for twenty years and even then I had hated him with a hatred that was as deep as it was mutual. 'Of course,' I said. 'Where are you staying? Maybe we can meet for a . . . Oh no.'

Noleen was signalling furiously behind his back. 'He's staying here, of course,' she said. 'Room 105. Do you have much luggage, Fartcar?'

'I travel light,' he said, opening the passenger door and lifting out a case half the size of Thursday's turkey. 'I've invested in a Wooland wardrobe. I wear my clothes for one hundred days at a time. It saves on water, soap pollution and pointless decisions about what to wear.'

Looking at his case, something sparked inside me. Or maybe it's a stretch to call it a spark. It was more like the final pitiful pulse from the moribund Mars Rover, but it was definitely there.

'You wear your clothes for a hundred days at a stretch and yet you picked those clothes?' said Todd. 'Interesting.'

'The life of the mind,' said Farquhar. 'It's very freeing.'

'It's Steve Jobs's dumbest schtick,' said Todd. 'And that's a deep bench, wouldn't you say?'

'I'll take that to your room,' Noleen said. 'And Todd can take care of refreshments, if his Tourette's doesn't get in the way.' She hadn't gone so far as to smile but it was still distressing to see the rudest woman in California grovelling at a customer like this. Business really must be terrible. 'You sit down and have a visit with your old friend, Lexy. I'll bring you a cup of coffee and a nice slice of pie.'

We all waited for Farquhar to say he didn't drink coffee or eat pie, but he wasn't so deep into Silicon Valley as all that just yet, and he merely gave another of the tight smiles and strolled towards the lounge.

'What kind of pie?' I asked Noleen. The creamy ones were gone, the fruity ones were gone, and the cheesecakes were surely – *surely* – in the bin by now.

'Pecan for you,' Noleen said. 'It's good till after New Year's with the amount of corn syrup and all. Peach for Dickless over there. It's been sitting out and it's getting fizzy. What a . . . What a . . .'

'Dick?' suggested Todd.

'Ironically enough,' said Noleen, and stamped off dragging the case behind her.

'Are you joining us?' I asked Todd.

'Tempting,' he said. 'It's been such a long time since I was down in the city soaking up shallowness that deep. But I've got HRT board queens to bring to heel. Find out what he's really doing here,' he hissed, as he was kissing me. 'He doesn't strike me as the helpful sort.' Then he melted away.

'So,' I said, as I joined Farquhar in the plastic seats. 'What do you need to get done and get gone?'

'You haven't got time to reminisce about our old friend?'

'I try not to speak ill of the dead,' I said. 'My memories of Menzies are not the sharing kind.'

Farquhar nodded sagely. 'You always were a sharp one,' he said. 'Do the police have any suspects?'

'How would I know?'

'How about a motive?'

'Same.'

'You're not giving much away.'

'I've got nothing to give,' I said. 'Which makes one of us. What exactly is going on, Vaseline? What are you doing here?'

'I hadn't heard that for years,' he said. 'Such an offensive nickname.'

'Hadn't?' I echoed.

He ignored me. 'Schoolboys are the worst.'

'When they're in their twenties, I agree,' I said. 'Or thirties. Or are you forty now? I know you repeated a couple of years but I'm not sure how many.'

'*You're* not mellowing much,' he said, and I detected the first whiff of the old Farquhar in both the drawl I could hear and the sneer I could see. He got hold of them both pretty sharpish, mind you.

'You must remember the night you and Lassie broke up,' he said. Another nickname I'd forgotten. Now I remembered someone shouting out 'Good girl!' as he mounted the stage at graduation.

'What about it?' I said. 'It was a long time ago and I've lived a lot of life since.'

'Menzies was pretty shit to you that night.'

'You all were. The BOLS Boys.'

He had the grace to bow his head. 'I can believe that, although my memories are hazy. What a bunch of wankers. God, when I think of how much we all drank! No one in California has ever drunk so much in their lives.'

I felt a pang then. The old suck and tug of shared experience in a strange land. 'No one on St Patrick's Day in Boston has ever drunk as much as we drank back then,' I said, and the same recognition put a smile in his eyes before he spoke again.

'But you've got to believe me, Lexy. I didn't know what had happened at that party.'

Was that true? They were like blue-arsed baboons back in those days. Not a single obnoxious, pathetic, unfunny prank went untrumpeted. 'I don't believe you,' I said. 'But I don't really want to talk about it.' I could taste red wine, and cheese and onion crisps, and the rank flavour you get left with when you kiss someone who's been smoking. And I could smell the damp of an old Victorian tenement flat, the sourness of towels that didn't get washed often enough or dried properly when they were. I could hear the thump of Shaggy singing 'Boombastic' in the living room and the hiss of rain in the roan pipes outside the window, the swish of tyres on wet road, the groan of a diesel engine as a late bus pulled away from a nearby stop. I could feel the rasp of a wool blanket against my back and the start of a bruise where my ankle bone had knocked against the legs of the high bunkbed I was lying under. I couldn't remember seeing anything, of course, because it was pitch black. That was the point of the game, after all.

'You didn't know what had happened until when?' I asked him. 'I'm guessing up till whenever you heard "Vaseline" again.'

He nodded. 'Until Menzies came banging on my door two weeks ago demanding an audience.'

'The trouble is,' I said, 'I remember you laughing and egging him on.'

'Me?' he looked genuinely astonished.

'One of you,' I said, although to be fair I didn't have a clear memory of Farquhar himself saying much at all. He really was spectacularly drunk that night.

'Interchangeable, were we?' he said.

I nodded, unconcerned about offending him. 'Do Perdita and Anselm know you saw him two weeks ago?' I asked.

'Why?' said Farquhar.

Such a shifty answer to a straight question. 'Because surely if you're a suspect, you can't ID the corpse.'

His face turned so white his stubble popped out. He looked like one of those iron-filing magnet heads. 'Haven't *you* done that?' he said.

'That's how I know suspects can't,' I said. 'I was one. But I've ID'd someone before and it's not so bad. Did you know they put paper underwear on corpses in the morgues here? Todd calls it the long tail of puritanism.'

'Todd?'

'The guy who thinks you're a racist. He's my best friend.'

Farquhar took that in and rolled it around a while. 'Nice for you,' he said at last. 'Weird place to live though, Lexy. What exactly are you doing here?'

'Oh no no no no no,' I said. 'No way. I'm not saying we won't get to me eventually, but only after you tell me why Menzies came to see you.'

Farquhar nodded. 'Of course,' he said. 'And then you tell me about his visit to you and we can compare notes.'

'No we can't,' I said. 'He was killed before I even knew he was here. Believe me, I've been wracking my brains about what brought him all the way from Edinburgh in the middle of an international travel ban. I'm assuming whatever you've got to tell me will make it all clear.'

'Can I trust you?' Farquhar said.

'To do what?'

'Keep it quiet.'

'No. As soon as you've dished, you need to go back up the road five hundred yards and dish to Molly. Sergeant Rankinson. She's in charge of the investigation. She's definitely going to want to talk to you.'

This time when his face went white, it went shiny with sudden sweat too. He looked more like an egg than ever. A peeled one.

'Can't,' he said. 'Won't. You wouldn't ask if you knew what I know.'

'Tell me and let's see,' I said. I'd had too many coy clients over the years to fall for a line like that.

'My wife,' he said. 'Hortense.' And then he stopped speaking.

'Congratulations,' I put in, at last. 'You're married? That's nice. Potentially.' My job had given me a jaded view of marriage. As had my marriage.

'My wife,' he said again. 'Hortense.'

'Left you?' I guessed. 'Didn't want you to do this favour for the Lassiters? Knows something about Menzies?'

'Bingo,' he said. 'Knows something about Menzies that you know too. In fact she found it out the same way you did. Because it happened to her too.'

'What?' I said. 'When?'

'When she was going out with Laidlaw.'

'Who the hell is Laidlaw?' I said, as anyone would.

'Tall, red hair, smoked roll-ups, useless at shaving? He always had nicks and scabs all over his face. You know. Laidlaw.'

He really didn't get that they all looked the same to me. They were *all* tall and smoked something and none of them was that spectacular at personal hygiene.

'Or maybe it's better if you *don't* have a mental picture of him,' said Farquhar, weirdly. 'Anyway he and Hortense went out briefly. More of a fling but there was plenty time for the game. And, here's the thing, Lexy. She hasn't got an alibi.'

'*What?*'

'I've got a horrible feeling,' he said. 'I mean, I'm not sure, but I think, she came up here and killed him.'

I stared at him. 'You're not sure? Aren't you pretty much still locked down together?' I said. 'In sunny Palo Alto?'

He nodded. 'We are. We have been. But then she took off suddenly.'

'Wait,' I said. A woman had come to Cuento to kill Menzies? 'When was this?'

'What do you mean? Overnight after Thanksgiving.'

'No, I mean when did she leave home?' Was it in time, I was thinking, to tail me round town and frame me?

'Wednesday.'

I sank back in my seat. That was far too late. The mysterious stranger had been knocking about the Lode, the Browser, the Thrift and Odic's long before then. Farquhar was waiting for me to speak. 'Well, it was Thanksgiving like you said. She probably needed to see her family. Where's she from?'

'St Helen's,' said Farquhar.

I sat up again. She was British? 'Can I just double-check?' I said. 'When you say Wednesday, you mean last Wednesday? The last Wednesday before today? That one?'

'Yeah,' said Farquhar. 'Why?'

'And when you say St Helen's, you mean in England? Not a place in the Caribbean?'

'That's St Helena,' said Farquhar. 'Why?'

'Small world,' I said, lamely. 'So you're married to an Englishwoman. Did you bond over the terrible tea? Did you meet when you both reached for the last jar of twelve-dollar Marmite in the ethnic food aisle?'

He frowned. 'What are you talking about? What have I just been trying to tell you? She was at uni with us. You *know* her. Hortense.'

I couldn't have picked whichever golden lass he had married out of a line-up but right enough I did remember giggling uncontrollably about the idea that someone had called their baby 'Horse's Tonsils', Hortense for short. Even Menzies, who had no room to talk, smiled a bit.

'Right,' I said. 'So. Not Thanksgiving with her family then.'

'No. Last Wednesday I got home from a training session and there was a scribbled message in the foyer saying she'd had a cri de coeur from her best friend and she was going to offer succour, not sure when she'd return.'

I nodded but behind my eyes my mind was whirring. Because that was the most bogus sentence anyone had ever tried to get past me, Simon included. If that was Farquhar's best attempt to say, 'I got back from the gym and she'd left a note saying her pal needed her and she'd gone to help', he should stick to whatever it was he did in Palo Alto and definitely not move south to break into Hollywood with a screenplay.

'Did you phone her?'

'Her phone was off.'

'Is that something she does a lot?' He didn't need to answer. His look was enough. No one under eighty ever switches their phone off, not in Silicon Valley anyway.

'Well, did you call her friend?'

'Yeah, she tried to cover for Hortense but it was clear she wasn't there.'

I spent a minute taking that in. 'And you think Hortense came on a road trip to Cuento?' He was silent. 'To kill Menzies Lassiter?'

He hesitated. 'I wouldn't say I *think* it. I would say I hope it's not true and I'm scared it is.'

He didn't seem scared, but then he'd probably been sent to boarding school when he was seven to make sure he never seemed anything.

'Why would she do that?' I asked.

'I told you. Because the thing that happened to you happened to her. I just said this, Lexy.' I stared at him. 'BOLS.'

'BOLS,' I said, trying to work out what he meant. I failed. 'The BOLS Boys, you mean.'

'I don't understand what you don't understand,' Farquhar

said. 'Unless . . . you do know what B-O-L-S stands for, don't you?'

'I do not,' I told him.

'Right, right,' he said to gain some thinking time. 'Well, it stands for Black Out Love Shack.'

'Jesus,' I said. I understood now. BOLS meant box rooms and cupboards and windowless bathrooms. It meant crying and shaking and scornful laughter. It still didn't sound like a motive for murder though. 'That's pathetic, Farquhar,' I said.

'If you think the acronym's bad, you should hear the anagrams,' he said. Then his face clouded. 'Actually, don't ask. But yeah, BOLS. They named the game first and then they started calling themselves the BOLS Boys because they played it. And the rest of us joined in because we were . . .'

'Wankers,' I reminded him.

'Such wankers.' Farquhar put his head in his hands. He was pressing hard against his stubbly skull. I could see his fingers turning white at the tips from the pressure.

'But you need to get your story straight,' I said. His fingertips grew even whiter. 'Because first you said you only found out about this two weeks ago and then you said you joined in.'

'I joined in on the entry level,' Farquhar mumbled into his hands. 'The bunny slopes. I mean, yeah, I tried to get girls in cupboards – harmless enough – but I didn't do the rest. That was top tier. Menzies . . . Well, you know he did that bit. *Not* harmless.'

'You know something,' I said. 'When I heard he'd been to see my parents, I guessed it was some kind of redemption tour.'

Farquhar looked up, letting his hands slide down, pulling his features out of shape. Clearly the pandemic hadn't cured him of the habit of touching his face. We Ditchers had all been trained by Kathi who would have administered mild shocks with an electric cattle prod if she could have found one online.

'Redemption tour?' he said. 'Is that what he told your olds?' He took a deep breath and let it go in a long wavery whistle. 'Because it wasn't that at all,' he said. 'It was the dead opposite. It was a containment exercise. Damage limitation. Someone back home had been speaking to someone else, you see. About the game. The not-entry level. The black diamond run. And they challenged him. Threatened to report him. They said they were going to go public and when they did then all the others – they guessed there were others – would come out in solidarity.'

I whistled. 'He'd have lost his job,' I said.

'He'd have lost fifteen to twenty years of his freedom,' said Farquhar.

'Really?' I said. That seemed excessive.

'Of course,' said Farquhar. 'How can you be surprised?'

'How can you not?'

We stared at each other for a minute or two. I cracked first.

'Are you sure?' I said. 'It was a long time ago. What's the statute of limitations on sexual . . . What would you even call it? . . . gaslighting?'

Farquhar stared some more. 'Anyway,' he said at last. 'He brushed off the first accuser. Maybe he *paid* them off. And then, like I said, containment.'

'Did he try to pay Hortense off?'

'We're too rich,' Farquhar said. 'No, with us it was threats. We weren't angels back in Edinburgh and we're here on green cards. Well, you know.'

I did. You can speed down the freeway, park by a hydrant or punch someone in a bar when you're here at the pleasure of the US government. But there are some things you're not allowed to do: drugs, drink-driving, and domestic abuse are the most common. Murder, kidnap, and espionage obviously. Arson, burglary, assault with a weapon. That kind of thing.

'Moral turpitude,' I said.

'Our little boy calls it moral turtle 'tude,' Farquhar said.

'How does your little boy know it's a thing?' I said.

He stared at me then said, 'Hortense is a lawyer.'

'And a mother?' I said. 'So not likely to risk prison. I mean, how old is your wee one?'

He started as if he'd just remembered something important, then he dug out his phone and started scrolling. 'Carmine,' he said.

I did that charmed snake thing with my neck, trying to get rid of the glare on the phone screen. 'Sorry,' I said. 'The light's not great. I'm sure he's lovely.' Which is never enough gushing for a parent. I should know that by now. He handed his phone over and

I saw a photo of a toddler in Batman pyjamas standing in a double-height foyer. The very foyer of the bogus note, I imagined.

'What a cutie,' I said dutifully.

'Swipe left for my daughter,' he said. 'As it were.'

I moved to the next picture back and saw a chubby baby in a bouncy chair with one of those bows attached to her head, the ones that I always think look like lick-and-stick window clingers.

'What a sweetie,' I said. It wasn't my best work.

'They both are,' he said, nodding his chin at the phone. And I swear to God I thought he meant for me to swipe again and see a picture of them both together. So I did. And he snatched that phone out of my hand quicker than a lizard's tongue can grab a fly.

'Don't worry,' I told him. 'It was your wife.'

'What?'

'The photo,' I said nodding *my* chin at the phone now. 'It was only your wife. Anyway, it's no skin off my nose what pictures you take. I'm unshockable.'

'Right,' he said. 'Right. Hahahahaha. Caught me, eh?'

'I think I do remember her, you know,' I said, trying to put him at his ease. It's an occupational hazard.

'Hortense?'

'I think so. She looked familiar.' I had only caught a fleeting glance of a tall and sturdily built woman with honey-coloured hair, standing make-up free but still attractive in front of one of those cute Spanish-style bungalows you get in Los Angeles. That was exactly what one of the slim, baby blonde, golden lasses would look like twenty years and two kids later.

'Sorry,' he said. 'To freak out. It's just – we still – even with Carmine and Hosanna we try to keep things spicy.'

Spicy, I thought. Ew. Then I willed my brain to turn away and focus on something else. 'Carmine and Hosanna, eh?' I tried to keep the tone of wonder out of my voice but, seriously, you'd think a Farquhar and an Hortense would have more empathy. 'And yet she just took off and left them?'

'Well,' he said, 'we've got the nanny. And the babysitter. And the housekeeper. They're doing pretty well between them.'

'But she hasn't come back yet?'

'I'm going out of my mind with worry,' he said. He didn't look as if he was going out of his mind with worry. He looked as if he was running lines for a play he'd been miscast in. If I ever had a kid and fortune to spend on school fees, I'd spend it on clothes instead, let the kid live at home and grow a heart.

'But if Menzies didn't mention Hortense,' he was saying, 'that means you haven't said her name to the police and that means . . .'

'What?' I said. I wasn't following his train of thought.

'Well, it means I can approach a private detective to try to find her without it alerting anyone who should probably stay unalerted. You know.'

'You're assuming I'm going to keep quiet now,' I said. 'About murder. That's quite a big assumption.'

He studied me for a while. 'And *you're* assuming he was only coming to speak to you,' he said at last. 'That's even bigger.'

'As opposed to what?' It was what passes for a cold day in Cuento, a day we'd have gone to the beach in Scotland, and I felt a little shiver.

'Because he hinted at more,' Farquhar said. 'So, you could say Hortense – possibly, conceivably – saved you.'

'If he was going to *do* something to me?' I said. 'That doesn't seem . . . I mean, I hadn't even thought about Menzies for years. Anyway, if he was coming here to do me harm, he *wouldn't* hint, would he?'

'True.'

'And why would Menzies want to kill me? I'm not too rich to buy off.'

'Maybe,' said Farquhar slowly, 'if he wasn't going to tell you something and he didn't mean to harm you, to kill you . . . Maybe he was going to . . . I don't know . . . *show* you something.'

There was a red flash in my mind's eye. A Kit-Kat wrapper. 'Well, he didn't,' I said.

'And he didn't leave something behind for you?'

He hadn't, I thought. He had binned it. 'Nope.'

'Are you lying, Lexy?'

'Yeah,' I said. 'He brought a souvenir of our doomed romance. Stupid. Pointless.'

Farquhar sat back. I hadn't noticed that he'd been inching

forward until I saw what a long way he had to go to get properly in his seat again.

'Did he bring anything to show Hortense?' I asked.

His brow creased again. He shook his head and turned his mouth down. If it hadn't been insane, I'd have said that, for a moment, he'd forgotten about her. About why he was here. About what trouble his little family was in. I didn't get the chance to unpick any of it. Noleen was approaching at bloody last, with a tray bearing two wedges of the unfinishable, unbreakable unchewable pecan pie, and a pot of coffee.

'Think it over,' he said. 'About reporting any of this.'

'I'll sleep on it,' I told him.

'It's three o'clock in the afternoon,' he pointed out.

But then he had never tried to get outside a slice of Noleen's pie.

TWENTY

I definitely needed my people this time. Ordinarily we'd gather on board, but the boat was beset with butter churns. We sometimes went to Todd and Roger's room because Todd had the best snacks, or the back office behind Reception if Noleen needed to keep an ear out for the desk. But Todd was on flat-out HRT preparation and hadn't been to the Lode for days, and the back office was full of all the crap Noleen had moved from the front office to make way for the mid-century-modern makeover, so there was barely space to squeeze through to the supply cupboard. The owners' flat was out. Kathi had made great strides during the lockdown: she now lived in her flat instead of sleeping in one of the rooms and only going home to clean, but she wasn't quite at the visitors' stage yet. That left Della's place.

It was where we all wanted to be anyway to coo at the baby.

Man, she was cute. She had little white dots – milk spots, said Noleen; milia, Della reckoned – all over her nose, as if her face had been snowed on, and her hair fanned over her forehead in tiny black spikes that moved up and down when she wrinkled her brows, which she did all the time in her outrage at the change in conditions since her birth. 'What the hell happened?' she seemed to be asking us. 'Things were fine. What's this bullshit?'

But then her ears were like tiny little carved beans and felt warm when you stroked them. And her lashes had doubled in length already and settled on to her cheeks when she finally fell asleep, fluttering with every breath until she was deeply gone. Then whoever was holding her felt her compact little bud of a body loosen and grow heavy until her cheeks rested on her bib and her fists fell open and her legs unfurled and her feet waggled in time with her snuffly little snores. And if you were trapped under her then work, food, drink and bladder be damned, you sat there barely breathing until she woke up, smacked her lips together and took up her grievances again.

Not that I was smitten or anything. Anyway, I was only half paying attention to Hiro. My antennae were tuned towards Della and Dylan, slumped in mutual exhaustion on the two-seater couch and looking as contented as I'd ever seen them. I didn't know Della was that kind of actor, truth be told.

'Where's Diego?' I said. They weren't acting for him, because he was nowhere to be seen.

'Walking math,' Della said.

'Cutest thing you ever saw,' said Noleen. 'Twenty seven-year-olds going two by two to the arboretum, chanting prime numbers.'

'What next?' I said. 'Therapy, book club, maths with an s . . . they'll have to reinforce the path soon.'

'Stop avoiding the subject,' Todd said. 'What is it? Why've you brought us here? I've got a lot of staging and trimming to do and this could surely have gone in an email, whatever it is.'

He really *was* busy, I thought, if he was looking a gift gossip in the mouth. 'I've got a problem,' I said, once he had handed round drinks – sherry for some reason, as if the balance of Brits had tipped, even though one of them was dead and in the morgue now.

'Farter?' said Noleen. She clicked her fingers and added, 'I have to be sure Diego meets him while he's here. Kid'd get a kick out of that name. How did the poor schlub get through grade school?'

Hiro, lolling fast asleep on Kathi's lap, tensed up as if she was about to wake. The rest of us tensed up right along with her. Then she relaxed again with a long, thin and muffled-by-nappy drone of baby flatulence.

'Exactly,' Noleen said.

'Not Farquhar as such,' I said. 'But related to him. I don't know what to do.'

'Let him take care of it,' Todd said. 'Take the win. Unless you *wanted* to fill out the paperwork to repatriate remains.'

'No, not that,' I told him. 'He thinks he knows who the killer is.'

'You?' Della said. At my look she went on, 'I'm not saying you are but is that what he thinks?'

'No,' I said. 'Not me. But not a million miles away. I mean, it could have been. It wasn't. But if I'd taken a different path away from the end of our relationship, who can say? But, no.'

'I like the "no" part of that word salad,' Todd said. 'But the rest of it is kinda troubling. Care to expand, Lexy?'

Not really. I tried tackling it from a different angle. 'The thing is I don't think he's going to report it. To the cops.'

'So you report it for him,' said Noleen. She looked around the room. 'Right?'

Everyone did some mix of nodding and shrugging, as if to say of course and why was I making such heavy weather but, since I *was* making such heavy weather, what were they missing?

'Well,' I said. 'Like I was trying to explain: there but for the grace of God, you know.'

Todd narrowed his eyes, the better to scrutinize me. Noleen took a huge slurp of sherry – she always claims that alcohol sharpens her wits and she likes busting people. Kathi gave me a searching look, scouring my face for clues. She doesn't mind busting people either. Dylan was gazing at Hiro with his whole attention. Della was also gazing at Hiro, but besotted and knackered as she was, she managed to flick a glance my way and twitch a smile at me.

'Tell us,' she said. 'For my brand-new baby girl, Lexy. Even if she has a man-soul.'

'She doesn't have a—'

'I'm too tired to argue,' said Della. 'Tell us for all the girls.'

'Well, shit,' said Noleen.

'That's what I was wondering,' said Kathi. 'Am I right?'

'You're all witches,' said Todd. 'I have no idea what you're talking about and it's not fair to exclude me from your sorcery this way.'

'Huh?' said Dylan, which at least lightened the mood.

'Farquhar,' I paused to let Noleen snort, which she did, 'thinks his wife murdered Menzies. Hortense.'

'What does that mean?' said Noleen.

'It's her name,' I said. 'Hortense Vass, poor cow. Farquhar thinks she murdered Menzies. He only agreed to do the boxing up and shipping home to give him a legitimate excuse to come up here and find out. And he doesn't want to go to the cops. Can you believe it?'

'That he doesn't want his wife in jail?' said Kathi. 'Yes, I can. Who would?'

'There's a bit more to it than that,' I said. 'Like I was trying to tell you.'

'Try harder,' said Todd. 'Come on, Lexy.'

'But before I do,' I said, 'I need your word that you won't make the decision for me. I know it's a lot to ask.'

'No it isn't,' said Della. 'No es nada.'

'Um,' Noleen said. 'I don't think I'd go that far, Dells.'

'If we want to go to Molly and tell, Lexy will too. If Lexy thinks this is a righteous kill, I guess we will too.'

No one said anything for a moment or two, except Hiro who said 'ftssssh' and woke herself up.

'Her first sneeze!' said Della.

'Fuck my first sneeze!' Hiro seemed to be indicating, by the way she responded to it.

'Oh my God she sneezed!' said Dylan, raising his voice to be heard over her screams. 'Is she OK?'

'Yes!' said everyone else in chorus.

'She eats lying down,' Noleen added. 'It's a miracle she's not chewing Tums already. A little reflux in the nose is nothing.'

'Can I hold her?' I asked.

'If there's reflux on the cards, be my guest,' said Kathi, depositing the baby in my lap. She was drowsing again after the enormity of the sneeze, her glare beginning to dim as her blinks lengthened. I took a good look. Della had excellent instincts. Looking at a brand-new proto-woman was indeed helping me.

'OK,' I said. 'Tarts and vicars.'

'Fictitious,' said Todd.

'As you spotted from the off,' I said. 'I didn't get the dress code wrong at the party the night Menzies and I broke up. And I didn't get slagged off by his obnoxious friends for over-dressing either. That's not what happened.'

'Wait till we pick ourselves up from off the floor,' Todd said. 'What *did* happen?'

'I got tricked into playing a game,' I said. 'Sort of.'

'Twister?' said Noleen. 'Strip poker? Truth or dare?'

'Worse. This game was called . . .' I felt my mouth start to taste sour as the adrenaline flowed through me. 'Wow, it's hard to say it. This is worse than I thought it would be. The game, as I've just discovered from Farquhar, was called Black Out Love Shack. BOLS for short.'

'I'm out,' said Noleen. 'Play on without me.'

I gave her a grateful smile. 'And it went something like this. I mean, I only played it once but that was enough to piece it together. The male half of a couple would get amorous at a party and start asking the female half to come with him to a nice dark place he had found where they could be alone.'

'At a party?' said Kathi.

'Students,' said Dylan.

'A box room, or an internal bathroom with no window,' I said. 'Even a cupboard would have done, I suppose. It was a box room with me.'

'How is this a game?' said Dylan. 'It just sounds like a party so far.'

'But to be discreet, the two people go separately instead of together,' I said.

'What kind of party is this where people care about couples going into closets?' Todd said. 'Church picnic? Focus on the Family holiday potluck? The kinds of parties I went to at college we didn't even walk away. Right there on the dance floor was just dandy.'

'Tell us less,' said Noleen.

'And this one night, Menzies persuaded me to go and get

comfy in the box room and he'd score a bottle of wine or something and join me as soon as he could.'

'And you did?'

'I did. I was young and in love. And drunk.'

I remembered giggling and kissing Menzies on the tip of his nose before I slipped away into the hall and opened the box-room door. No one paid any attention to me. It was a feature of Menzies's friends I had noticed before. They were always completely absorbed in what they were doing. They never noticed anyone outside the charmed circle of whatever joke, or argument, or bantering session they were the centre of. I thought right then that night, even through a haze of drink, that we could both have slipped away together and it would have been absolutely fine.

'But of course that would have defeated the point of the game,' I said. 'So I went on my own and I waited a while, maybe five minutes, then he joined me.'

'And?' Noleen said.

'And,' I confirmed.

'I don't get it,' said Noleen. 'How is that a game?'

'Me either,' said Dylan.

'And then he left,' I went on. 'Before me, like we'd said. Like we'd agreed. And I was supposed to wait a couple of minutes and then discreetly rejoin the party too.'

'I still don't get it,' Dylan said.

'But while he was in the box room,' I said, 'he didn't say anything at all. It was completely silent.'

'Oh shit,' said Todd. 'Oh jeez, Lexy.'

'Oh my God,' said Kathi. 'But didn't you notice?'

'What?' said Dylan. Della kicked him. For someone halfway out the door she was certainly still using all the marital shorthand.

'Wait,' I said. 'There are more twists to come.' I took another slug from my glass and crammed a handful of peanut M&Ms into my mouth. It was a toxic combination but I needed the booze and the sugar for what was ahead. 'So I waited a few minutes. Or it might have been quite a few. Like I said, I was really hammered.'

'Why?' said Della. She'd never been to Scotland.

'But eventually, I got up and straightened my dress and all

that. I tried to put my knickers back on but I was wearing massive high heels and I couldn't balance, so I just kept them in my hand. That doesn't matter for the story. It just got embarrassing later.' I closed my eyes as the scene replayed behind them. 'Anyway, I went back out of the box room and rejoined the party. Menzies was in the kitchen talking to some gimp I didn't know and, when he saw me, his face fell but like it fake-fell, you know? And he looked horrified, but fake-horrified, you know?'

'What? Why?' said Todd.

'And he goes "Oh my God, Lexy! I'm so wasted. I'm so sorry. I totally forgot." And by now he's giggling and trying not to – covering his mouth with his hand and all that – and I'm just staring at him. He kept apologizing and saying he was an idiot. But he kept laughing too and asking if I had really stayed in there all that time waiting for him.'

'Oh my *God*!' said Dylan, catching up at last. 'It wasn't *him*? Who *was* it?'

'Wait,' I said. 'I'm nearly finished. He's giggling and Farquhar's sniggering away in the background too, and the rest of them. So I started shaking, and I told him what had happened and said I needed to go to the hospital and then the police station and he was like "Whoa! Whoa whoa whoa!" with his hands up and backing away. Then he said he should have known I'd be on it like a fly on shit but hold on there a minute.'

'What?' said Noleen.

'He said it was a joke. Of course it was him. He said pretending he forgot was a wind-up. That was the game.'

I closed my eyes again. The kitchen had been full of drunk people and the worktops were getting that end-of-the-party look about them – fags stubbed out in wine bottles, nothing but crumbs left in the crisp bowls, and the stink of booze and tobacco couldn't quite cover up the fact that someone had puked somewhere. Despite the crowd, as far as I was concerned there was no one else there except Menzies. His face swam in front of me inside a smeared nimbus of light from the anglepoise clamped to the cooker hood behind him.

'You're saying it *was* you?' I asked him.

'Couldn't you tell?' he said again. 'Jesus, Lexy. What does that say about you?'

'What did you just say to me?' I asked him.

'No!' He clamped his hands over his mouth again. '*Me!* I meant to say "What does that say about *me*?"! About my prowess. Last of the red-hot lovers. Jesus, I'm so pissed. I'm so sorry.'

'So it was you, but you wanted me to *think* it was someone else?'

'It's just a joke,' he said. 'It's just a game. A bit of fun.'

'And you only came clean because I was talking about going to A&E and reporting the rape.'

'Whoa! Whoa!' he said again. 'What's that word doing in this conversation?'

'If someone came into that box room and had sex with me without consent, what would you call it?'

'But you did consent,' Menzies said. 'We agreed.'

'Yeah,' I said. 'Because it was you, there was no rape. The joke was making me think there was. And the joke was going to carry on as long as you could spin it, only I spoiled it by thinking about an STD test and the morning-after pill and a police report.'

He smiled and leaned in to kiss me. 'I forgive you.'

Noleen choked on a mouthful of sherry. 'He *forgave* you? He forgave *you*? Jesus Christ, I'm sorry he's dead and I can't go and kill him.' She took another mouthful, more carefully. 'What then?'

'Then I screamed at him like a fishwife, embarrassing him in front of all his friends. I threw my knickers at him, threw all the little trinkets he'd given me that I was carrying round like a numpty. Cursed him to hell and left.'

'So it *was* him?' said Dylan. 'It's a mean prank even so. But thank God it *was* him.'

'It was him,' I said. 'The game had two . . . parts. The first thing was to shag your girlfriend at a party. Even Farquhar did that. They all did. Struan, Strathpeffer . . . But then there was an advanced level. Only for when the girl was drunk and it was really pitch black. It was gaslighting is what it was.'

'I'd kill him with these two hands,' Noleen said.

'Or maybe if the girl wasn't a regular girlfriend it wouldn't have been hard to pretend to be someone else, you know. *We'd* been together less than a year. Not long enough to get into a comfy rut.'

'Speak for yourself,' said Todd.

'Yeah, yeah,' said Noleen. 'We know, reinforce the light fittings: it's the Todd and Roger show.'

'Guys?' I said. They sobered and settled again. 'What I'm saying is that Menzies did the full works to me. Farquhar didn't do that bit. Then there was another bloke I don't actually remember, Laidlaw.'

'For fuck's sake,' Noleen put in.

I shrugged. 'It's the name of a place. It's like calling a kid Tennessee or Savannah.'

'That doesn't help.'

'Anyway he did it too. But the thing is, Menzies did it to Farquhar's wife. Or . . . wait, did Laidlaw do it to her? Or maybe they both did. But anyway, she's a lawyer and she reckons it's a great big deal. It's a crime with serious time.'

'Really?' said Kathi.

'That's what I said!' I said, then quietened down again as Hiro threatened to wake. 'Shush-shush-shush,' I said, rocking her. 'That's what I said,' I whispered, 'but Farquhar seemed pretty clear about it. And he thinks his wife took a shortcut, missed out all the reporting and affidavits and court time and just drove up here and killed the guy.'

'Over a prank?' said Dylan. 'I mean, a nasty prank but still a prank. That's pretty unhinged, isn't it?'

'It really is,' I said. 'And it's even more unhinged that Farquhar thinks I might be onside for a cover-up. The whole thing makes no sense at all.'

'Lexy,' said Todd, 'you're not thinking straight.'

'What do you mean?' I said.

'Farquhar didn't make it clear whether it was Laidlaw or Menzies with Hortense?'

'So?'

'OK, well, consider this,' he said. 'Black Out Love Shack has two levels?' He waited and then eventually went on. 'One, bang your chick at a party. Two, bang your chick at a party and make her think it wasn't you. And . . . that's it? The rule of . . . two?'

'Todd,' Noleen said, 'Lexy's the one it happened to, and she's the one that heard the facts about what a big deal it is from this lawyer woman's husband. We go with that, until we hear different. OK?'

Todd's eyes opened very wide and he sat back in his seat as if Noleen's words were blasting at him like hot wind. 'Absolutely!' he said. 'You got it!'

I looked at both of them. 'Why are you being weird?'

I glanced at Kathi, who shrugged. 'If either of them ever starts being normal I'll text you.'

'I'm lost again,' said Dylan.

Della was staring at me and she had tears in her eyes.

'What's wrong?' I said.

'Hormones,' she told me. 'And my breasts hurt too. Hand her over before I burst, Lexy.'

I looked down at Hiro who was grunting and struggling, almost ready to start crying again for real. 'You got any clue what they're on about, baby?' I said. 'Or are you as lost as me?'

Hiro gave me a withering look – I swear she did – then opened her mouth and started screaming.

TWENTY-ONE

I was woken up in the morning not by Taylor taking me in his arms and kissing my closed eyelids (which is actually not as annoying as it sounds), nor by Todd bringing coffee (which is exactly as wonderful as it sounds; we're messing when we moan about it), and not even by Hiro crying (although I had been aware of non-stop grumbling and squeaking through the wall during the night), but by a hammering on the door and Farquhar's voice calling my name.

I stumbled out of bed, shaking off the twisted sheets that were wound round my legs, and opened up.

'She's back!' he said.

'Yay,' I croaked. 'Who's back?'

'Sedona,' he said. 'She went to Hortense.'

'Hortense went to Sedona?'

'Sorry, yes! That's what I meant to . . . She was on a retreat. In the desert. No phones. But she's home now.'

'Look, come in,' I said. 'It's too cold to stand here in my nightie.'

Taylor gave me a filthy look and disappeared off to the bathroom. I got back under the covers and sank against my pillows. 'So she didn't kill him?'

Farquhar put his head in his hands. 'I can't believe I said all that. Of course she didn't kill him! She was shaken up by the visit. So she decided to take off and do a cleanse. She said you should try this place, by the way. It's like a five-star monastery.'

'My favourite kind. How come she didn't say that's where she was going?'

'She did!' Farquhar said. 'She left a detailed note but the new maid tidied it away before I saw it.'

'She left a short note in the foyer saying she was going to her friend's and a detailed note somewhere else telling the truth?'

'She was hoping her friend would join her.' Farquhar shrugged. 'Women!'

I didn't take the bait. Instead, I said, 'Does she know where you've been? What you thought?'

'No, because I don't want to tell her about Menzies,' he said. 'She doesn't need to know. She thinks she saw him off with her counter-threats and now, when she never hears from him again, she'll just carry on believing that. Fine by me.'

'And where does she think *you* are?' I said.

'Dealing with a work emergency. I'm setting off home now anyway. I'll be back in time for brunch.'

'What about the job you took on for Anselm and Perdita?'

'Oh that,' said Farquhar. 'Task Rabbit. Sacramento Task Rabbit is the bomb. Even San José doesn't have notarized bunnies. Someone's taking the whole thing right off my hands for forty dollars an hour.'

'Except the ID'ing of the corpse presumably,' I said. 'So is that coming back to me?'

'COVID amendment,' Farquhar said. 'Sergeant Rankinson said the Lassiters can do it over Zoom. She's stretching a point because that was supposed to end after the lockdown. I think it helps that you saw him already and did an unofficial one. So!' He clapped his hands together and stood up from where he had been leaning against the credenza.

'But,' I said. I'm useless before my coffee. 'So you're just leaving? What about . . .? I mean, if Hortense didn't kill him, we're kind of left with the problem of who did.'

'Do you really care?'

'I do,' I said. 'Of course I do. Even if I didn't care about Menzies particularly, I care about people not breaking into rooms where my friends live and murdering people while they sleep.'

'Why *do* you live in a motel?' he said. 'You graduated. I remember seeing you walk up on the stage. Why aren't you doing better for yourself? Is it *drugs*, Lexy?'

I squinted at him. Something about the way he had said 'drugs' in heavy italics like that had finally sparked an actual memory. Not of the whole lot of them, the undifferentiated mass of them with their sniggers and their stupid signet rings that they didn't know were funny, but of him, Farquhar himself. He had arrived at a party, it might even have been *that* party, and stood in the doorway declaiming at the top of his voice. 'I have a very sensitive nose and I detect "drugs" in this dwelling.'

'What?' he said. 'You're looking at me as if you're going to dissect me and pin me to a card. What is it?'

I could hardly tell him I thought I had finally recognized him at long last. That wasn't a kind way to leave things between us.

'Nothing,' I said. 'Memories. Well, happy travels, Farquhar. All the best to Hortense, Carmine and Hosanna.'

'Well done,' he said.

'Comes with the job,' I explained. 'Terrible thing for a therapist to forget a name. We can't call people "dear" these days.'

With that we made our goodbyes. I saw him out, watched him wheel his tiny suitcase across the car park to his four-by, felt once again that mild but deep sense of unease stemming from God knows what, and then waved as he drove away.

What *was* bugging me? Still his coldness yesterday? Because his relief this morning was enormous and very real, making his earlier lack of panic even weirder.

Taylor came out of the bathroom as soon as the coast was

clear and stood behind me with his damp arms around my waist and his wet hair trickling down my neck.

'You're very affectionate this morning,' I said, and even I could hear the accusation in my voice.

'I spoke to Todd,' he said. 'Or rather, Todd spoke to me.'

I puzzled that out for a beat or two and then groaned. 'I didn't mean anything by it,' I said. 'I didn't say *we* were in a rut. I'm perfectly happy. I'm ecstatic. I'm dangerously fulfilled. I might need some downers to save putting strain on my heart. God sake, Taylor.'

'I haven't got the first clue what you're on about,' he said, and kissed the top of my back just where the lace on my nightie neck makes it feel tickly.

'So he's gone, has he?' said Noleen. 'And we're none the wiser about this murder.'

'I'm starting to get an inkling about the next one,' I said, staring at the plate of pie she had banged down on the breakfast table in the lounge. 'It'll be a poisoning. How the hell can this still be OK after all these days?' It was a wedge of cobbler this time, the cornflour-buttressed fruit bit as solid as a well-done steak and pretty much the same colour, the scone top looking like a house-brick.

'Get real,' Noleen said. 'You think Kathi would let food stay in her refrigerator once it's no good?'

'Thursday to Monday?' I said.

'Listen, you maybe have flour weevils and rancid fat back in the old country, but we got the FDA on our side. Every damn thing in this pie is so super-ultra-hyper-pasteurized you could have it for dessert after Christmas dinner. You want cream?'

'You can't have kept the cream!'

Noleen produced an aerosol can from her back pocket and, pulling down her glasses to focus, read from the label. 'Best before July 2023,' she said. 'American know-how, baby.'

'OK,' I said. 'Squirt me. But why are you being so nice? You're freaking me out.'

'It won't last,' she said. 'Get it while you can. What you doing today? You booked up? You hanging here?'

'You care why?' I said, matching her tone. She really was unsettling me with this act of kindly interest.

'I don't want Todd to go to the HRT on his own,' she said. 'Every time he gets loose he comes back with more and more crap he reckons we "have to" do to make our mark on this goddam tour I wish I never heard of. You know the latest, don't you?'

I would have said I did. I would have said the latest was that we'd been bumped from the HRT because of outsize rodent activity in the forecourt dumpsters. But it didn't seem so from what Noleen was saying.

'Should I?' I replied, craftily. 'Does it concern Trinity? Please say no.'

'Good guess,' Noleen said. 'Flash makeovers on the way out the door.'

'Oh!' I said. 'The latest from *Todd*?'

'What?'

'Nothing! I mean. He can't be serious. Scratch that. Of course he can be serious. This is the man who tried to get nuns into better lingerie.'

'And that's not all,' Noleen added. 'You didn't escape. He's offering flash therapy too.'

'He—'

'—never met a boundary he'd admit existed,' Noleen agreed. 'And speak of the devil.'

Todd had appeared on the upper walkway. He stood for a while gripping the rail and taking deep breaths with his eyes closed and a beatific smile on his face. There was no one around except Noleen and me, but he always did this with the air of a newly married royal emerging on to the balcony at Buckingham Palace to roars from the gathered crowd. Plus a touch of Mussolini.

'Flash therapy, Todd?' I called up. 'Really?' I had shifted pretty rapidly from hoping Ews One and Two had got over themselves to praying Todd was for the chop.

'Not therapy via flashing,' he said, walking along to the stairs and trotting down to join us. 'Not some crazy exhibitionism supposed to free the psyche.'

'Yeah I know that,' I said. 'I didn't think that even of *you*.'

'Just an ecologically responsible parting gift at the end of our tour. No one gives *stuff* any more, Lexy. No one wants clutter and dreck. People who're tuned into the moment give experiences.

And what better experience for our guests to take away from their visit here but a gift of your expertise or mine? They get to choose. Either I tell them one thing to change about their look. Or you ask them what makes them most frustrated, or anxious or upset. And boom.'

'How'd Kathi wriggle out of this?' I said. 'And boom what anyway?'

'Boom, you fix it,' he said.

'That is not how therapy works,' I said.

'Yeah, yeah, I know. Without repeat business, you'd be on the corner with a cup. But this is the genius of my plan, see? No one's actually going to tell their deepest fear on a holiday home tour, are they?'

'You never said fear.'

'They're going to pick something they kind of know the answer to anyway. That's what I would do. "My husband works long hours" or "My mom is irresponsible with her health". And you'll say what they already know anyway. And they'll think you're a genius and then, when they're looking for a therapist, they'll come right back to you.'

'And your bit?' I said.

'Same,' said Todd. He was carefully dissecting the cobbler in a way that was intensely annoying but impossible to look away from. He had isolated the pumpkin seeds and the blueberries from the rest of the cornflour mush and now he was scraping them free of fat and syrup. 'They won't say "My neck" or "my waistline", will they? They'll say, "I'm not sure this is my colour" about some scarf they're only wearing because it was a gift and they'll have to donate it if they don't use it before another Christmas rolls round.'

'Eh?' said Noleen.

'Those are my rules of closet management,' said Todd. 'They're sweeping the nation.'

'Sounds like a pile of crap,' said Noleen. 'I've still got my band uniform.'

'And I'll say something like, "a less busy pattern would bring out your eyes more" and they'll agree and then I'll slip them a business card and see them in January.'

'Is that ethical?' I said.

'Are you kidding?' said Todd. 'All the caterers are going to be giving out coupons like candy on Halloween. Anyone who's had any work done on their home is going to have flyers from the contractor. And the organizers themselves insist on displaying the names of florists, stagers, designers, event planners and music directors prominently. Haven't you read the literature?'

'Music . . .?' I said. 'What . . .?'

'Our choir is coming tomorrow for a rehearsal.'

'Our choi—? Todd are you laying out a ton of money? Have you had final confirmation from the HRT that—?'

But he wasn't listening. 'I worried about the "crime scene recent death" angle, I'm not going to lie. Because I don't know if you've ever seen the Cuento Gay Men's Choir, but they tend towards the exuberant. However, they've agreed to keep to the respectful end of their repertoire for us: "Santa Baby", "Jingle Bells", "Despacito" . . .'

'"Despacito"?' I said. 'You can't get them to take a swing at "So Mi Like It"?'

Noleen started laughing on an inhale, ended up coughing and had to slap herself in the chest.

'Don't be ridiculous,' said Todd. 'The CGMC would never culturally appropriate Jamaican reggae.'

'I believe my point stands,' I said. I winked at Noleen. 'Hey Todd, since I seem to be a wee bit behind the step on the HRT ramp-up, what would you say to me coming with you on your next recce? Depending on when it is and what I've got on?'

'It's this morning.'

'I have one client,' I said. 'And not until after lunch. I *was* hoping to have a word with Della . . .' I left that hanging, expecting one or the other of them to dish. Assuming Todd knew. Which of course he would. Because Todd knew everything first. It was a policy.

'Well, OK then,' he said. 'Let's visit our competitors at ten o'clock.'

'Collaborators, surely,' I said. 'We're all stops on the same tour, aren't we?'

But when I saw what Todd was wearing to go and inspect this other house that had been plucked from obscurity to feature in the HRT pantheon, I could tell he had dressed to win, even to kill. Or rather he had *swathed* to kill, wearing a garment that was not quite a scarf and not quite a jumper, but more of a Möbius strip cum cowl that looped around him and left tantalizing glimpses of ribcage and clavicle uncovered as he moved.

'Isn't that a bit draughty?' I asked.

'I'm baking hot from the pants,' he explained.

'They're not real, are they?' I asked him. They looked like snakeskins and not many snakeskins. There were no tucks and puckers where they disappeared smoothly into his ankle boots. It was as though a pair of mammoth snakes had eaten one leg each.

'In this town? Are you kidding?' he said. 'The PETA SWAT team would be out before I could say they were all dead anyway. No, it's fake skin. That's the problem: real skin would breathe. These are like sausage casing.'

'I feel I'm letting the side down,' I said, looking at myself in my black jeans and red hoody.

'Oh totally,' Todd said. 'I've got an outfit hanging in the back of the Jeep for you. You can change on the way.'

I knew it was futile to argue so I got into the back seat and had wriggled out of my jeans before we were beyond the underpass. The outfit Todd had picked out for me was 1970s by way of 1870s, the kind of sprigged frock with flounced hem that the Ingalls girls wore as they tumbled around on the telly in my childhood.

'What's the explanation for this?' I said. 'I'm not complaining. Just asking.'

'The prairie dress?' said Todd. 'Fashion forward. Wait and see.'

There was a pair of wet-look-patent fifty-hole Docs and a biker jacket too.

'This is surely fashion backward,' I said, bent double struggling with the laces. 'Early Kate Moss at Glasto.'

'Exactly,' said Todd. 'Keep 'im guessing.'

'Keep who guessing?'

'All of 'im.'

I took a beat. 'Oh "them"!' I said. 'Keep *them* guessing?'

'What did I just say? Did you find the face wipes? Can you scrub off all your make-up? I don't have time to fix it and what you've got there is worse than nothing.'

I didn't say my habitual 'none taken' though, because I was lost in thought. Something – a memory, a notion, a wisp of a thread of a forgotten idea – was wafting about me like someone else's leftover fart when you walk into an empty lift. But unlike someone else's fart it was gone too soon.

We were threading our way through the streets of Old North Cuento now, the dream streets, as I called them, since they were neither cramped nor obnoxious, neither student-infested nor ruined by the bolshy vigilantes of an over-zealous neighbourhood watch, neither down on their luck nor up their own backsides. If I didn't have the boat, I would love to live in one of these tree-lined blocks. Of course, I'd have to go back in time and screw a better divorce package out of Brandon to raise a down payment. So I accepted that a nose around one of the houses today was going to have to do me.

And what a house it was! These HRT types certainly knew how to pick a plum. As we passed the familiar illegible lawn sign and feasted our eyes on the building behind it, I wondered again how the hell a few bits of kitsch furniture and a spinning wheel had ever got the boat and the Ditch into this exalted company. It was an eye-popping futuristic marvel, so well-hidden from the street by a hedge of Cyprus trees, like Sleeping Beauty's castle, that I had never guessed it was there in all my meanderings while I was getting to know Cuento that first spring of my residence here.

'Wow,' I said. As I continued to study the place, it began to look a bit more like Sydney Opera House, if Sydney Opera House was made of soap and someone had dropped it in the bath and it had lost all its corners. Or if Sydney Opera House and the Moomins had had a love-child. It was smooth and pale shell-pink, glittering with tiny panes of glass, and it rose out of a bed of moss and boulders like the centrepiece in a Japanese garden.

'Wait till you see inside it,' said Todd, striding up the white marble pathway as if it was a catwalk and he was the model who got to wear the wedding dress and close the show.

He rapped on the door, and an elderly man in a boiler suit answered. He had a spotted hanky tied round his neck, which he moved up to cover his nose and mouth as he clocked the strangers. Todd, likewise, pulled up his trousers-matching snakeskin mask – that had to be real, surely. Or how could he breathe? – and introduced himself.

'We're on the tour this year too,' he said. 'Lexy here has an Art Nouveau houseboat and I was responsible for developing the mid-century rooms in an iconic Cuento inn.'

The guy pursed his mouth to speak, but Todd sailed on.

'We're sure the Brewster Mansion and that sweet little Victorian stick, not to mention the Mission entry and the Queen Anne reproduction won't overlap in any way with our aesthetic, but we did want to be sure we weren't stepping on your modernist toes.'

'I wouldn't let the Hiddlestons hear you call their Queen Anne a reproduction,' the man said.

I smiled ingratiatingly at him from behind my own mask, hoping a bit of humility would balance Todd's galactic hubris. He was overplaying his hand even for him: I could see past the guy in the boiler suit and my oblique view of the inside of this place told me it was the Brewster mansion all over again. There was a waterfall in the hallway just behind him. An actual effing waterfall, silent and sleek as it coursed down a sheet of copper into a shallow pool of glass and steel.

'Have you had any trouble about safety waivers?' I said. I was just making chit-chat, wondering how the litigious locals of Beteo County would react to tipping headfirst into that pool if they came to gawp at the Moomin Opera House after a stirrup cup at one of the other stops on the tour. But my remark turned out to be code for 'Open Sesame'.

The boiler-suit guy stepped back and ushered us in, ranting about the committee, the gutlessness of his beloved country, the nature of lawyers, the impossibility of safety guards because of the unique and priceless nature of his floor . . . He was still talking when we were way past the water feature and into the living room behind it.

'Wow,' I said. 'This is incredible. Is there any way to make sure no one comes from your place to my place? Because the comedown would give them the bends.'

'I'm sure that's not true,' the guy said, beaming behind his bandanna. I didn't argue. I was too busy drinking it all in. For one thing, it was huge. You could definitely play a game of tennis in this living room without having to push any furniture back. Maybe even basketball. But it wouldn't be a hardship either way, because there wasn't a lot of furniture to push; just a low, Japanese-style table with moulded kneeling pads all around it that made me think of bite guards. It could probably seat – kneel – twenty diners but it was pure white and totally empty. A devil on my shoulder wished I could add a fruit bowl when Bandanna Man wasn't looking.

Besides the table, there was a pale pearly grey . . . couch, I suppose, although in size and structure it resembled a levee more than a seating solution. The clue was the remote that was resting on one of the . . . arms, I suppose, since it was higher than the rest . . . just like it would on an ordinary couch in an ordinary room. God knows where the telly was, mind you. Not visible, for sure. I gazed up in case it had shot into the rafters when the bell rang, like a sci-fi version of how my mum could clear the dishes off the table and get the centrepiece back on its doily in one movement when she heard footsteps on the pink gravel.

There was no telly in the rafters like a big flat-screen bat.

'Where's the TV?' I said.

Bandanna Man looked at me as if I'd brought a dog in and that dog had just scraped its arse along the floor to wipe some worms off.

'I don't own a television,' he said, in a waspish voice.

'You starting with the buttons and saving up?' I asked him, pointing at the remote. I thought I'd caught him out. I'm an idiot.

'That device regulates temperature and humidity,' he said, 'and plays music. I don't have any interest in mass culture being piped into my home.'

'We are kindred spirits,' said Todd, for all the world as if he had never seen a celebrity chef whose signature dish he hadn't immediately committed to memory. 'Now, how did you persuade the board to allow you to express this delectable aesthetic? Without sullying it for the season?'

'The board?' said Bandanna Man.

'The board members of the HRT,' I said.

'The what of the who?' said Bandanna Man.

'The members of the board of the Historic Residence Tour,' I said. 'There's a sign outside on your lawn.' I would have blamed my accent but he had started quibbling when it was Todd. This was getting weird.

'You mean the committee of the History and Holidays Tour?' said Bandanna Man.

'The font is not well-chosen,' I said. 'But . . .'

'Shouldn't you know the name of the organization you're involved with?' said Todd.

'That,' said Bandanna Man, 'is exactly what I was thinking.' He whipped a phone out of the bib of his denim dungarees and hit a speed-dial button.

'Jode?' he said.

'Who?' said Todd.

'Do we have a mid-century motel and a Beaux Arts houseboat on the tour this year?' he paused. 'I didn't think so. No, no, nothing.' He hung up.

Beside me I could see Todd's chest rising and falling rapidly as he tried to process what was happening.

'Do I need to dial 911?' said Bandanna Man. 'Or will you leave quietly?'

'*What?*' I said.

'You talked your way into my home under false pretences, and while I don't know what your scam is exactly, I know that you need to leave. Now.'

'Before we half-inch your knick-knacks?' I said, putting a curl on my lip as I looked round the yawning emptiness of this – now I looked a bit closer – weird and chilly hangar of a building.

'Is that gang speak?' said Bandanna Man. Bugger. It wasn't the first time a perfect put-down was ruined by Brit slang.

'Now look,' said Todd. 'Clearly there's been some breakdown of communication here. "Jode" is either ignorant about aesthetic movements or wasn't listening. The board – committee if you will; let's not split hairs – approached me weeks ago to ask if we were willing to join the tour and I've been preparing ever since. If you would like to visit the Last Ditch, perhaps this evening for a cocktail—'

Bandanna Man broke in. 'The Last Ditch Motel? The place that makes the Rosebud look like the Ritz? Under the tracks? By the self-storage facility? The one with the chain-link?'

'Snobbery says so much more about the snob than the

snubbed,' I said. In perfect Standard English. I was thrilled with myself.

'*Snub* and *snob* are etymologically unrelated,' said Bandanna Man. 'And anyway, the board approached *you*? Weeks ago? Either you're lying to me or you've been lied to. There is a waiting list of more than twenty to be considered for this tour. This year's tour was finalized before last year's tour began. You've been played, my friend. But you're done playing me.'

Todd opened his mouth to speak but Bandanna Man sailed on. 'So are you leaving or am I calling the cops? Our Neighbourhood Watch has a hotline.'

'We're leaving,' I said, dragging Todd with me. 'I just want to say two things. One, how does a cultural monk such as yourself know that the *Schitt's Creek* motel is called the Rosebud? Got a forty-inch flat-screen opposite your Barcalounger in the basement, eh? And two, Neighbourhood Watch? Soooo suburban.'

'Thank you, Lexy,' Todd said, as we scurried down the path to the Jeep with the slammed door echoing behind us. 'I was rendered momentarily snarkless there. What the fuck is going on?'

'Nothing good,' I said. 'Let's go.'

TWENTY-TWO

I had laid the whole thing out before we were back under the shameful tracks, past the mortifying self-storage and beyond the despised chain-link. Todd was speechless.

'I can't believe how elaborate it was!' he said. 'All that detail! All that effort! Just to get into the motel and onto your boat?'

'To get keys and steal a phone and plant a gun and get away with a murder?' I said. 'Yeah right, why would anyone go to any particular effort over that? And anyway, it was you who did the grunt work. Moving furniture and snapping up spinning wheels.'

'You've got a real problem with that spinning wheel, haven't you?' said Todd. 'You keep mentioning it. Like it's the centrepiece or something. What about the butter churn? Or the apple press?'

'You're not making the point you think you're making,' I said.
'But you know what? It *was* pretty elaborate, actually. It included
ostentatious double-buffing. I even overheard two of them talking
themselves out of letting us join the tour. And now you're saying
there *was* no tour and we were never joining it anyway.'

'What in the name of Ru Paul and the memory of Divine are
you talking about?'

'I was hiding in a dumpster and I heard two women saying
they'd get called bad people for dumping us off the tour.'

'And then you woke up?'

'I know, right? But no. They hated you, Todd. They called
you a deluded do-gooder.'

'Hm,' said Todd. 'Bitches both. But are you sure? Because I
didn't meet with two women. I dealt with just one. Like you
guessed. And she was ready to have my babies. Like you guessed,
I flirted us on to the list. Except I didn't, of course. I flirted for
nothing,' he sighed. 'What a waste of talent.'

'They hated me too,' I said. 'And I never even *met* them. They
called me your sidekick and said I was rude and obnoxious.'

'Or maybe they hated Kathi and Noleen was the obnoxious
sidekick.'

'No, because they were worried about being called racists if
they flaked on the deal.'

'And you thought they meant because you're Scottish? Or
because I'm Chicano? Scottish isn't a race, is it?'

I shrugged. I had no idea. We don't really care about all that
'23 & me' stuff so much when we still live along the street from
our grannies. 'Whatever,' I said. 'We need to tell Molly all of
this. Once she stops laughing, maybe it'll help with the case. I'll
do a sketch of the dumpster women—'

'Why were you in the dumpster, by the way?'

'What? I was getting my binbag, remember? And don't change
the subject. Could you do an Identikit of the people who
approached you and the people who came to do the final . . .' I
paused. 'When was the first . . .? The first I heard was— Oh my
God! I am *such* an easy mark!'

'What is it?' said Todd, not very convincingly.

'You let them on my boat before you even asked me, didn't
you?'

'No!' said Todd. I waited. 'Noleen might have.'

He was right: it *was* Noleen who had said 'final walk-through' to me on the day when, as far as I was concerned, this whole HRT thing started. And it was Noleen who got so aggressive about me leaving my phone lying around. She must have known it was sitting on my boat the day she let strangers crawl all over. The day she let murdering scumbags on to my boat to frame me. I was going to kill her. Well, I was going to speak sternly to her. But I would definitely raise my voice. After she had got used to the news that the lucrative HRT tour was a pile of fool's gold and she'd been had. While she was getting used to the news, I would be kind.

'You should really have known, Todd,' I said. I saw no reason to be kind to *him*. 'Didn't it strike you as slightly too good to be true? Bandanna Man back there was right. They shouldn't have come to you. You should have had to go to them. Didn't that ever occur to you?'

'I find Bandanna Man offensive as an epithet,' Todd said. 'Homophobic.'

'Sod off,' I said. 'What makes you think he was gay?'

'Puh-lease,' Todd said. 'But that's not the point. Double-denim is an anti-lesbian slur no matter who you direct it to.'

'You're nuts.'

'Mental illness is not a joking matter.'

Thankfully he had now parked the car and I got to walk away. But, before I had gone five paces, I found myself turning back. 'Something's bothering me,' I said.

'Fraud, murder, political correctness gone mad so you can't say all the things you used to say?' Todd asked me.

'None of the above,' I replied. 'Something about the board coming to you when you should have gone to them. Something about them courting you when you should have had to grovel to be considered. It's ringing bells.'

'I have no idea what you're talking about,' Todd said.

'Me neither,' I said. 'And you know something else? I *should* have let you change the subject to the dumpster and why I was in it. Because something about that is bugging me too.'

'You'll know for next time,' Todd said. 'Don't interrupt the flow. Everything I say is worth hearing.'

'It wasn't the Kit-Kat wrapper,' I said. 'That was a distraction. It was something else.'

'Unlike you,' said Todd. 'You often open your mouth and let total garbage out.'

'Garbage, garbage,' I said. There was something there, if only I could remember. 'Boarding passes, luggage labels, handi-wipes, mint wrappers . . .'

'Great poem,' said Todd. 'I never knew you were so lyrical. Come and help me break the news to Noleen,' he added. 'Stop her eating me up and spitting out my bones like an owl.'

She was still shouting when I had to extricate myself from the scene and go to meet my two o'clock. Even Kathi hadn't managed to calm her down.

'Look at it this way . . .' she'd said. 'Reception looks a hell of a lot better than it ever has before. Instead of putting this place and that one room back to normal we could do the rest. Rebrand ourselves as a hipster destination.'

'Kathi,' Noleen had said, in a voice that could flash-freeze lava mid-eruption. 'If I have to count to ten and keep drinking not to rip our standard-issue crazy-making road-trip families a new one when they start their shit with me, what the hell makes you think I could deal with fucking *hipsters*? I'd do hard time if I even tried.'

And so I slipped away.

Della was walking round the forecourt with a wailing and wriggling Hiro strapped to her chest. 'Shush-shush-shush,' she said, her voice hoarse enough to make me believe she'd been saying it a while. She was walking funny too, like an astronaut, bouncing slowly down on each step and rising ponderously every time she lifted a foot.

'How are you?' I said.

'Still bleeding, leaking milk, bone-tired and stinky,' she said. 'You?'

'You're not stinky,' I said.

'I've got puke down my back and poop up my arm.'

'Not stinky from here,' I amended. 'Can I say something?' Hiro's squeals grew more piercing and her legs kicked like paddles. Perhaps she sensed her mother's attention was drifting

– or maybe she was missing the moonwalk, since Della had stopped pacing to talk to me. 'Jesus, what a bloody racket,' I said. 'Sorry. That popped out. But can I just say one thing?' I crashed on without waiting for permission. 'I know this advice is from after a death, not a birth, but I think it stands. Don't make any big decisions for at least a year.'

'I can't even get in the shower to wash the puke and poop off me,' Della said. 'I'm good.'

'I overheard you talking to Noleen,' I told her. 'About feeling like you can't cope and deciding to simplify your life?'

'Oh,' Della said. 'You heard that, did you?'

'And I'm saying don't make any big decisions rashly.'

'It's not a big decision,' Della said. 'And I'm not being rash. It was a rush of blood to the head that made me think it would ever work and I've calmed down now. No biggie.'

'That's a pretty callous way to put it, frankly,' I said. Even though I was slightly horrified at myself for scolding a mother so new she was still bleeding. 'There's more than you involved in this now.'

'They'll live,' Della said.

I stared at her. Wasn't childbirth supposed to make you emotional? Weren't all those hormones flooding through Della's body designed to make her fierce and vigilant, to protect the tiny human? This blankness made no sense to me.

'Well, OK then,' I said. 'None of my business anyway, I guess.'

'Not really,' Della said. 'Your business is Trinity and I've been very clear about what Trinity could do for me.'

'What Kathi's wing of Trinity could do for you,' I said. 'Wait. I mean, it wouldn't be for you, Della. Just because Menzies died the night Hiro was born—'

'And she bears the same mark he did.'

'Oh,' I said. 'Someone told you that?'

'Yeah, you. Thank you. It was driving me nuts how Dylan wouldn't say where the bullet went in.'

'That was low,' I said. Then I took a minute to try to choose my next words carefully, respecting her sincerely held beliefs. 'Dell, you do know you are talking absolute bat-shit crazy nonsense, don't you?' She raised an eyebrow but said nothing.

'And speaking of crazy . . . I'm late for my client. So I'll be on my way.'

The novelty wasn't wearing off the arboretum any: it was busier than ever and the gateway was positively thronged with people, all of whom had, of course, decided to meet up on the hour and rendezvous at the most obvious spot. I was going to have to think about starting my sessions at quarter past.

I spotted Minerva waiting as far from the crowd as she could get and still be able to see me coming. She was a tall, rail-thin woman who looked even taller than she actually was from years of yoga leaving her with the posture of a ballet dancer. I had never seen her standing out of 'mountain' pose. I waved.

'How's your daughter?' I asked, once we were under way.

'She ate half a potato and five peanut M&Ms for dinner last night,' she said. 'Two blues, two greens and a yellow.'

'Mm,' I said. That was a lot of detail.

'She left the potato skin under the lip of her plate.'

'Ah.'

'She went upstairs afterwards, but I followed her and waited outside the bathroom door.'

'And?'

'There was silence from inside.'

'Oh.'

'Yeah.'

We had a shorthand now. If Niamh went to the loo and there was silence that meant she had gone to evacuate and was thwarted by her mother's presence. No visit at all or a visit with audible peeing were what we wanted.

'But she did ask me to buy san-pro.'

'OK.'

'But I've been going through her trash can every night and she hasn't used any of the last lot. Or if she has I don't know where she's putting them. I did wonder if she's been flushing them. So I asked her.'

'Very straightforward of you,' I said. 'What did she say?'

'Went nuts at me for going through her trash and refused to answer.'

'Ah,' I said again.

'Do you know, Lexy,' Minerva said, after a pause, 'you only say "good" and "bad" about straight-talking and subterfuge. You don't say "good" and "bad" about eating itself. Unlike the damn doctors.'

'Is that right?' I said. I didn't mind someone pointing out how effortlessly great I was. 'Wait, though,' I added. 'They don't say "bad" about eating, do they?'

'They say "concerning",' said Minerva, 'which is worse. You are much easier to talk to.'

'Good,' I said. 'To coin a phrase.'

'So can I *really* talk?'

She had just given me a colour-breakdown of her daughter's M&M consumption so, to my mind, she was already really talking. 'That's the idea,' was all I said.

'It seems like time. I've been watching all this new content, see? I think it's good for me.'

'Does it help you stop fretting?' I said. 'Do the shows enlighten and empower?'

'I wouldn't call them shows,' Minerva said. 'Clips maybe. Uploads.'

'From doctors?' I said. 'From recoverees?'

'It's not . . .' she began, and then we walked in silence again for a bit, just the tramp, tramp, tramp of our feet keeping perfect time on the bark chips.

'Not what?' I said, at last.

'The best sites are pro,' said Minerva.

'Professional help sites?' I said. 'Well, probably the content there would be broadly positive and worthwhile, no?'

'Nooooo,' said Minerva. 'I mean they're pro-ana. Some of them are pro-mia. Or just thinspro generally.'

'You're going to have to help me out with the jargon,' I said. But, even as I was speaking, the code started to leak. 'Pro-ana?' I echoed. 'Pro-anorexia, you mean?' Minerva nodded. 'And pro-mia is pro-bulimia?' Another nod. 'Wow. Um, well, I suppose knowledge is power. What's thinspro?'

'Inspiration from skinny pics,' said Minerva. 'And, you know, it really is helping.'

'OK,' I said. 'Helping how?'

'Well, some of these girls are gorgeous.'

I quite often get mildly dizzy walking in the arboretum. There are so many roots underfoot that you have to look down to stop yourself tripping, and there's something about the flash-flash of my feet appearing and disappearing from view that makes me feel as if I'm falling forwards. But, if I look up, the flash-flash of the branches overhead makes me feel as if I'm falling over backwards. This was neither of those things. This was actual reeling from not being able to believe my ears.

'It's helping me see things from Niamh's point of view,' Minerva said. 'I've been pretty judgemental up to now.'

'Let's sit,' I said, diving for a bench before I crashed to the ground, which seemed like a distinct possibility.

'Have I shocked you?' Minerva said. That's when I had to put my head in between my knees. It was her voice. It was the *relish* in her voice, the knowing delight that rolled out of her mouth like a nasty little string of puked-up M&Ms.

Suddenly everything was clear. Her obsessing about the details of Niamh's meals and purges, the way she regaled me with the minutiae of her avid concern over and over and over again. Until we had a shorthand, for God's sake! Her slow tiptoeing to where she'd got to, taking me with her – or so she thought! And then, with one neat twist, she was barely pretending to wring her hands any more. She was openly – almost openly anyway – revelling in the wonderful world of . . .

'What's the overall term for this point of view?' I said. I knew there was one. I was sure I'd heard it somewhere.

'Ana-mia,' Minerva said. 'It's niche but it's nothing to make a fuss about. I'm relieved I've finally found a therapist who's open-minded enough to let me discuss it.'

Ah yes, I thought. I'd asked Minerva about her history of therapy right back at the start of our association, long before the chummy reports and the birth of the shorthand. She said she'd been trying for five years to find the right person to open up to. I sat up again and gave her a bright smile, the sort of professional smile I learned in training but didn't actually hoist on to my face that often. The problem was, five years ago Niamh would have been nine.

'Can I ask you one question?' I said. She nodded. 'Do you actually have any children?'

She sat stone still for so long I wondered if she'd had the quietest stroke in human history; if she'd maybe died when she happened to be perfectly balanced, her spine held in place by bands of muscle and her head sitting on her neck like a Fabergé egg on its stand. I was almost ready to reach out and poke her, see if she'd topple, when she blinked. 'Is this a deal-breaker for you and me?'

I shook my head. 'Not at all,' I said. I think I managed to say a few words about the many paths to honesty and the need for trust to build as a process by whatever means blah blah blah. The truth was my mind was whirring like a minute to midnight in a clock-mender's workshop. I could feel something coming, oiled cogs about to click into place, puzzle pieces about to snap together airtight. Minerva wasn't anxious about a beloved daughter; she was neck-deep in her own illness. Her point of view was a full one hundred and eighty degrees from the way she'd been playing it to me. And that was an unsettling echo of something else that had been going on all around me. It was so close I could almost taste it but, as I reached, it retreated, starting to dissolve even as it came into view.

Della, I thought. She got the mood wrong, just like Minerva had. She got the tone wrong. She should be distraught and she wasn't. Like those women I'd listened in on at the pizza place that day. I couldn't work out which one of them had the narcissist boyfriend and which one was sympathizing. The tone was wrong. The mood was wrong. They were like bad actors in a weak play.

But even that wasn't really what was bothering me. There was something else. Who goes to whom. Who speaks and who listens. Who offers and who accepts. I had made a humongous error somewhere. The clocks were about to chime, the cogs were going to catch, the puzzle pieces were going to click like an alligator's jaws.

And I was far from sure that I could deal with the shape of the thing I was straining to see.

TWENTY-THREE

I f there's a sadder sight than the trimmings for a holiday tour being dismantled and trundled off days before the grand gala opening, I've never seen it. The piles of vintage crap stacked on my front porch – kitchenware, crocheted knee blankets, kitschy little paintings – were as sad as they were solid. And boy were they solid; I did not like the way the boat was listing to one end.

'Todd?' I called out. 'You might want to move some of this on to the bank before you add to it.'

'I'll start with the spinning wheel,' he said, appearing in the doorway carrying it uplifted in his arms like a sacrifice. 'Unless you want me to throw it overboard since you hate it so much.'

'I don't hate it!' I said. 'If you don't need to give it back, I'd be happy to keep it. I'll even look at a YouTube video and work out how to use it. Knit you a jumper.'

'Asshole,' he said, not quite smiling.

'OK, I'll knit you an asshole. Anything you need.' That got a real smile. 'But first, I'm going to talk to Della. Again. I need to stop pussyfooting about. My last client has put me in the mood for some straight-talking.'

Round at Della and Dylan's room I could hear Hiro through the door. I had found her newborn cry pretty convincing, but the full, lusty fire-alarm now replacing it was the real deal. This was how our species survived all these millennia.

'Jesus!' I said, letting myself in at Della's shouted invitation, 'What a bloody racket. What's *wrong* with her?'

'Well,' said Della. 'Menzies' murderer is still at large, so there's that.' I refused to dignify this with a response. 'Or maybe she's got indigestion.'

'Here,' I said, reaching out. 'Does she like patting or rubbing?'

'She's easy,' Della said. 'And I'm mixing it up so she stays that way. Question is, do you care more about your shirt or your pants?'

'Neither,' I said.

'So free choice then,' said Della. 'Lie her face down over a forearm or put her up against your shoulder.' She had struggled to her feet and now she went waddling off to the bathroom. The sight of her bulky maxi-pad, like a loaf of bread in her baggy leggings, made me feel very tender towards her and I considered not having the difficult talk I'd come here to have.

While I tried to decide, I lay Hiro face down on my arm as suggested, like a waiter with a trio of plates, and started rubbing her back with the flat of my other hand. Within seconds she stopped crying, which made me feel quite god-like. Within another few seconds, she let out a thunderclap of a burp with no follow-through. I upgraded myself to Zeus and cuddled her in against my shoulder.

'Did you hear that?' I asked Della, who was returning.

'I felt it shake the floor,' she said. 'Her burps are nearly as loud as her farts. And her farts, when there's no diaper to muffle them? Mi pequeña pedita.' She sat carefully, lowering herself into the chair with both hands gripping the arms. She managed not to wince; I didn't.

'Shoot,' she said. Then, 'Sorry. Lexy, will you ever get used to the guns up here? Over here for you, I guess. But will you?'

'Nope,' I said. 'You sound wistful. Are you thinking about going home?' Bad as Della dumping Dylan would be, dumping him and taking the kids over the border would be ten times worse. Dylan wasn't sharp enough to handle international travel. He'd end up stateless in an airport like that movie.

'This is home now,' Della said. So that was something.

'Good,' I said. 'Glad to hear it. Right. Don't shout at me, OK? Because I think she's falling asleep.' Hiro's head was resting on my shoulder and she was drooling – I hoped – into my neck with every snuffly little exhalation. 'Please don't leave Dylan,' I said. 'Let me help you work it through. No charge, as many sessions as you need. But please at least give it a try.'

'What are you talking about?' Della said. 'Of course I'm not going to leave Dylan. Why would I leave Dylan?'

'Because he's selfish and immature and you can't stand him and all his romantic mierda?' I said.

'What?' said Della again. 'Why are you saying nasty things about my husband? About *her* papa?'

'You said them,' I said.

'I didn't,' said Della. 'That's the best part of being honest, Lexy. You don't have to remember what you said, because if you don't think something you know you never pretended to.'

'But I heard you,' I said. Hiro was deeply asleep now and she seemed to have turned on some kind of gravity enhancer. She suddenly weighed a ton in my arms. I kneed a pile of washing off the nearest upright chair and sank down on to it. 'I overheard you telling Noleen. But fine, have it your own way. If you've changed your mind, no one is going to be more delighted than me. Great. Subject closed. Let's move on.'

'Nice try,' Della said, in a voice I'd only ever heard her use to Diego. 'When did I say these untrue, unkind things I never said?'

'Sunday,' I said. 'To Nolly. In Reception. You were practically in tears. Saying you couldn't cope and you were foolish to think you could and you just wanted to be left alone at night to sleep.'

Della's face split into an enormous grin and her eyes flashed with what I hoped was merriment. It could have been malice. The grin was certainly wolfish enough. 'Don't think for a moment I'm not still angry,' she said, but then she burst out laughing. 'But my hormones are shot. Lexy, you idiot. Look at my side of the bed.'

'Which side's yo—?' I began, but one bedside table had a pile of books and magazines, a box of breast pads, a tube of some kind of emollient cream and statue of Santa Maria de Guadalupe. The other bedside table had an empty Coke can and a framed photo of Della. 'What am I looking at?' I said.

'On top of the pile,' said Della.

'The book?' I said. It was a thick one, probably the latest baby-wrangling advice, I reckoned.

'The book,' Della said. 'My choice for my book club. Nine hundred pages about a selfish little boy who never grew up that I imagined I wanted to read.'

'*Don Quixote!*' I said.

'I was wrong,' she said. 'No one wants to read *Don Quixote*, Lexy. People are leaving my book club like . . . alma que lleva el diablo.'

'Rats on a sinking ship?'

'*Greased* rats,' Della said. 'Half my first sign-ups staged a protest. They said he was a fantasist and a controller and they get enough of that in real life.'

'OH MY GOD!' I said. Hiro spasmed and I rocked her feverishly. 'Oh my God,' I whispered when she had settled. 'I heard two of them! They hated him! I thought they were talking about a boyfriend.'

'And they weren't the worst,' Della said. 'There's another little clique that thinks I only chose the book because it was Spanish.'

'OH MY GOD,' I said. Hiro woke up properly this time and started grizzling. 'Oh my God,' I whispered again. 'Shoosh-shoosh, baby girl. Sorry. But, I heard them too! I thought they were talking about Todd. I thought . . .'

'What?'

'I thought,' I said, 'they were . . . weirdly . . . disengaged.'

'They *were* disengaged,' Della said. 'They point-blank refused to engage. They said we should have a two-hundred-page maximum and nothing before the twentieth century.'

'Yeah but,' I said. 'That's not the only . . . it was . . . Hang on. There's something wrong somewhere. Something doesn't add up. Nothing's . . .'

'Are you OK?' said Della.

'I don't know,' I said. 'I think I've been derailed somewhere along the way. I just don't know how exactly.'

Della gasped. Then she started speaking very fast. 'Don't dwell on it,' she said. 'Look forward. Where's Taylor? When's the wedding? Do you want Diego to bear your rings? He would love to. Don't you want to get started on one of your own?' She nodded at Hiro who was settling again, sucking hard on my collar and restarting the gravity machine.

'Why are you babbling?' I said. 'Are you trying to distract me? What for? It won't work, you know.'

And it wouldn't have. Hiro suddenly delivering a hot jet of semi-digested milk down the inside of my shirt did wonders though.

I decided to deal with it immediately. Quite a bundle of my clean clothes were waiting in the Skweek after a service wash so I knew I could undress directly into Kathi's 'bio-hazard' washing machine, the one she keeps for, as she calls it, mud, blood and party crud.

'Why are you walking like that?' she said, as I glided in. My shirt was tucked in and my belt was cinched tight but I could still feel a distressing amount of trickle headed down from my waist anytime my hips did more than shuffle.

'Hiro,' I said. 'Can I stand on a binbag and strip?'

'Jesus,' said Kathi. 'It's a good thing she's cute.'

She wiped me down thoroughly. I tried not to breathe in and I didn't complain that the wipes were supposed to be for floors and hard surfaces. The tingling was just shy of what you'd call an actual burn and there was no denying I felt clean afterwards.

As I slipped some fresh clothes on, I tried to share my state of mind. 'You know,' I said, 'I think I've made a fundamental error about Menzies. And I'm pretty sure that if I could straighten it out in my mind I could help Molly solve the case.'

'Or,' Kathi said, 'you could just be glad that Molly knows it wasn't you and forget all about it. That would work too.'

'Have you been speaking to Della?' I said. 'She just tried to distract me by dangling my wedding in front of me like a ball on a string. What's with you both? Actually, what's with you *all*? Because Todd and Noleen were at it too, now I think about it.'

'That doesn't seem likely,' Kathi said, but she's a terrible liar.

'Nothing is hanging together,' I said. 'Nothing is making sense to me. Everything Menzies did is such a massive over-reaction. He played tricks when he was a student. So what? It was mean but it was one step up from a Tide pod challenge actually. I don't believe Farquhar's wife knows what she's on about in terms of sentencing and statutes either. It's crazy. OK, some women get in touch with each other and compare notes and then they track him down and give him a scare. Good for them. But what he's supposed to have done next? Gone to my mum and dad and found out where I live, and outwitted the travel ban to get here and then stopped off in the Bay to threaten another victim of his silly pranks? That's insane. And then he comes up here to threaten me too, only he doesn't? He goes to bed and lets me party outside his room because it's Thanksgiving? Which is a holiday neither one of us actually gives a stuff about, by the way. And then, to crown it all, someone kills him?'

'It does sound bonkers when you put it that way,' Kathi said. She gave me a great big fake smile. 'Oh well. People are weird.'

'You certainly are,' I said. 'I just don't get anything about this. Someone was setting me up to take the rap for this days before I even knew Menzies was coming: faking the HRT, planting the gun, adding the app, going all over town asking after me like they were a long-lost friend, doing that big bogus backwards walk into the Thrift to keep their face off the camera. Why go where there are cameras at all? How does any of that make any sense?'

'It doesn't,' said Kathi. 'Actually, yeah, you're right. It doesn't. Even . . . it really doesn't.'

'Even what?'

'Nothing.'

'But it doesn't, right?'

Kathi did something unprecedented then. She stopped halfway through folding a load and swept it all, folded and tangled alike, back into the plastic basket. When the folding table was clear she took a pad of paper from her desk (one of the big yellow ones that are 'legal' in some way I've never worked out, because why the hell would any paper be *il*legal) and uncapped a serious-looking Sharpie.

'A stranger comes to town,' she said. 'And prepares a story where you kill Menzies, because *he* is coming to town to bribe or threaten you out of reporting him for an old crime—'

'I don't think it *is* a crime.'

'OK, an old pattern of shitty behaviour.'

'Which I wasn't going to anyway.'

'Right,' Kathi said. 'But he gets murdered.'

'Yes. And then the husband of one of the other women who got messed about by one of the other BOLS Boys comes to see me because he's convinced that she killed Menzies.' Kathi frowned. 'See? You've that "no way" feeling too now, haven't you?'

'I totally have. Even if . . . Yeah, I have.'

'Even if what?'

'Nothing.'

'Also, Farquhar . . .' I paused as Kathi snorted.

'I'm sorry. It's never going to stop being funny.'

'Also Farquhar,' I said again, 'was adamant that Menzies coming here wasn't a truth and reconciliation thing. He said it was a containment exercise. But Menzies didn't contain it. He blabbed it. And Farquhar truly believed his wife – who is a lawyer, remember – would risk a long prison sentence to pay Menzies back about a million times too much for what Laidlaw – not even Menzies now I think about it – did to her. Instead of just #Metooing his shitty arse all over the internet and telling his boss and all his friends and doing what a normal person would do. No one is doing what a normal person would do!'

'No one?' said Kathi. 'You mean both the Vasses?'

'I mean no one! That's what was bugging me so much about Della leaving Dylan—'

'*What?*'

'She's not, she's not, don't interrupt me. And the same thing bugged me when I couldn't work out which of these two bints was going out with Don Quixote.'

'You've lost me.'

'Or why these other two bints were so furious with Trinity.'

'That would be because of Todd, wouldn't it?'

I took a beat to give that the little smile it deserved, but I was on a roll and I wasn't going to let anything stop me now. 'It's because no one was saying or doing what a normal person would say or do. Because it wasn't real. It wasn't personal. It was a book. And it's the same with Whatserchops. Hortense. She wouldn't go all John Wick because of a bad boyfriend in the Nineties! It's just not real.'

'Well, to be fair, she didn't,' Kathi said.

'Yeah, but she wouldn't take off to a spa retreat in New Mexico either. Not when she's got a full-time job and two little kids as well. It doesn't ring true.'

'She might,' said Kathi. 'I would.'

'Yeah but I don't think she did. I don't think she—'

I broke off as the door opened. It was Todd. 'Kath . . .' he began. 'Oh. I was going to ask if you knew where Lexy was.'

'Tah-dah!' I said.

'Not in that outfit,' Todd said. 'That is not a tah-dah compliant assemblage of garments. What the hell?'

'Hiro puked on me and Kathi picked these off the top of a bundle.'

'You look fine,' said Kathi. She turned to Todd. 'What is it?'

Which was the moment I realized he was pale and his jaw was quivering.

'What?' I said.

'I've been putting your boat back to rights,' he said.

'I know,' I said. 'I saw you. Oh my God, Todd! Did you keep piling stuff up on the porch? Have you capsized it?'

'No,' he assured me. 'I took away all the trimmings and I put back all the crap and clutter. Not that you need a quarter of it but that's for another day.'

'Right,' I said.

'See the thing, is,' said Todd, 'I did it in a bit of a rush on Friday. I wasn't really paying massively close attention to what I took. I just dollied it off and locked it in a storage pod. So don't get mad at me.'

'I'll try,' I said. 'But you're not making it easy. Spit it out, will you.'

'I brought back various boxes and bags,' said Todd. 'And I unpacked them and put everything where I'd found it to the best of my recollection. With, you know, a little extra attention if I thought you had it in stupid places before.'

'Todd, seriously,' Kathi said. 'Get a move on.'

'And then so I started to unpack this suitcase I'd taken away . . .'

'I haven't got a suitcase,' I said. 'I donated my suitcases because I've got nowhere to store them and yours are nicer anyway.'

'But I was on autopilot,' said Todd. 'I opened it up to unpack your pitiful shit and replace it where it makes your home look lame. Only it wasn't your shit. It wasn't any shit that I had packed up.'

'Whose was it?' said Kathi. 'Did the self-store fuck up and give you someone else's bag?'

'No,' I said. 'No, that's not what happened at all.'

'How do *you* know?' said Kathi.

'How *do* you know?' said Todd.

'Because it's been bugging me for days,' I told them. 'The suitcase you're talking about belonged to Menzies, didn't it? He put it on my boat and left it there, didn't he?'

Todd nodded.

'I was supposed to go through the contents before he spoke to me. That's why he didn't make himself known the first night he was here, right?'

Todd nodded again. 'Seems like it.'

'I knew it,' I said. I had known it since I was crouching in the dumpster. A Kit-Kat band, boarding passes, a handi-wipe sachet, receipts from airport shops, mint wrappers. And the thing that shouldn't have been there. A luggage label, from a checked bag, thrown away by a man who only had a carry-on. I took a long breath. 'What's in it?'

Todd shook his head. 'Come with me,' he said. 'You need to see.'

TWENTY-FOUR

The boat looked as if someone had been disturbed mid-burglary but I only had eyes for the suitcase lying open in the middle of the messy living-room floor. Inside it were a neatly packed, I mean Tetris-neat, collection of . . . coloured cardboard folders. I was more disappointed than I had words to express.

'Any chance that's a thin layer of fake work product with treasure underneath?' I said.

'It's a thick layer of treasure,' said Todd. 'Upsetting treasure but treasure nonetheless.'

I reached out to take one of the folders, but Todd laid a hand on my arm. 'Really upsetting treasure,' he said. 'Names and dates and full descriptions.'

'Of?'

'BOLS,' he said. 'Black Out Love Shack. Nearly ten years' worth. Don't read it, Lexy.'

'For God's sake!' I said. I might have shouted. 'Why is everybody being so bloody weird? It was a game. It was a joke. And it was years ago. What the hell am I going to read that's going to be beyond my ability to cope with? And why the hell did Menzies get killed for it? Why the hell did Farquhar think I'd cover up a murder because of it? It was a prank, Todd! It was a bluff! It was—'

My boat is wide and flat-bottomed. And the slough is shallow and sluggish eleven months of the year. So there's no chance that it actually moved underneath us. It was much more likely a bout of vertigo.

'Shit,' I said.

'Shit,' agreed Todd.

'It wasn't,' I said.

'It wasn't,' Todd confirmed.

'It was a double bluff?' I said. 'The "oops, I forgot" act and the switch to "I was kidding" wasn't the truth? The truth is . . .'

'I think it is . . .'

'. . . that it wasn't Menzies in that dark little room with me.'

'It wasn't,' said Todd.

'Who was it?' I said.

'I don't know,' said Todd. 'They used nicknames. It might have been anyone. Except Menzies. Other nights with other women it might have been someone else who set it up and Menzies who . . . did . . . the . . .'

'Rape,' I said. 'With the twenty-year sentence and the long statute of limitation, making it an excellent motive for murder.'

'Yeah,' said Todd.

'I can't believe I didn't know!' I said. It came out like a howl. 'What does that say abo—?'

'No!' said Todd. 'Absolutely not. Apart from anything else, I think they might have spiked your drink.'

He nodded at the folders again and I remembered Farquhar – if it was Farquhar – saying 'drugs' in that bogus voice and Menzies glowering at him.

'Are you OK?' said Todd. 'Sorry. Scratch that. Would you like a hug? Wait, no, sorry. Scratch that. Would you like me to get Kathi or someone to come hug you?'

'I'm here,' Kathi said, from the porch. 'I followed.'

'I don't want a hug,' I said, which was total bollocks and

thankfully Todd and Kathi knew that and came at me in a pincer movement, squeezing me so hard my bra squeaked. When I struggled out of their grip at last, I said, 'So everybody worked that out except me? That's why you've all been so weird? You?' Todd nodded. 'And you?' Kathi nodded. 'Never try to get work as a spy, Kathi, by the way. Definitely Della.'

'And Taylor and Noleen,' said Todd.

'And who decided not to tell *me*?' I said. 'Whose brilliant idea was it to carry on where Menzies left off and not let *me* in on what was happening?'

'Well, all of us,' said Todd. 'We had a meeting.'

'Ha ha,' I said, before I realized he was serious. 'What?'

'To be fair,' said Kathi, 'we didn't think of that angle. That we were doing the same thing again. Sorry. But yeah we had a meeting. It took five minutes. And I'd do the same again.'

'But why?' I wailed.

'Because every single damn thing you found or heard or thought from the minute this started, your only response has been to tell Molly. And that would have been incredibly dumb, we decided. Right, Todd?'

'Incredibly dumb,' Todd said, nodding. 'To go mincing off to Molly and tell her you had the mother of all motives. Also . . . Jesus, Lexy. Why would you want that news after all these years anyway?'

He potentially had the beginning of a small point and so I decided to leave it. 'I would have worked it out in the end,' I said. 'I was getting there. The HRT tour helped. Everything was the wrong way round. They don't come to you; you go to them. Like a guy who got away with something really bad doesn't come looking for his victims. They go looking for him. And I see it all the time at work too. I've got these clients right now who are classic cases: there's this psycho and every accusation is a confession; this really broken woman who turns it all out so every caring query is really a cry for help; then there's this woman with a monster eating disorder and every bit of handwringing is really her secretly revelling in it. Poor cow. It's the same thing. And with the book club too. Everyone was far too bloodless talking about terrible boyfriends and imminent divorce, because they weren't, you see. It was all pretend.'

'I *don't* see,' Kathi said. 'I mean, yes, Menzies came to you like an HRT committee chair. But you didn't speak to him, so how do you know he was projecting? That's what you call it, right? Projection? And how do you know he was bloodless and fake, when he died before you even saw him? Do you mean when he went to see your mom?'

'Oh for God's sake,' I said. 'I'm not talking about Menzies! Don't you see? It never made sense that he came to intimidate me – or worse! – but he got killed before he could do it. I was right all along. Menzies came to set things straight. He came to hand over evidence. For redemption. He came to do the right thing.'

'Of course he did,' said Kathi. 'The *other* one came to kill him before he got the chance.'

Todd was nodding. Then his eyes narrowed. 'What other one?' he said.

'Farquhar!' I told him. 'Catch up. Farquhar's story was insane. I think he might be married and it might be to someone he met at Edinburgh, because I recognized her photo on his phone. But I don't think she's a lawyer and I definitely don't think he's got kids or, if he has, those pictures he showed me weren't of them. Batman pjs and a lick-and-stick head bow? Those were not the moppets of a Silicon Valley entrepreneur. No way. And he freaked all the way the fuck out when I scrolled on his camera app and saw a photo he hadn't set up for me. I wondered why but now I get it. He even lost a unit of his shit when I told him Menzies had brought something to give me and I'd found it. Then he relaxed when he heard what I thought it was. A daft wee token from when we were together. I mean, I'm saying he relaxed, but it was more like a puncture in a lilo. I missed all the signs! I'm supposed to be good at this. It's my job!'

'Except you missed nothing,' said Kathi. 'You stored it all away and you just dredged it back up again. Give yourself a break, Lexy. Todd's the one who's had the lobotomy.' She prodded him with her toe. '*What other one?*'

But Todd wasn't listening. He had started flipping through one of the folders from the suitcase.

'I've found the key to the nicknames,' he said.

I took a big breath. 'So I'll be able to work out who it was? In the box room with me?'

He nodded. 'You don't have to—'

'Hit me.'

'Lachlan,' he said. 'Is that how you pronounce it? With a "hghrlrghlch"?'

'That's how you pronounce it,' I confirmed.

'Wow,' said Kathi. 'I thought Della was nuts about all that reincarnation crap, but why else would Hiro say that very name every time she pukes her milk up?'

Which is why, despite all of it, when Taylor came home I was laughing.

They had me bang to rights, those friends of mine. As soon as I'd told Taylor and had a bit of a cry and a stiff whisky I was all for trotting up to the cop shop, with the suitcase banging off my legs, and handing it over. Noleen, arriving with a jug of sangria and the very last of the pies as if she'd smelled trouble in the air and didn't want to miss it, talked me down.

'We shouldn't touch it again,' she said. 'This way it's their fault they never asked to go through your stuff. If we take it up there they'll twist it round and end up blaming us for fingerprints and God knows what. Drink up, Lexy. Do you want some squirty cream?'

'OK,' I said. 'Oh, Noleen!'

'I know, honey.'

'I'm going to need to talk to someone about all of this. And I really hate talking to therapists. It doesn't work on me. I get bored and arsey.'

'I believe you,' Noleen said. 'It was always a mystery to me that you *were* one, to be honest. It's not as if you're hell-bent on helping people, is it? But this makes it clearer in a way. It was subconscious. Somewhere deep inside you knew.'

'Wouldn't that have made her a police officer?' said Taylor.

'I could never have been a police officer,' I said.

'No argument here,' said Molly, letting herself in the door.

'I phoned her,' said Todd. 'Don't kill me.'

I wasn't even tempted to kill him. For once. I knew I had a boulder inside me that could flatten Indiana Jones and I needed to roll it away. 'Settle in, Sarge,' I said. 'This could take a while.'

'Pie?' said Noleen.

'It's Tuesday,' said Molly. 'Give it up, Muntz. It's time to compost the remains and let it go.'

It took quite some time to fill Molly in on the sordid history of the BOLS Boys, the late attempt at redemption by one of them, and the last-ditch effort at containment by another. She mostly listened but she was gratifyingly loose-lipped at odd moments. 'Fuckers!' she said, more than once. 'You OK to keep going?' got an airing too. And 'Are these names as stupid as they sound, Lexy? These guys are going to be soooo easy to pin once we get the alumni office on it, right?'

When I finally ran dry, she snapped her notebook closed with a twang of elastic that rang out across the boat. 'How sure are you that it was Menzies who went to your parents' house?' she said. 'That's been worrying me. How he got his travel arranged so quickly after he found out your address. But if it wasn't him, if it was someone on his tail, that clears it right up. And so I'm thinking . . . they hadn't seen the guy for twenty years, right? If some dude rolled in and claimed to be him, would they know?'

I felt my face drain. 'Oh God,' I said. 'Do you think they're safe? Because it could absolutely be any single one of the bastards at all. I don't even know if it was Farquhar who came here yesterday. It could have been Laidlaw, or Struan or Strathpeffer or another one I've forgotten. It could have been . . .' I didn't say Lachlan. I wasn't sure I could get the word out without a Hiro-style follow-through.

'An alias would track with their old MO,' Molly said gently.

'He really could have been anyone!' I said. 'That's kind of the point, after all. That must be where they got the idea from, the scumbags, the monsters. They're all the bloody same!' I was getting hysterical. I knew I was. But I'd had shock after shock after shock and I didn't think there was any way to stop myself from unravelling completely. So, instead of fancy breathing and stoicism to squash it down, I leaned in. Which is to say I shook and sobbed and ripped up tissues into tiny pieces and threw them on the floor.

'You could phone home,' said Todd. 'Ask your mom for a proper description of "Menzies". See if it was actually "Farquhar".'

I cleared my throat, stopped shaking, fanned my shirt to dry my sweat, and started picking up bits of tissue. 'Nah,' I said. 'You're OK.'

TWENTY-FIVE

S it tight. That was Molly's advice to us all. She had a colleague from Police Scotland headed for my parents' house to take another statement and try for a description, which they hadn't bothered with before because everyone assumed the visitor was Menzies. She had told Noleen to lock the gates and report any unexpected guests. She took the suitcase away in the great-granddaddy of all plastic evidence bags and left us with those instructions: sit tight.

'Sit tight,' said Todd. 'God, that's infuriating when we broke the case for her.'

'Sit tight,' said Kathi. 'An impossible task for any anxiety-prone person at the best of times.'

'I can only dream of it,' Della said. 'I had no idea how totally my body would lie down and give up after a second birth. I feel like a bundle of laundry.'

'You're perfect,' said Dylan, the genius. Then he followed it up with, 'More of you to love,' the idiot.

'But what could we do anyway?' I said. 'The police are better equipped to find Farquhar. Or whoever he was.'

'Let's sit tight,' Taylor said. He'd been looking at me in much the same way Dylan looked at Della when she was elephant pregnant. It was thoughtful but very annoying and there was to be no break from it, because he had called in sick to work. I'd smiled and said thank you when he told me, knowing he'd grab any excuse to skip a shift in the phone shop, but then I overheard him talking his sub through the tasks on the docket and realized a well-nigh incredible thing. He wasn't plunking the phone shop. He had called in sick to the bird sanctuary. For me.

'You know what I still don't understand?' I said. 'This is not not sitting tight, by the way. This is just sitting tight and chatting while I'm at it. But I don't understand who it was who was looking for me. All over town. In the Thrift. In the Browser. In the Lode. Who was that and what did she want?'

'Definitely a "she"?' said Noleen.

'Definitely,' said Todd. 'Multiple people confirmed that.'

'So not Menzies,' I said. 'And not Farquhar.'

'Maybe it was just a friend,' said Dylan. 'Unrelated to all this. Maybe it really was just an old friend from home looking you up because she happened to be in town.'

'In the middle of a global pandemic when all international travel is being administrated by minions of Orwell,' said Noleen. 'Right.'

'Although,' I offered, 'there *was* someone here from home. I saw her in the Lode. I cornered her in the Lode actually.' I looked up, surprised by the silence that met this. They were all staring at me. 'You met her,' said Taylor. 'And you didn't think to tell anyone?'

'Wh—?' I began.

'You actually saw the person who stole your phone? And broke into your place? And tricked us all into thinking we were on a Christmas tour?'

'And this is the one thing you don't tell Molly?' said Kathi.

'No!' I said. 'I only knew she was from back home because she had a Tesco bag. She wasn't a friend. She's never going to be a friend either. She didn't brush me off – we ended up having a coffee – but she couldn't get rid of me quick enough when she finally stopped eating.'

'Funny that,' said Noleen.

I frowned at her. I had no idea what she was getting at.

'And it was after this chance encounter with someone stupid enough to be trolling round Cuento with a Tesco bag that a mysterious stranger started asking for you all over town?' Todd said.

'So what?' I countered. I could tell I'd been an idiot, somehow or other, and I wasn't looking forward to finding out more.

'Almost as if she was here to plant evidence,' Kathi said, 'but you busted her. Her and her bag. And so she had to lay a false scent about someone *else* knocking around so as to throw you off. In case you remembered her when the shit hit the fan.'

'What did she look like?' said Todd.

'Random Brit,' I said. 'Bog-standard middle-class English woman in early middle-age.'

'Thick streaks like fruit straps?' said Todd. 'Gold over brown?'

'I suppose,' I said. 'I'd have called it honey-coloured but yeah.'

'Ill-advised stretch jeans one size too big so the wrinkles go right round like the threads on a screw-top jar and don't hide the spread?' said Todd.

'Since you mention it,' I said. 'Although I'd have said she was sturdy rather than spreading. Where are you getting this?'

'Eyebrows too wide from overplucking the middle and too thick from under-plucking the top line?'

'No Brits pluck the top of their eyebrows,' I said. 'So probably.'

'I knew it!' said Todd. 'The so-called advance inspector of the so-called HRT board!'

'She was?' I said. 'Huh. You never said the inspector was British.'

'She was doing an accent,' said Todd. 'She said she'd lived here for years. But then when I said I was born in Cuento and I didn't recall ever seeing her, she changed her story and said "here" meant down south of the city.'

'South of the city?' I said. 'Hang on . . . something's . . . honey-coloured hair, sturdy figure like from having kids . . . Oh my GOD! I *knew* I recognized her!'

'You recognized her?' said Kathi.

'Not when I met her at the Lode,' I said. 'I recognized her when I saw her on Farquhar's phone.'

'His wife?' said Todd.

'God knows,' I said. 'She might be. She might even be called Hortense and maybe she once lived in Edinburgh. But that's not where I knew her from. What an idiot I am.'

'But would any woman help an asshole like Farquhar plan a murder to get away with a rape?' said Kathi. 'That's what we're saying, isn't it? Menzies went to Farquhar to say he was blowing their old crimes and Farquhar and the Tesco bag lady set out to foil him?'

'That's what *I'm* saying,' said Todd. 'Menzies knew where you were and let it slip to Farquhar that he was coming to confess to you. So Farquhar sent Aslan or Numbnuts to get your addy and followed Menzies here.'

'And between the two of them, Bonnie and Clyde got the murder done and a suspect framed,' said Noleen.

'And but for one ill-judged reusable bag, they would have gotten away with it,' said Della.

'Oh my God, Lexy,' said Taylor. 'You must have made her bum squeak when you accosted her.'

I gave him a nod for excellent use of slang but most of my attention was elsewhere. In the far distance I thought I could see a glimmer of light. 'I think I know how to catch her out,' I said. 'If I'm right about this.'

'You *are* right about this,' said Della. 'Look at Hiro. She's smiling.'

'She's too wee to smile,' I said.

'And yet she's smiling,' Della said.

'It's wind,' I said. 'She'll burp in a second.'

We waited in silence for it to happen. When Hiro had drifted into a deep sleep without so much as hiccupping, Della said, 'Menzies is at peace now because you've cracked the case.'

'OK,' I said. I was not going to touch any bit of that with a pole. It was creepy. 'Now, who wants to come on a last ditch outing. I mean a Hail Mary type last ditch. Not a *Last Ditch* last ditch.'

'You really mean a Trinity last ditch, don't you?' said Todd.

'Would this come under the heading of sitting tight?' said Taylor.

'It would not,' I told him. 'Don't you love the way I never lie to you? Isn't that one of the best things about me?'

'Where are we going?' said Kathi, standing. 'Do we need snacks? Change of clothes? Passports?'

'None of the above,' I said. 'This is local. And quite unlikely but still – I want to try.'

I explained it in the Jeep as we headed under the tracks to the business district. 'She definitely bought something in the Casual Browser,' I said. 'They told me so. And she was intending to buy something in the Lode the day I met her, because she had the bag. So she might have bought something in the Thrift, right?

I caught a look at her wallet as we were having our coffee that day, see?'

'You saw her ID?' said Kathi.

'No, I saw her extensive collection of loyalty cards. Her purse was fat as a tick with them. And I'm pretty sure there was one from the Browser in there. They're that horrible cat-food pink, you know?'

'She wouldn't have signed up to the loyalty scheme in a town where she came to commit a murder!' said Todd.

'Unless she was a world-class tightwad,' I said. 'Which she might have been. I know she piked me for basically a full meal when I suggested a coffee, plus she pocketed multiple creamers and sugar sachets too. So, even though it's a long shot, I think it's worth checking. If we're lucky Pat will be working and she might take pity on us.'

Pat was nowhere to be seen at the Thrift though. Instead we found a young man – floppy hair, chunky boots, grungy clothes – holding the fort alone.

'What now?' said Kathi as we huddled near the shoes, out of luck.

'Bribery?' I suggested. 'Honesty?'

'Don't be ridiculous,' said Todd. 'This is a job for precision bullshit. Watch and learn, ladies.' He went swaggering up to the kid who was mesmerized by the vision approaching.

'Sweetie,' said Todd, then clapped a hand over his mask. 'I am so sorry. That just slipped out.'

'Putty in his hands,' Kathi murmured to me as we drew near.

'I need to ask you to do something for me,' said Todd. He reached into his back pocket and drew out a business card. He smoothed it flat – it was shaped like a shoehorn from the curve of his perfect glutes – and pushed it across the glass counter-top. This is highly irregular,' he said. 'So I'm just going to ask you. We think someone was in the store some time fairly recently and signed up for a customer loyalty account.'

The mesmerized assistant nodded but said nothing.

'And we would like to know what that person's name is, and their email address and a phone number if you have one.'

'That's not possible,' the assistant said, obviously pained to refuse Todd anything, but also obviously a man of principle.

'Not possible?' said Todd. 'Literally impossible? Or not legal? Not ethical? Because we know that, but we'd like you to overlook it just this once. Please. We'd be very grateful. I'd be *super* grateful.'

I watched as a blush the colour of undiluted pomegranate cordial suffused the assistant's face.

'Because this person is a killer,' Todd said. 'The police are after her. But the police need warrants. We don't.'

'I can't,' said the assistant. 'I'm sorry.' There was a pause. I opened my mouth to break it but Todd kicked me. 'Who'd she kill?'

'Who did she not!' said Todd. 'The last time I saw her she was wearing snakeskin boots and a rabbit-fur jacket, carrying a crocodile handbag.'

Three minutes later we were in the back office behind a locked door – in case his boss came back from lunch early – looking at the spreadsheet of new customers.

'The snakeskin boots were a nice touch,' I said. 'Always put some truth in every lie, right?'

'I think you over-egged it,' said Kathi. 'Damn near said she was eating a foie gras veal burger. I can't believe he didn't see through you.'

'We're here, aren't we?' said Todd, scrolling and scrolling. 'Who knew this place was so popular. You think it's a front for money laundering?'

'When did you get so cynical?' I said. 'Stop!'

But there was no need to tell him. He had seen it too. Right there in dark green and lighter green – it was a very old computer – was a lie that read 'Becca-Lou Klatshovk'. The same last name Menzies had used to check in at the Ditch. And, while centuries of immigration from Eastern Europe and the confounding effects of Ellis Island made for some very strange American monikers, the three of us recognized an anagram for Black Out Love Shack like the online Pub Quiz regulars COVID had made of us all.

There was no address, and I didn't doubt that the email was bogus, but it's hard to make up authentic phone numbers off the cuff and, besides, I knew the Thrift ran its loyalty scheme by texting coupon codes to your phone while you stood there so I crossed my fingers and gave it a go.

'Hortense?' I said, when the call went through.

'What?' said a voice. It's hard to make out an accent from that one syllable alone. I ploughed on.

'Hosanna?'

'*What?*'

'Farik? Farquhar? Carmine? Oh wait, this'll work: Menzies? Or can't he come to the phone?'

'How did you get this number?' she said.

'Doesn't matter,' I told her. 'Tell the nearest BOLS Boy I found the thing he was wondering about. I've got it with me right now. It's very interesting. But I don't have much storage space at my place so I'd be willing to hand it over to someone for safe-keeping.'

'What the—?' I heard, before I hung up the phone and dropped it on to the cluttered desk of the Thrift's back office, wiping my hand on my jeans to dry a sudden rush of cold sweat that had popped out all over me.

'*Now* we sit tight,' I said, squeezing in between Roger and Taylor on a couch that's really only made for two. We three had the smallest bottoms but it was still just as well we were good friends.

'Do you think he'll come?' said Kathi.

'Definitely,' I said. 'He's too confident and too stupid to consider the possibility that this is a trap. And he's too venal and too self-centred to imagine that not everyone is the same as him, willing to sell evidence.'

'Do you think the woman on the Thrift cam will come too?' said Noleen.

'No idea,' I said. 'She was dumb enough to go shopping and take a Tesco carrier with her. It puts a whole new twist on "bag for life", eh?'

'Did you speak to your parents?' said Taylor. 'Are they OK?'

'They're fine. There's a cop car parked at the gate and my mum's baking for them, ferrying out cups of tea. If someone does turn up they'll be too fat and sleepy to chase him.'

'Did you tell them?' Todd said.

'No. I will, but the news that I went into a cupboard to have sex with my boyfriend would floor them anyway, never mind the . . . way it went wrong.'

'Are you going to speak to a professional?' said Todd. 'At least until you can say the word?'

'Dunno.'

'Because can I suggest that I'd be perfect?' he went on.

'As a "long ago trauma" counsellor?' I said.

'Absolutely,' he said. 'And I can do your nails at the same time.'

I took the finger I was chewing out of my mouth and turned to Roger with my eyes so wide I could feel them drying.

'He'll never change,' Roger said. 'You should just love him the way he is. It works for me.'

'Can you hear something?' said Kathi, sitting upright in her chair. 'Is that Hiro?'

'Maybe,' I said. The wailing didn't sound like Hiro but I kind of hoped it was. The fact of her stopping crying at the exact moment she'd stopped crying was still giving me the wig.

We listened some more.

'Definitely not Hiro,' said Noleen, as the wailing resolved itself into sirens and was joined by squealing tyres and shouting.

I held my breath for what seemed like an hour and only let it go when my phone rang.

'Got 'im,' Molly said. 'Cuffed and carred.'

'Just him?' I said. 'Just Farquhar?'

'What did I tell you?' said Molly. 'We've got 'em.'

'Right!' I said. 'Right! Gotcha. Thanks.'

I hung up my phone. 'That's not the first time that's happened,' I said. 'I thought you were telling Della "Fuck him", Noleen. I thought you were talking about Dylan. I thought you were breaking up a family. But you were saying "Fuck *them*", weren't you?'

'Always,' Noleen said, raising her glass. 'Words to live by. Fuck 'em all.'

FACTS AND FICTIONS

Cuento is not a real place. But anyone who knows Davis, CA, might well get a faint sense of déjà vu whilst reading this book. (And if you go to my website, www.catrionamcpherson.com, you will find an Easter Egg quiz about all the reasons for that.) None of the staff at the Beteo County SPCA, the Casual Browser bookshop, The Lode supermarket, or Odie's Ovens are based on real Davis residents, though; nor are any of the participants or volunteers in the 'HRT'. The Last Ditchers have no close counterparts in real life. Unfortunately. The pies? That's all true.

ACKNOWLEDGMENTS

I would like to thank: Lisa Moylett and all at Coombs Moylett Maclean Literary Agency; Carl Smith, Joanne Grant, Rachel Slatter, Penny Isaac, Jem Butcher, and all at Severn House; my friends Eileen Rendahl and Andy Wallace, who included me in their Thanksgiving feast when I was so green I could only be trusted to bring Martinelli's and are still inviting me; all my other California pals who meet round that big table in November and who schooled me on the menu; my friends and family across the rest of the country, up beyond the border, and over that ocean – I missed you all so much while I was writing this in late 2021 and getting to see you again has been a joy; the booksellers, librarians, reviewers, bloggers, bookstagrammers, podcasters and readers who make this lonely job far from lonely every day; and finally Neil McRoberts – we weren't locked down together quite so completely while I wrote this one but he was still pretty much right there and yet again we survived it.